NAKED TALES
tails

EDEN WINTERS

ROCKY RIDGE BOOKS

Naked Tails

Copyright © 2012, 2020 by Eden Winters

Cover Art by Perie Wolford

Print ISBN 978-1-62622-081-2

Printed in the United States of America

First Edition Dreamspinner Press

Second Edition Rocky Ridge Books, Broomfield, CO 80021

Many thanks to the following wonderful people: Carole, Pam, Chris, Feliz, Jared, Doug, and John R., for your friendship, unwavering support, and wonderful insight. You helped me turn a scary night of critter home invasion into an adventure.

Hugs,
Eden

- Jack—A male opossum
- Jill—A female opossum
- Joey—A young opossum
- Kit—Young fox
- Passel—A group of opossums
- Possum—Casual form of "opossum"
- Reynard—Leader of the skulk
- Skulk—A group of foxes
- Sweet tea—Traditional Southern beverage served over ice, containing too much sugar
- The Jack—Male leader or co-leader of the passel
- The Jill—Female leader or co-leader of the passel
- Vixen—Female fox

EIGHT-year-old Seth McDaniel drew in his knees and elbows, completely concealing himself behind a massive armchair. He'd been scolded often enough for sneaking uninvited into his great-aunt's bedroom, where Auntie Irene and Nana disappeared to have grown-up talks. But he'd overheard his name mentioned more than once and, worried he'd gotten into some kind of trouble (again), couldn't help his curiosity. Whenever his parents spoke his name when they believed him out of hearing range, he'd either later been punished or received a surprise. Seth swallowed past the lump in his throat. *I won't cry like a baby!* he told himself.

Footsteps grew ever closer, the slow, shuffling gait of Auntie's sensible shoes, followed by the clip-clop of his grandmother's high heels against the polished wooden floor. "Tomorrow morning I'm taking Seth home with me to Chicago, away from this place." Nana's words struck fear in Seth's heart. What? Chicago? Why?

"You cannot deny the child his heritage," Auntie Irene stated, far sterner than normal.

"If not for that… that *man*!" Nana spat the word like something vile. "If not for that man, my daughter would still be alive! Hit by a car! At thirty-one years old! Run over by a damned Buick like a stray dog!"

"That *man* was my nephew Aaron, and he went back for her. Gave his life trying to save your daughter!" Irene snapped back. Her voice softened, taking on the same gentle tone she used to comfort Seth when he'd skinned a knee or woken from a bad dream. "Please. Your grandson also happens to be my nephew's son, and the last living member of my family. Don't take him away from me."

Seth took a chance and peered around the back of his refuge, normally the anchor post of tent forts. The black stuff his nana wore around her eyes now ran down her face, leaving blotchy trails. Both women brushed back tears with their fingertips, only Auntie's were clear, not black. "I'm sorry," Nana said. "I cannot allow my daughter's tragic end to happen to Seth. He's coming back to Chicago with me."

Auntie asked, barely above a whisper, "Summer? School holidays? Can he at least visit me occasionally?"

Nana sniffed, steel leaching into her words. "I don't believe contact with any of your kind is in the boy's best interest."

Seth's heart sank. "Your kind"? What did she mean by "your kind"? No visiting Auntie? No playing fort with his friend Dustin? Nana didn't play fort, and anyway, her apartment wasn't big enough for a soldier to hide in. He choked back a sob.

"How is denying who he is, who his parents are… were… serving his interests?"

"I'm sorry, Irene. But I've made up my mind and I won't let you or anyone else convince me otherwise. He'll live with me, and that's final. None of this… this… nonsense."

"But I have visitation rights! He's my great-nephew!"

"In light of your family's... issues, I'm afraid I'll have to say no. And if you make any attempt to contact him without my permission, I'll guarantee your entire family's dirty laundry becomes public knowledge. Do I make myself clear? How my daughter ever...." Nana's voice rose again. "How she ever allowed some freak of nature to *change* her!" Between sobs, she added, "I won't let you corrupt my grandson! I won't, I won't, I won't!"

"Victoria, Seth's only half blood; chances are he'll never change. He's not at risk...."

"My daughter wasn't any blood, until... until...."

Auntie dug her heels in. "My nephew didn't force her. Your daughter made a choice."

Seth suddenly wished he'd stayed in the living room with the others who'd come to his parents' memorial service, even if they had confused him by saying, "There was barely even enough to bury."

"And she chose wrong! Why couldn't she return to Chicago after college? What brought her here to this godforsaken place?"

"She and Aaron fell in love."

"Love! Ha! You see where their *love* got them."

"Yes, it got them Seth."

The rest of the conversation was lost on Seth, who fought the urge to both comfort his grandmother and demand that she not keep him from Auntie's house. Who'd feed the hens and help gather the eggs? Who would Dustin tell secrets to if Seth lived in Chicago?

The two women left the room, one after the other, Auntie's pleas apparently falling on deaf ears. Seth spread his legs out in front of him, tears dripping down his cheeks. First he'd lost his parents, now it appeared he'd lose Auntie and Dustin too. What did Nana mean about Daddy's family?

3

"Seth? You in here?"

Dustin made a beeline for the chair. He always seemed to sense where Seth was, making hide-and-seek an unwinnable game.

"Oh, Seth. Are you alright?" Dustin squatted beside the chair, wiping tears from Seth's face with the tail of his Sunday best shirt.

Red-haired, freckle-faced, and green-eyed, ten-year-old Dustin Livingston was Seth's best friend. Many nights they'd stayed at each other's houses, chatting until the rooster crowed. The prospect of never seeing Dustin again broke what little remained of Seth's heart.

"I want Mama and Daddy back!" Seth wailed, afraid to tell what he'd overheard. If he didn't tell, it might not be true, right?

"Shhh...." The hands normally used to tickle him, give noogies, or playfully punch an arm lifted Seth's sopping face. "You got me. I ain't going nowhere."

The dam broke and Seth wailed in earnest. "Nana's taking me away! Says I can't come back here, ever!"

Dustin held him while he cried, murmuring, "You'll come back one day. And when you do, I'll still be here—waiting." He reached into his pocket and then pressed something into Seth's palm.

Through a glaze of tears, Seth stared at his friend's prized possession. "I can't take your lucky arrowhead. What will you do without your luck?"

"You need luck right now worse than I do, I reckon. Maybe it'll make you lucky enough to get to stay."

The arrowhead didn't work.

The next morning Auntie Irene woke Seth early and made his favorite pancakes, served with homemade blackberry syrup. She didn't smile or sing like usual, and the corners of her mouth turned down in a frown.

Seth finally worked up enough nerve to ask, "Am I in trouble?"

Auntie looked up from the fork she pushed around her plate, rearranging her meal without actually eating. "In trouble? What on earth gave you that idea?"

"I dunno." Seth shrugged. "You don't look happy, and when I'm bad I make you sad."

"Oh, you sweet boy. You sweet, sweet boy. No, you haven't done anything wrong." She dropped her fork to the plate with a clatter and scooped Seth into her arms, sniffling into his hair. "Oh, baby. I love you so much. Never forget that. Promise me."

"I promise, Auntie."

A car horn sounded outside and Auntie Irene straightened, wiping her cheek with the back of her hand. "Your grandmother is here. We have to get you ready to go."

"Go? Why can't I stay here with you?"

"I want you to, but you can't. You have to go with your grandmother."

Panic seized Seth's heart. "Why, Auntie? I don't want to go! I wanna stay here with you and Dustin! I'll be good, I promise! Please don't make me go! Please!" Tears flooded his eyes, spilling over onto his cheeks.

"I'm sorry, sweetie. I really am. But you have to go."

She said nothing more as she loaded Seth's suitcases into Nana's rental car. Auntie dropped to her knees and pulled him close one more time, squeezing the breath out of him. "I love you, sweetie," she whispered into his hair. She buried her face in his neck, whiffing deeply.

"Love you too, Auntie," he mumbled weakly, his heart about to split in two.

Auntie Irene released her hold and stood, giving Seth a strained smile. Nana bustled him into the car, ignoring Seth's, "No! I wanna stay here! I don't wanna go!"

Nana kicked up dust from the red Georgia clay in her hurry

to get to the Atlanta airport. Seth spotted Dustin on the side of the road on his bicycle as they whizzed by. Dustin turned when he saw the car, pumping the pedals to try to keep up. Through the back window, Seth watched a copper-crowned head growing smaller and smaller, finally fading from view. He didn't stop crying until he reached Chicago.

CHAPTER 1

DR. DUSTIN LIVINGSTON finished his shower. How ironic: showering and grooming when, in a few hours, he'd be ambling on four legs through weeds, hunting earthworms and other munchable critters, and exploring vacant burrows. "If you're going to act like an animal, at least be civilized about it," his mother always said. Of course, his mother would likely root around the yard of her Florida retirement home tonight too.

He missed his mother, yet missed his dad more, for a simple phone call connected him with Mom, but Dad was beyond reaching out to now. Dustin sighed. After tonight, he'd have one more person to miss, one who directly affected the path of his future.

Since his birth, Irene McDaniel had played a huge role in his life: mentor, leader, teacher, friend. Tonight would be her last. After far more years than most folks realized, her strength finally reached an end. She'd not survive another full moon.

Heart heavy, he drove to Irene's in silence. Several cars crowded the yard of the old woman's farmhouse, and Monica Sims's beat-up Silverado proved a welcome sight. He'd need her support tonight.

He parked next to Monica's truck and entered the house he'd practically grown up in, his gaze automatically landing on the photos displayed on the mantel. By rights, Irene's great-nephew should assume the torch at her passing, but Seth McDaniel hadn't darkened her door in twenty years. Out of long habit, Dustin paused a moment by Seth's picture, a knife twisting in his heart. Damn, but he wished his childhood friend were here.

Through a crowd much too large for even the spacious farmhouse, Dustin sought out a familiar blonde. He found her in the kitchen. Normally Monica kept her thigh-length tresses bound in neat braids, but not tonight. Tonight her hair, like the woman, would run free, golden waves flowing over her broad shoulders. Even without the beacon of her shiny locks, the six-foot nursing assistant towered head and shoulders over many gathered tonight.

She noticed Dustin and fought her way through the crowd, pressing her lips tightly together.

"Hey!" shouted a red-faced man, industriously slapping sandwiches together in an assembly line for a woman to place on the floor. "Mine's the one with mustard and pimiento. Don't step on it!"

Monica ignored him. Every eye turned to her, even while young and old scrambled out of the way of a woman on a mission. "The tension in here's so thick you can cut it with a knife," she said after finally elbowing her way to Dustin's side.

Dustin, at five foot seven, rose on his toes to hear her better over the others' chatter. "Well, it's not every day the passel loses a leader after fifty years." If the shifters who made up the passel were a family, tonight they'd lose their mother.

Dustin and Monica shared a quiet, eye-to-eye moment, tuning out the chaos around them. Monica's "all business" expression softened. "She's asking for you."

He forced a smile. "I'd best not keep the lady waiting. Can

8

you manage things out here?"

"Short term? Yes. In a few hours? Not on your life. I wish we'd shift in the field. Less mess and a whole lot more room."

Dustin agreed wholeheartedly. Soon, all hell would break loose, turning Irene's house into a disaster zone. "Yeah, but tonight will be her last. She wants the passel with her, and she wants to spend her last night in the house she grew up in."

Dozens of eyes followed Dustin's progress down the hall, where he quietly knocked and then entered Irene's room before closing the door behind him.

"Ralph." He nodded to the elderly man sitting at Irene's bedside, tenderly stroking her arthritic fingers.

"Doctor." Ralph Mason, county coroner, rose from his chair. Dustin didn't miss the bittersweet smile the two seniors shared. Though not passel, Ralph and Irene's friendship ran deep; the old man would miss her upon her passing—as would half the county.

"Is everything in order?" Dustin pretended not to notice Ralph drawing Irene's hand to his lips.

"Yes. I've got the papers ready, waiting for your signature." The coroner reached his free hand over and tapped a manila envelope lying on a dresser. "And per Irene's instructions, I'll wait until after her official burial to contact her next of kin. Less explaining to do that way."

"It'd be a whole lot easier if what we see in movies was real and we turned back human if we die in shifter form."

"Yeah, Doc, but you know as well as I do that this is how she'd want it. The moon will help her make the change, but she's too weak to change back on her own."

In a few short hours, Dustin, a medical doctor, would pronounce Irene legally dead, verified by the county coroner. They would bury her body in the wild, with the funeral parlor in town providing documentation of a burial in the local churchyard, should any curious parties ask questions.

Such had been the way of Possum Kingdom since the town's creation. A world within a world, playing fast and loose with human laws while hiding in plain sight.

"Promise me?" Irene's raspy voice ended both the spoken and unspoken conversations taking place between the two men.

Dustin stepped closer to the bed, bending his slight frame to better hear Irene's whispered plea. "Promise you what, my Jill?" he asked, though already suspecting the nature of her request.

"It must be you; there's no one else."

Dustin's heart sank. "But the title should be passed to your family. I love you like my own mother, but we're not blood kin. What will the passel think?" The passel, one-hundred-fifty-odd strong, were a fickle bunch, ranging from the easily led to die-hard traditionalists. His leadership wouldn't be accepted without a challenge or two. Challenges became messy, as he'd witnessed before with other groups. No one had ever second-guessed his Jill, however.

"They'll agree with my decision. You're the best man for the job." The wizened lady lying in the bed, formidable despite her advanced years, leveled him with her steely eyed gaze, the same one that had backed down many a young joey.

"Besides, the only kin I have is partial blood. Had *that woman* allowed contact over the years, it might be a different story. Because of her meddling, Seth grew up with no idea of his legacy. Even if he did, he'd have a decision to make. Not every half blood chooses to become a full-fledged passel member, especially at his age."

Dustin clearly remembered Seth's tear-streaked face the day his maternal grandmother had taken him away from the house twenty years ago. Twenty years. Had it truly been two decades since they'd last seen each other? "She's been gone for a couple of years now. Have you even contacted Seth and asked him to come home?" Dustin clutched at one last straw, his heart filled with longing. Thoughts of Seth McDaniel brought to mind shaggy brown-and-gold hair and dark-brown eyes, hazed by tears. Even now, after so much time, the memory brought a lump to Dustin's throat. Seth, ripped away from his life by "the evil harpy from the north," the label Dustin had given Seth's closed-minded grandmother. Oh, how he'd cried, wanting his friend back.

"He comes from a different world and has his own life there. We can't expect him to understand his true path since no one's been there to teach him who he really is." Irene lifted a trembling hand to stroke Dustin's cheek. "He doesn't even know about the passel, so how can he love them like you do?" One heavy-lidded eye winked. "Though he might make a good coleader one day, if his inheritance manages to lure him down from Chicago."

"What do you mean?"

"I've left him the house in hopes he'll decide to live here. If he's here, he'll need a friend." She lowered her voice, adding, "And possibly more."

"Are you telling me Seth's gay? How could you know such a thing?" No matter how strong her power to know the truth in people, truths most others would never see, surely her reach couldn't extend to someone so far removed.

The weak sound she made could have been a chuckle. "Down at the library, the Johnson boys showed me what they call a 'social media site' on the Internet. Seth is a photographer and takes lovely photos, he's interested in men, and he's single." A crease appeared above her brow. "He changed his status to 'it's complicated', once, whatever that means. Although I can't understand why folks tell everything about themselves for strangers to read, I did learn a thing or two about my great-nephew." An expression of sheer satisfaction momentarily smoothed her wrinkles. "He's the spitting image of his daddy."

What? The old lady lay on her deathbed, trying to play

matchmaker? "Are you suggesting I date your great-nephew? The passel won't accept such a thing! Remember what happened to the fox shifters when their leader chose a male mate."

Back in the sixties a handful of independent foxes had shown up seeking protection and guidance to form their own skulk. Their ranks swelled, close to fifty now, but without Irene's intervention, a battle for command of the skulk a few years ago might have raged out of control.

"Ah, but the old Reynard wasn't strong enough to retain power. Andy Coleman is much better suited for the job."

Dustin's stomach churned, as it always did when someone reminded him of the skulk's current Reynard, and what Dustin had personally given up to secure Andy's leadership. The vixen Andy had married to appease his people was expecting twins, due in late fall.

"You could always do as leaders have in the past," Irene murmured. "Name Monica your official mate and keep a male lover. If he doesn't interfere with passel politics, they'd accept such an arrangement. Plus, Seth's a McDaniel. They have to respect the name."

The mere thought soured Dustin's stomach. "Such an arrangement wouldn't be fair to me, him, or Monica."

"Ah!" The lady smiled, the uplifting of her mouth easing pain lines from her face. "You admit there is *someone*?"

"Not anymore," Dustin murmured.

Irene ran her knotted fingers gently against Dustin's cheek. "You still miss your Reynard."

No use denying. "Yes, ma'am."

"He chose tradition, took a vixen for his mate. It wasn't personal, and he still thinks highly of you."

Dustin nodded. "We remain friends, nothing more."

Irene tugged Dustin down to swipe her chapped lips against his cheek and whisper, "You deserve better."

Picturing Andy and his missus, laughing, happy, and planning the arrival of their twins, Dustin closed his eyes, willing the residual hurt from his mind and heart. "Yes, I do."

Dustin stayed at Irene's bedside until the sun began to set. He didn't need to see the moon edging over the rim of the world—lunar power pulsed deep within him. Irene's widened eyes and her fingertips scrabbling against Dustin's face told him she sensed the moonrise too.

"One more time," she whispered. "Help me!"

Having seen her naked on most full moons, and being her doctor, Dustin didn't hesitate to help the elderly lady disrobe. The coroner, on the other hand, suddenly found the drapes of great interest.

"I have to go," Dustin said, slipping off his jeans and T-shirt. He wore nothing underneath. The less clothes the better. The passel had no problems with public nudity.

"Dusty! You better get out here!" Monica shrieked from outside the door.

Torn between his duty to the passel and the need to be with his leader when she breathed her last, Dustin hesitated.

Irene relieved him of a tough decision. "You go on. In a few moments, they'll need you more than I."

"I'll be with her," Ralph said, stepping up to the bed.

Pressing his lips to Irene's forehead, Dustin replied, "Until we meet again, my Jill."

A transformation that years of med school couldn't explain rippled through Dustin's body, shortening his limbs, elongating his snout, multiplying his teeth, and judiciously applying a tail. He squeaked and scurried off, grateful to Monica for pulling the door ajar while she still possessed human hands.

Outside the door pandemonium reigned, furry bodies scampering around Irene's kitchen, devouring any food in sight. Two fat, gray possums scuffled over an olive. Dustin ordered, "Follow me," and barreled through the hole in the wall, sidestepping a puddle of water from the leaky water heater. He blazed a trail outside, where the passel would engage their beastly sides until dawn. "June bugs beware!" Dustin chirped, wading into a moveable, or rather, moving, feast.

From sundown to sunrise, Dustin reveled in his animal nature, keeping a cautious eye out for others of his kind. Unseen, nonshifting guards hovered around the perimeter, alert for predators.

The sixteen-year-old Johnson boys, the passel's newest full-fledged members, had shifted for the first time six months prior. They'd proudly visited Dustin's office to show off their recently learned ability to shift at will. Dustin only hoped he wouldn't be called to the county high school anymore to explain when one accidently lost control in gym class. He'd done a heck of a lot of lying to the other students to convince them the three brothers had merely played a prank, and Eddy Johnson hadn't actually turned into an animal during a volleyball game. A bit of fast-talking and a little smoke and mirrors involving the foot-ball team's mascot, Petey the Possum, had effectively covered the trio's shenanigans—for the time being.

One other needed watching over too, and Dustin moseyed over to the spot where he'd sensed a relatively new member snuffling around in the grass. One night a pretty young bride, wanting to share everything with her new husband, had said, "Bite me," a phrase with a literal meaning in Possum Kingdom.

Those not born with the Channing-Frost virus—colloqui-ally referred to as the changeling virus—in their blood were prone to more animalistic instincts, resulting in unfortunate accidents like the one involving Seth's mother. Without her human knowledge, she'd merely stood in the middle of the road, mesmerized by a car's headlights. Seth's father had raced back to save her, too late. Both died in possum form. Empty caskets lay buried in the First Baptist Church of Possum King-dom's cemetery, a proper burial held to appease Seth's "Yankee" grandmother. As an added precaution against history repeating itself, Dustin had put this bride to work in his practice as his receptionist, maintaining an ever-watchful eye.

Not for the first time, Dustin wondered where Seth was, what he was doing, and hoped he was happy doing it.

Daylight came and Dustin straggled back to the house. He crept naked into Irene's bedroom and slipped on his jeans.

Ralph sat beside the bed in a brocaded chair, eyes red from a combination of tears and lack of sleep. He stroked a still, furry body on the bed. "She went quickly," he said. "Without pain."

A stack of forms lay on the dresser, and Dustin, heart heavy, signed on the appropriate lines, making Irene's death official before shoving the documents back into the envelope and handing them to Ralph.

"Would you like to come with me?" Dustin scooped up the tiny body, hugging his beloved leader's remains to his chest and lightly stroking an ear. A single tear slipped down his nose, splashing against her fur.

"Yes, please."

Together the two men stepped out into an early summer day. Men and women in varying degrees of nakedness fell in stride beside them. Dustin's steps slowed as he trudged toward his destination, a small pond situated on the back of Irene's property. Beneath a pin oak, he placed the body into a prepared hole and then paused to take a deep breath. While her second-in-command had every right to tend her body, the moment Dustin lifted the waiting shovel and tossed the first bit of earth into the hole, he announced his intention to provide a successor for Irene, either by choosing a viable candidate or assuming the role himself. He heard a few murmurs from various passel members, some favorable, some not, but chose to ignore them for the time being.

After flinging in the ceremonial shovel full of dirt, he relinquished the tool to Monica, who vouchsafed him by adding her own contribution to Irene's burial.

The elders stepped up, one by one, saying their good-byes. After each member of the passel had spoken their piece and tossed in dirt, they drifted away, leaving only Dustin, Monica, and the coroner. Dustin placed a stone marker over the grave, to keep other creatures from digging up the remains, and then stood, brushing his hands on his jeans.

A light breeze cooled his sweaty brow and he gazed down at the new grave, kept company by several others. Though gravestones in a cemetery in town bore the names of Seth's parents, their actual bodies rested here, along with Irene's brother and his wife, Irene's father and mother, and an uncle. Dustin had paid for a marker for Irene in town, in keeping with tradition, to preserve shifter ways from the blissfully ignorant.

"It's peaceful here," Monica murmured.

"The family chose this spot for a reason," Dustin replied.

"What do you suppose will happen if Irene's great-nephew inherits and sells the farm? What will happen to her and the rest buried here?"

"I reckon I'll have to buy the place." He'd go in debt up to his eyeballs to keep Irene's heritage from falling into the wrong hands.

Dustin, Monica, and Ralph stood over the grave, each lost in their own thoughts, sniffles and the occasional sob marking their shared mourning.

PICKING his way through tall grass back to his truck, Dustin spotted one of the Johnson boys. "Hey," he said. "How about you and your brothers clean up Irene's house before her nephew arrives?"

"Sure," the boy said. "Let me go find 'em."

CHAPTER 2

"Must I wear this hideous sack of a dress? I look fat!" A string bean of a woman stood in front of a green screen in Seth McDaniel's studio. No way in hell could anything make the chiffon-swathed waif look anything but underfed. As Seth's Aunt Irene used to say, "Someone give that poor child a biscuit."

"Jut your hip out a little more, and remember, smile!"

The spoiled rotten brat of a model sneered.

Seth used a threat he'd often employed in the past. "Do you want to make the cover, or wind up buried on page thirty next to an ad for adult diapers?" The model's overbleached teeth made a strained appearance. "Much better. Now, a bit more to the right...." Seth clicked off a series of shots, weighing the time spent playing nursemaid against money earned for the magazine spread and wishing he'd never taken the assignment.

When a friend first suggested the shoot, photographing high fashion seemed a great way to get his name out to the right people, possibly help him graduate from weddings and bar mitzvahs and take a step up to more serious work. Besides, the friend hadn't specified male or female models, allowing

Seth to indulge in many happy fantasies before the first arrived, tapping high-heeled stilettos and screeching demands. Each model he'd worked with had complained bitterly about everything from his studio being two degrees too chilly to him not supplying a diva's favorite chocolates. After he'd special-ordered the expensive treats for the next day, his *diva du jour* spotted the distinctive satin-bowed box and squawked, "What are you trying to do, make me fat?"

He'd bitten his tongue, dreams of advancement reduced to simply hoping his business survived the women's scathing complaints. In contrast to diva tantrums, providing photographic evidence of bar mitzvahs seemed like a dream job.

Once he'd shot enough pictures to hopefully prevent ever having to deal with the woman again, he dismissed her, poured himself two fingers of tequila, and sank into his favorite chair, grabbing his phone.

For the entire shoot, the damned thing had chirped and vibrated, making Seth antsy to connect with the outside world. He'd received several texts, mostly message board entries, e-mail notifications, and a few hits from the social media sites he belonged to—idle chitchat, nothing directly for him. He'd also received two phone calls: one from a number he didn't recognize, the other from a number he did.

Hitting redial, he prepared for the latest installment of "The Michael and Seth Show," as he privately called their sporadic relationship; a pattern of on-again-off-again dating with more twists and turns than the Tour de France. A month had passed since they'd even spoken. Seth's erstwhile love interest picked up on the first ring. "Hey, Seth. How's it going?" Michael's voice didn't quite offer the welcome Seth hoped for.

Seth took a deep breath, trying not to appear overeager. After all, Michael had broken up with *him*, not the other way around. "Good. How're things with you?"

"Better than good, actually. Listen, I have something I'd like to talk to you about. Are you free for dinner?"

A shared dinner sounded promising. "Sure, what do you have in mind?"

"Pick whatever you're in the mood for."

"I've got the perfect place in mind," Seth replied, determined to keep an open mind and hear the man out. "I'll text you after I make reservations."

"Okay. Any place you choose will be fine."

"You'll like this place, I promise." Seth hung up the phone, already planning to change his *All About Me* status from "single" back to "it's complicated."

Seth banged on the strings of his air guitar, belting his heart out with the AC/DC tune firing from his stereo speakers.

Rap, rap, rap, came from the wall in his living room. "Okay, okay, I'm turning it down!" he hollered, crossing the floor to reduce the window-rattling volume.

His favorite playlist now barely audible, he boogied his way into the kitchen in socked feet, grabbed a bottle of water from the refrigerator, and downed the contents in one go. "Ahhh…," he exclaimed, wiping his mouth on the back of his hand. He tossed the empty bottle in the general direction of the recycling bin, missing completely.

He shimmied into the bedroom and entered his seldom used closet in search of a button-down shirt, totally at odds with his normal attire of band T's and blue jeans. Tonight was a special night, and he'd even taken extra time showering and shaving, hoping Michael might appreciate his efforts.

He paired a light-blue dress shirt with dark-blue slacks, then slid his feet into a pair of loafers to complete the outfit. Next, he picked his way over piles of laundry, both dirty and clean, a discarded paperback, and four pairs of shoes on his way to the bathroom mirror for a cursory inspection. His normally straight and cooperative short brown hair stuck up at odd angles. Seth wet his hands in the sink, attempting to rearrange the mess to acceptable levels. He pulled back his lips and performed a "teeth and nose" check, or rather, in his case, a "teeth and beak" check. Both passed muster.

A splash of cologne and then Seth darted across town, parked two blocks away, and trotted to the front door of Swanky's—a place he'd normally consider out of his price range. Michael arrived by cab a scant moment later. "Perfect timing." Michael pulled Seth into a somewhat stiff hug. "Let's go in, shall we? I'm starving!" He held the door open for Seth. "I've missed you," he said, voice dropping to a murmur. "I'm glad you agreed to see me tonight." The unique combination of familiar soap, shampoo, and cologne scent brought back memories of past sleepovers.

The maître d' tilted his head to the side, regarding Seth with interest. "Do you have a reservation?"

Seth shook the man's hand, passing over the tip he'd promised for securing a reservation on such short notice. "McDaniel. Table for two."

"Right this way, gentlemen," the man said after taking a discreet glance at Seth's payment. He led the way to a table at the rear of the restaurant, snapping his fingers at a passing waiter.

Michael muttered something to the waiter too low for Seth to decipher no matter how hard he listened. The waiter shuffled off. "I ordered us a bottle of wine," Michael replied to Seth's raised-brow query.

"Is this a special occasion?" Seth scrolled through his mental appointment calendar, hoping he hadn't somehow missed a birthday. Nope, they'd celebrated Michael's birthday in March, three months ago, the last time they'd been out on an actual date. Maybe Michael intended to come back for good. A flush crept up Seth's cheeks. Maybe he should have cleaned up his apartment a bit.

"Maybe." A smug smile played around Michael's full lips.

Seth loved Michael's smile; it certainly boded well for later. "What're you going to order?" Seth stared at the handsome man seated across from him.

The waiter approached with a bottle of wine. "Sir," he said, holding out the bottle for inspection. Seth glanced up, nearly swallowing his tongue when he noticed the vintage. He wasn't well versed in wine, but any bottle bearing such a fancy label had to cost well over a hundred bucks. What could be special about this evening?

They sipped wine and studied their menus over a plate of crudités. "How have you been?" Michael asked.

"I've been okay, I guess. It's been awhile. What've you been up to?"

The waiter returned and Michael placed his order. "I'll have the veal scaloppini with braised asparagus and artichokes, and a baby field green salad with raspberry vinaigrette. Hold the olives."

That was one thing Seth liked about Michael—except for their now-you-see-it-now-you-don't love affair, he always seemed to know exactly what he wanted, even if those wants changed rapidly and without notice.

Throwing caution to the wind, Seth pinched the extra inch around his middle. He could always put in extra time at the gym tomorrow. "I'll have the same."

They enjoyed pleasant small talk over dinner. Michael showed pictures of his sister's new baby, and Seth shared a few anecdotes from his model shoots.

At the end of the meal, Seth grew impatient. "You said you wanted to talk to me about something," he prodded.

Michael didn't quite meet Seth's eyes. "Do you remember me telling you about Luther?"

"Luther from New York? The older guy who broke your heart?"

A sheepish smile crept across Michael's face. "Yeah. I wanted commitment, but he never quite seemed ready."

"And?" Seth felt certain this story came with an "and."

"And he wants me back. I'm leaving next week to move to New York. We're getting married. I wanted to tell you face-to-face." He reached across the table, grasping Seth's hand. "I want you to be happy for me."

Married? What the fuck? Seth bit back a confused jumble of hurt and anger. Married?

Noting the pleading look in Michael's eyes, Seth swallowed his wounded pride, dreams of getting back together vanishing. "Of course I'm happy for you," he lied.

"And you're not angry with me?"

"Angry? Why would I be angry?" Seth ventured, forcing a smile.

"Well, you knew I liked older men…."

And I hoped I'd be the one who changed your mind. "I'm happy for you, I truly am," Seth managed to say, fighting a grimace.

"Good, you don't know how much that means to me." Michael insisted on picking up the tab, despite Seth's half-hearted protests, and practically skipped out of the restaurant, a weight lifted from his shoulders. Too bad that weight fell directly on Seth. A nearly empty wine bottle (much cheaper than the bottle Michael had ordered at Swanky's) sat on the coffee table. Seth sprawled a few feet away on the couch. Married. Michael was getting married, dashing any hopes Seth had of them together on a more permanent basis.

Okay, honestly, he'd never actually believed they'd be together on a lasting basis, despite a bit of bliss-induced post-coital pillow talk. Michael came and went like a breeze. And he wanted to get married? He'd never mentioned marriage to Seth.

Just for a moment Seth allowed himself to dream of a large house with a huge front porch, himself and some phantom man sitting side by side, a child or two with them. The perfect little family. Try as he might, though, he couldn't seem to work Michael into the picture. The mystery man remained a vague shape. Whoever he turned out to be, he'd be honest and dependable. And for some strange reason, he seemed to have red hair. Why would Seth fantasize about a man with red hair? Michael's hair was blond.

Then again, if Seth paused a minute to think with the right head, Michael had waltzed into his life while on the rebound from the mysterious Luther, a high-powered New York attorney who'd spoiled Michael rotten until Michael had gotten it into his head that he wanted permanence. And now he'd get it.

"Ha! Won't last a month!" Seth proclaimed to the wine bottle.

His phone chirped, announcing a message. He raised his head and stared at the offending gizmo with bleary eyes. "Not now!" he yelled, dropping his head back to the couch arm. What the fuck would he do? He should be enjoying makeup sex right about now. Instead, he lay on the couch in his tiny apartment, wallowing in self-pity and cheap wine.

I'd better check my messages. Who knew? Maybe he'd gotten an out-of-town job offer. He'd love to get away for a week or two. Or longer.

Eventually he summoned enough energy to unlock his phone and access the message. Smashing the tiny iPhone to his ear, he heard, "Mr. McDaniel? I'm Richard Clooney, of Clooney, Anderson, and Gentry. I represent your aunt's estate."

CHAPTER 3

SETH reread the documents he'd been sent, while crammed into a coach-class airline seat. Some things he understood, others he'd definitely need to speak to his aunt's attorney about. And while the papers hinted at money coming his way in addition to a house, they hadn't named a specific amount. The one thing he knew for certain was that he needed to spend time in the South, unraveling the details of his aunt's will and deciding what to do with all she'd left him. He reread the lawyer's last letter: "I received your itinerary and an associate of your aunt's will pick you up when you arrive." The lawyer hadn't specified who or how Seth would know them. Oh well, he'd find out soon enough.

He'd demolished the last of his airline pretzels by the time his Samsonite case came into view on the luggage claim carousel at the Atlanta airport. He received a few appraising glances. The curious stares might have been for him, his over-sized case, or the distinctive rainbow strap that both announced his sexuality to savvy individuals and made his black, expand-able spinner bag easier to find.

A six-foot Valkyrie straight from the Wagnerian opera his

grandmother once dragged him to—minus the horned helmet
—bore down on Seth as he wrestled his luggage off the
conveyor. Had the darned thing put on a burst of speed to
taunt him? With one hand on the handle, he followed his
runaway suitcase around a bend, chorusing, "Excuse me,
pardon me" to anyone in his way. Without slowing down, the
Valkyrie swooped in, grasped the strap, and hauled the at-
weight-limit-bag to the floor. "You Seth McDaniel?" she asked,
extending the handle on his suitcase.

Seth glanced up. And up. And up. He gulped. The woman
possessed the body of a professional wrestler and the attitude
of a sentencing judge. "Y… yes."

"I'm here to take you to your aunt's." Without another
word, she turned on her heel and strode toward the door with
Seth's luggage.

"Wait! Miss! Miss!" Seth grabbed his laptop case and
jogged after her, puffing for breath by the time they'd made it
curbside. The battle maiden tossed an annoyed *Keep up, why
don't you!* glare over her shoulder.

"Out of shape, are you, city boy?" she sneered. Her long
gold braids and the stern set of her shoulders brought to mind
a Girl Scout on steroids.

Everything about the woman seemed built in squares, from
her firm jawline to her blunted fingernails. Dressed in worn
blue jeans, a "Southern by the Grace of God" T-shirt, and flip-
flops, not a speck of makeup enhanced her carved-from-ice
complexion.

Without waiting for a reply, she resumed charging toward
the parking lot, dragging Seth's suitcase behind her and forcing
Seth to scramble in her long-legged wake. Apparently single-
minded in her determination to reach another state on foot, the
only time the Amazonian warrior bothered to glance up was
when a car approached. Each and every time, she froze in

place, shook herself, and then resumed marching across the asphalt.

She stopped next to an ancient blue-and-primer-colored Chevy Silverado and slung the suitcase into the back. The over-loaded luggage landed with a solid thud.

"My cameras!" Seth cried.

A glinty-eyed stare lowered down to Seth's level. "Next time, you can haul your own damned bag."

Seth narrowed his eyes and bristled. How dare she! "I would have taken it this time if you hadn't grabbed it. I don't even know you! Who are you?"

"Jill," she replied, folding her arms across her chest. "That's all you need to know." She stepped in, crowding Seth's personal space, and then sniffed, her nose buried in his neck. "You smell like passel, but weak. What the hell kind of soap do you use?"

"Hey!" Seth jumped back. "What the fuck? I don't know what a passel is, but I most certainly don't smell like one. I'll have you know my soap comes from an exclusive boutique in Chicago." And he'd never gotten complaints before, at least not from men.

Goldilocks reared back, teeth bared. "Well, stop using it!" She rounded the truck to the driver's side, flung the door open, and flumped down behind the wheel.

Seth waited for an invitation to get in, but when Jill fired up the engine and began backing out of the parking space—with his suitcase—he gave up any pretense of good manners and grabbed the passenger door handle, running beside the truck. When the woman braked to shift out of reverse, he hopped inside, stowing his laptop case on the floorboard.

"You might wanna fasten your seat belt," Jill warned, stomping the accelerator hard enough to slide Seth's suitcase down the truck bed to rap against the tailgate. Seth grabbed the "oh shit!" handle, hanging on for dear life.

Had he been abducted by a madwoman? "We haven't met properly but I'm—"

"—the no-account loser who abandoned his aunt and never even came to visit in twenty fucking years."

What the fuck? "Now wait a damned minute. My aunt didn't bother calling me, not once in all that time."

Jill stomped the brake, sending Seth jolting forward, and tossed a paper ticket at the parking lot attendant. His suitcase slammed against the cab. "Nobody needed to tell you to do the right thing. That'll be five bucks."

"Huh?"

Jill jammed a thumb toward the attendant. "My truck, my gas. You pay parking."

Seth perched on one ass cheek to reach into his billfold, grumbling while digging out a twenty. Jill handed it to the attendant, smiling sweetly. "Keep the change."

She floored the gas pedal, cutting off Seth's, "Hey! I got fifteen bucks coming back!"

He'd never met this woman before and yet somehow had managed to piss her off—not that he'd ever understood women, particularly his dour, demanding grandmother (God rest her soul!). However, usually he had some inkling of his error whenever one grew physically violent with a vehicle or other inanimate object on his behalf.

No denying Jill was right on one account. He really could have made an attempt to call Auntie Irene. With his grand-mother no longer around, he didn't run the risk of unleashing her hysterics. Somehow her warnings of "You'll end up like my daughter!" or "Please, please don't go there!" hadn't instilled confidence. For all her faults, she'd raised him. While lacking warmth, she had provided for him. He supposed she loved him, though she'd never been demonstrative with her affections. Yet she'd never once allowed him to call anyone with a Georgia area code.

Regardless of Nana's talk about "Irene McDaniel doesn't care about you," Seth had memories of being sung to, read to, and being allowed to help bake cookies. And when Aunt Irene died, she'd left him everything. That hardly seemed like the behavior of someone who didn't care.

Despite a handful of happy memories, why his aunt had never once contacted him remained a mystery. She'd told him she loved him the last time he'd seen her, and then… nothing.

"I—" he began, at a loss for words.

"Can't hear you," Jill yelled over the radio she flipped to full volume.

Seth winced. A forced discussion at this juncture might prove dangerous. With time on his hands and the ride having smoothed enough to allow letting go of his death grip on the grab handle, he pulled his iPhone from his pocket, desperate to communicate with someone familiar.

He punched the icon for his favorite site, sighing when he read message after message from his so-called cyber friends, congratulating Michael on the upcoming wedding. Adding insult to injury, Michael had hired a second-rate photographer to record the ceremony. A man who used a secondhand camera and hadn't a clue about proper backlighting.

Seth scrolled through the list of well-wishers, finding no love. Traitors. He pulled up short at seeing his own name: "Better keep Seth from showing up to ruin things. What you ever saw in the loser is beyond me." *What?* Oh, Michael's sister, Angela. Michael's social-climbing sister hadn't considered Seth good enough for her brother.

Screw them. Seth tried another media site, one more devoted to who did whom, and sighed again at his "friends" boasting of hookups and near misses. Not a single person mentioned him or even commented on his leaving. Didn't he have any true friends? Thumbs clicking across the phone's tiny keyboard, he wrote, *In Georgia, back soon.*

He let out the breath he'd been holding, relief washing through him when he received a response from some guy he knew only by a purple penguin icon, a screen name of "Squeaky," and a penchant for online gaming. *Nice hearing from you. Was worried.*

I'm okay, he typed back. *Settling aunt's estate.*

He received: *O good. Worried you jumped off bridge after M's engagement.*

Did his friends think him that distraught over Michael? *Michael's getting married?* he asked. No rejoinder came back, though he waited a few minutes.

Once the usual posters presumably assumed he'd moseyed off, they recommenced their prattle about who slept with whom, who wanted to sleep with whom, etcetera.

He shoved his phone into his pocket, more depressed than ever.

"You might try talking to somebody in the real world. You know, flesh-and-blood people. Folks who use actual words and not text-speak."

Seth hadn't even noticed the volume on the radio dropping enough for them to converse without yelling. And though Jill's arctic tones didn't actually approach anywhere near an open invitation to chat, at least she wasn't hissing through clenched teeth now.

"Thought you weren't talking to me."

"I meant you should have called your aunt every once in a while."

"She never called me!"

"The phone works both ways. Did you ever even try calling her?"

No sense in denying the truth. "No, but maybe I should have. Happy now?"

"I don't do happy."

Seth wouldn't argue the point. After turning off the interstate, they traveled a few miles on a state road, and then turned once again onto a much less cared for stretch of blacktop, weeds encroaching on either side. After a small eternity, they passed a town limit sign. *Welcome to Possum Kingdom, population....* Whatever number had once graced the sign now hid behind a blob of black spray paint, replaced by a smearily scrawled, *How long you staying?*

"The last get-together pretty much cleaned Irene's kitchen out. If you plan to stay at her house, you're going to need provisions." Jill parked the truck in the parking lot of an unremarkable mom-and-pop grocery store. They still made those? A vague recollection tickled Seth's memory—Auntie dropping quarters into the mechanical horse out front, Seth and his friend taking turns riding. Seth recalled red hair, crooked front teeth, and the laughing eyes of the best friend he'd ever had. His heart lurched. Could it be possible that Dustin still lived around these parts?

Before he could ask, Jill stormed out of the truck and into Phil's Grocery and Sporting Goods. Supposing he ought to heed her advice and get some food, Seth scrambled to keep up with her, straining his legs to match her ambitious pace.

"Grab a cart," Jill barked. She leaned beside the front door, mouth stretched in a yawn.

Irritated as much at his natural inclination to bend to her will as her surly demeanor—which he attributed to years of training from his overbearing Nana—Seth disentangled a shopping cart from its intimate embrace of a fellow and tried to keep up when she bounded off, squeaky, shuddering wheels notwithstanding.

"You're not one of them there vega-met-tarians, are ya?" she asked, with the same amount of disdain she probably used for the question, "You don't kick dogs and children, do you?"

"No."

"Good!" Jill proceeded to fill the shopping cart with broccoli, cauliflower, and other items Seth normally didn't include on his grocery list. What the hell? He'd said he wasn't vegetarian, hadn't he?

She bypassed steaks and ground beef to toss packs of chicken and fish on top of the veggies, apparently at random. "Jill!" called a female voice. A woman passed by, nodding at Jill and Seth.

"Jill," Jill replied in turn, wearing what Seth supposed passed for a smile on her otherwise stony expression.

"Her name's Jill too?" Seth asked.

"No, idiot. Her name's not Jill. She is *a* jill. I'm *the Jill*, for now, thanks to your sorry ass."

What the hell? Seth was so confused, it took a moment before he noticed he was alone. Once more, he pushed the cart after a shopping mercenary, who now approached the dairy section.

"Jill," a man greeted, inclining his head, the gesture, like the woman's, appearing to be a mark of respect rather than friendship.

"Jack," Jill replied, nodding to another man a few feet away. "Jack."

"Let me guess—they aren't *named* Jack, they *are* jacks, right?"

Jill snorted, rolling her eyes. "Right. Their names are Hank and Buster. But they're jacks."

Not understanding but game to adopt community traditions, Seth inclined his head toward the next lady who passed. "Afternoon, Jill."

The woman glowered and hurried away.

"No, she's not a jill, dumbass," Jill said, accompanied by an overly dramatic sigh. "Didn't your grandma teach you anything?"

"Apparently not," Seth replied to her retreating back.

He gave thanks that Jill bypassed the fly rods and camo

sections of the store, and caught up with his abductor/personal shopper/tour guide at the checkout. A harried-looking woman beat them to the conveyor, huffing bangs out of her eyes. The source of her obvious frustration, three teenaged boys so close in appearance they must have been triplets, tussled with each other while wrangling groceries out of the cart. "Noogie!" one cried gleefully, capturing another in a headlock and scrubbing knuckles against a buzz-cut scalp.

"Wedgie!" shouted the unoccupied youth as he reached inside noogie-boy's board shorts and hauled his briefs' waistband up to his shoulder blades.

"Jill!" the weary mother pleaded, her shoulders slumped.

The Valkyrie snapped into drill-sergeant mode right before Seth's astonished eyes. "What the heck do you boys think you're doing?" she barked. "This ain't no playground! Now you better cut out the crap and help your mother with the groceries!"

"Ma'am, yes, ma'am." As if someone had flipped a switch, the teens stopped antagonizing each other and carefully piled foodstuffs on the conveyor, where a gum-chewing teenaged girl methodically swiped items across a scanner.

"Hey, Lis…," one of the boys began, leaning across the counter into the girl's personal space.

She whapped him with a can of peaches. "Oopsie! Didn't see you there." The girl's eyes danced with mischief while the other two brothers sniggered. Yeah, Seth remembered his high school days. Young love was never pretty.

Jill chatted with the mom, and her imposing presence kept the boys on their best behavior. Seeing his guide was occupied, when their turn came, Seth unloaded the cart, paid for his, or rather, Jill's purchases, and single-handedly hauled them out to the truck and loaded them into the bed of the single cab.

Jill emerged from the store and crossed the parking lot in impossibly long strides.

"Are the boys jacks too?" he asked, nodding toward the trio, who'd resumed their Three Stooges shenanigans a few cars away.

"No, too young. They're joeys. Get used to them; the Johnsons are your nearest neighbors." She hopped into her unlocked truck and turned the key in the ignition, forcing Seth to rush to the other side before Jill left him again.

He pulled out his phone, planning to check the happenings in civilization, but Jill snatched the gadget from his hand. "Hey!" he hollered. "Give that back!"

"No way in hell. We're in God's country. The least you can do is pay some respect and enjoy the view."

With nothing better to do, Seth found himself staring out the window, which whirred open to emit a blast of summer heat, along with the sweet fragrances of honeysuckle and magnolia, stirring memories to life. Mountain peaks played peekaboo through the trees.

Jill turned the truck down a tree-lined dirt road, and for one split second, Seth expected to spot a freckled redhead pedaling a bicycle down the rutted lane. The truck bumped and bounced over the worn track, Seth's suitcase and groceries taking a beating in the back. He tucked his laptop case closer to the seat with his legs, shielding its precious contents from harm, and prayed that at least one of his cameras survived the journey.

Finally they came to a clearing, the scrubby pines giving way to a pair of stately oaks, a bloom-loaded magnolia, and the occasional crepe myrtle, time-honored symbols of summer in the South. Time stood still. Then it reversed. Seth's heart dropped to his stomach. His inner child surfaced, his eyes fixed to the front door, hoping to find his parents rushing outside to greet him and ask about his day at school, or Auntie Irene welcoming him and his friend inside to sample a fresh batch of cookies. His heart lurched.

"I used to play with a redheaded kid named Dustin. Any chance he's still around?" Seth asked, until reality caught up with him and he realized that if he'd grown up, Dustin must have too. "Man, I mean. A man named Dustin. No, that's not right." Growing flustered, he blurted, "He was a kid then, a man now."

"Dustin Livingston?" Something in Jill's voice made Seth turn her way. Wariness shone from her bright-blue eyes. "What you asking about Doc for?" She narrowed those eyes slightly.

"We were friends. Played together when I lived here. I wondered if he's still around. How he's doing."

Jill parked the truck and opened the driver's door, hocking a loogie onto the dry red dirt. "If you were truly friends, you'd know, wouldn't you? Or did you just stop thinking about this place after you hightailed it to Chicago?" She pronounced the name "She-cargo."

Once more at a loss, and taking her well-aimed accusation like a knife to the gut, Seth crawled out of the truck, lugging his computer. Jill leaned against the hood, offering no help while Seth struggled with his luggage and shopping bags, leaving them piled on the steps. "Do you have a key?" he asked, waiting patiently by the front door.

Jill rolled her top lip in disgust. "This is Possum Kingdom, Georgia, city boy. We don't lock our doors." Without further ado, she leapt back into her Silverado and flung up a spray of red dirt back to the main road.

"Nice meeting you too!" Seth snarled. He proceeded to cough, choking on airborne dried Georgia clay. When he reached for his phone to vent his spleen via the Internet, he realized Jill hadn't returned his iPhone.

~

"How'd it go?" Dustin asked, tidying up after sending his last patient home for the day. "Did you get Seth settled in at Irene's?"

"He's dumb as a rock and won't last a week," Monica replied, "but it went okay."

Dustin heaved a weary sigh. He'd held out hope of Irene's nephew simply being a late bloomer who'd somehow magically grown up to be the Jack the passel needed, come to claim his rightful place. *Better Indian than Chief* was Dustin's personal motto. He'd fought long and hard not to be Irene's second-in-command, and only the threat of her appointing an ambitious lesser male had convinced him to step up to the plate on a *temporary* basis—four years ago when he'd graduated from med school.

Monica pulled him close, momentarily cutting off his air. The woman didn't know her own strength. "Don't worry, he won't challenge you. He's not truly one of us."

"He is and he isn't. His parents had him tested early. His dad passed on a dormant strain of the virus. They hoped it would become symptomatic during puberty. Since Irene never mentioned any frantic calls from Seth's grandmother, I'm supposing it didn't. Another infusion of fresh virus might help, but since he was raised outside the community, I don't picture Seth volunteering to let someone take a bite of his arm anytime soon." Dustin's heart clenched at the memory of a younger Seth, and how close they'd been.

"If he's not the type to stick around, with any luck, maybe he'll sell the house and have his ass back up north by month's end."

"That's what I'm afraid of." Their leader's only kin being a naive half-blood left the passel up for grabs. And though Dustin didn't want to assume the title of "the Jack" and the mantle of leadership any more than Monica wanted "the Jill," if he didn't announce his intention to assume control or name a successor within three full moons, there'd be war. Dustin's hands were full enough with his looking after the health of the townsfolk, and Monica often asserted that "I don't want to even be responsible for a houseplant, let alone the likes of Junior Timmerman." She often added, "Though if I had to choose between the two, I'd pick a rhododendron, they're smarter."

A chirping sounded from the vicinity of his assistant's back pocket. "What's that?" he asked.

Monica stepped away, fishing out a sleek, state-of-the-art phone. "You've talked about him endlessly over the years. I figured I'd give you a reason to go visit while he's here. Get those old warm-and-fuzzy feelings out of the way the moment you realize the childhood friend you loved grew up into a heart-less asshole." She placed the still-tweeting device in his hand and sauntered away, whistling "Dixie."

CHAPTER 4

ONCE the roar of the Silverado's engine died, Seth found himself surrounded by the kind of quiet that could never happen in the city. Funny thing was, even though he'd lived in Chicago for most of his life, something about the rural setting felt like home. Birds chirped from the magnolia trees, and unseen things in the grass twittered and whirred. No honking horns, no constant rumble of engines, no people calling to each other from a distance. A breeze stirred the uppermost branches of the oaks he clearly remembered climbing once upon a time. After his initial fear of being alone eased, Seth found himself breathing deeply of clean country air. Home. This was home.

He imagined his eight-year-old self running through the side yard, or swinging from the front porch swing. If he took a short walk, no doubt he'd find the barn through the trees behind the house. His auntie had raised chickens when he'd lived here with her and his parents—he'd often helped his dad collect eggs. A faint recollection came back of asking Auntie why his parents lived with her, to which she'd replied, "I'm teaching your mother... things." He'd supposed she meant cooking and cleaning, since his mother's attempt to make

Auntie's homemade buttermilk biscuits usually resulted in rock-hard, charred stones of burnt dough.

With a resigned sigh, Seth scooped up his grocery bags. He took a deep breath and tugged on the door, half expecting to find the lock secured, despite Jill's assurances to the contrary. The door opened and Seth stepped through, immediately thrust back in time.

A funky smell assailed his nostrils. How long had the place been shut up? A few weeks? It definitely needed a good airing out.

The sitting room appeared precisely as he remembered, with an old rocker in one corner and firewood stacked neatly by the hearth. The settee had been old even twenty years ago. An elaborately carved grandfather clock used to tick off the minutes in this room. Seth remembered pulling the chains every morning to wind it.

He placed his bags on the polished hardwood floor, then crossed the room in six long strides to open the door on the clock's belly. A fine layer of dust marred the glass. The place begged for a good cleaning. Seth's slovenly reputation came honestly; however, even he had limits. He wound and set the clock, the steady *tick tock* sending yet another wave of nostalgia washing over him.

After putting the clock to rights, Seth explored the room at leisure, longing filling his heart as he examined the old family photos displayed on the mantel, several featuring Seth and his parents. His chest constricted painfully as he gazed at the man and woman who lived on in his memories. What would life have been like if they hadn't died?

A few newer photos appeared out of place among the old. One was a group shot, with Auntie in the middle, surrounded by what most might assume to be a large family grouping. But other than himself, she didn't have any relatives that Seth knew of. The pain in his heart grew, along with guilt. He'd been too busy living his life to spare much thought for the woman who'd once sung him to sleep, and had comforted him after his parents' death. His grandmother hadn't liked Aunt Irene, though he'd never quite figured out why. After his grandmother's death, he'd simply put off reaching out or visiting, telling himself, "Soon." He'd receive a fabulous opportunity for a photo shoot, catch a cold, or simply forget, and postpone the trip once more. Now it was too late.

"I'm sorry, Aunt Irene," he told the empty room. Shivers darted up his spine at having broken the quiet.

He studied the picture, spotting Jill standing to his great-aunt's right, a handsome red-haired man on the left. Another picture snagged his attention: a newspaper clipping, encased in a frame, containing his Auntie Irene, Jill, and the man. Bringing it closer he read, "Local leaders Irene McDaniel, Monica Sims (*Ha! Her name isn't Jill!*), and Dr. Dustin Livingston." What kind of leaders they were or what they'd done to earn them a spot in the newspaper remained a mystery. Chamber of Commerce, maybe? Why the hell hadn't he made more of an effort to connect with his father's only relative? *I'm the last. And alone.*

Wait! Dr. Dustin Livingston? Dusty? Seth stared, trying to reconcile crooked front teeth, dimples, an unruly coppertop, and freckles with the handsome man staring at him from his aunt's picture frame. Well, damn. It hadn't truly sunk in when Jill called Dustin "Doc." Even as kids Dustin had talked about being a doctor or veterinarian some day, or "maybe both." Well, at least one of them had fulfilled their dreams. Seth's childhood dream had changed constantly, from fireman one day to astronaut the next, but he'd never figured on taking people's pictures for a living.

After a few more moments spent indulging in the past, Seth retrieved his laptop and suitcase, and proceeded to pick a room.

He came to his aunt's first. Once again, memories flooded

him. Each new room held a key to events from his history. He left his things in the hallway and tiptoed inside, much like he'd done when he'd been a kid. Everything appeared to be the same. Ignoring the aching in his heart, he focused on why he'd come. This wasn't a visit home; he'd come to settle his aunt's estate, and then hopefully return to Chicago in a few weeks. Not that he had anything left to go back to.

Loneliness setting in, he reached for his back pocket out of habit, determined to connect with his sixteen-hundred-strong cyber friends, most of whom didn't even know his real name. Damn! No phone. Silently cursing Monica, he vowed to catch up with his real world later, via laptop, and set about viewing the room and his aunt's possessions with his eyes, not his heart.

The elaborately carved four-poster bed, matching dresser, mirror, and chest would net a fortune in a Chicago antique shop, if shipping didn't prove cost-prohibitive. A genuine St. Lawrence clock sat in its place of honor on the mantel. Later he'd need to catalogue the lot, but for now he'd simply make a mental inventory, astounded that someone hadn't crept in and cleaned the place out since the house had stood unoccupied and unlocked for weeks.

Tiny cut-glass perfume bottles and other knickknacks took up space on Auntie's dresser, and the old rolltop desk in the corner had most likely cost a fortune when new. If he took his time, sold each piece separately for maximum profit, not only would he keep his inner capitalist happy for about a year, he could afford to concentrate on photographing only what he wanted to, leaving bride and groomzillas, preening divas, and noisy bar mitzvahs behind for good.

Only.... A wooden frame hung from the wall, holding a picture of Auntie's parents. On the nightstand, a porcelain Labrador kept watch over a folded pair of glasses. He picked up the trinket and ran a finger over a hairline crack, from when he'd once dropped the little dog. Auntie had scolded him soundly and swept up the pieces in a dustpan to toss out. Seth, maybe six at the time, had cried over the poor thing he'd broken. In the end, they'd sat down at the kitchen table and glued the dog's ear back on. And she'd kept it. A broken, dime-store figurine, and she'd kept it all these years. How could he possibly part with any of her treasures?

Unchanged from his memories, the same patchwork comforter covered his aunt's bed. Upon closer inspection, the intricate stitches and tiny triangles of pieced-together fabric appeared hand-sewn. Like he'd expected, the backing consisted of joined flour sacks. He recalled using a similar quilt to build his tent forts over the backs of chairs on rainy days, or to curl up with when the weather turned cool, his mother nestled against him, reading or making him sound out difficult words while his father built houses in the next town.

He detected a tiny hair clinging to his thumb and shook it off. Yes, he needed to give the place a good cleaning. But wait! Many such hairs covered the quilt. He ran his hand over the surface of the bed. A feather mattress? A quick jab of a finger proved his theory, but didn't explain the gray, wiry hairs. Had his aunt owned a cat? If so, had anyone been feeding the poor creature?

Poking his head into the hall, he called, "Here, kitty, kitty, kitty." No furry feline rallied to his cry. Oh well, he'd ask around later. Maybe visit the neighbors. Surely they'd be able to tell him if he'd inherited a pet.

Tired and disoriented, now wasn't the time to make decisions about what to do with his great-aunt's possessions. He made his way to his parents' former room. Leaning his head against the cool wooden panel of the door, he drew in a deep breath, steeling himself for what might wait inside. Photo albums? Clothing he might remember? Personal notes to each other? Reminders of the happy life they'd shared? Once more, he reached for his phone, needing a friend, even if only a cyber one, to enter the room with him. Again he came up empty-handed.

"Here goes nothing," he murmured as he turned the handle and eased the door open. Inside he found... a room. Blue-checked curtains that appeared homemade hung over the window; a chenille cover neatly encased the bed. Unlike Aunt Irene's room, every flat surface crowded to capacity, giving the place a lived-in ambiance, his parents' room lacked personalization.

A pair of chifforobes stood against one wall, in lieu of a closet. Their hinges squealed protest at Seth's invasion. Nothing. Not a sock or a scarf left to mark the lives of the two people who'd meant the most to him. A cane-backed chair sat next to the double bed. Emitting a depressed sigh, he sank down on the bed, wishing he'd made more of an effort to connect with his aunt. Of course, the distance between them wasn't entirely his fault. If his aunt wanted anything to do with him, she would have come to Chicago, right? Or at least called him once in a while. Only, would his grandmother and her iron-handed control have allowed a meeting? He recalled the argument between the two women the day of his parents' memorial service. For some reason Seth had never comprehended, Nana seemed to blame Auntie for his mother's death. Why? She'd stepped into the path of an oncoming car while crossing the road, and his father had died trying to save her. Seth, having spent many years in Chicago, and understanding the treacheries of traffic, was no stranger to vehicular tragedies.

He rose from the bed to continue exploring. Neither his auntie's nor his parents' room would do for a new base camp. Slowly he approached the room at the end of the hall like he'd done, usually at higher speeds, in his youth. The knob turned effortlessly, and the door emitted no wail of disuse like he'd expected. Seth gasped. The room looked exactly as he remembered. The bed was unmade, a forgotten toy truck lying on the quilt, as though he'd recently put it there. A thin layer of dust coated the surface of the dresser and the airplane models he'd once painstakingly assembled.

With a trembling finger, he touched the delicate propeller of a World War II fighter plane. The twenty-year-old plastic popped loose, falling to the floor. Apparently, his aunt hadn't forgotten him, preserving the room as some kind of shrine to his childhood.

At that moment, he hated himself for ever thinking about selling even one piece of his tenuous connection to his family. But what would he do with all this stuff?

Stumbling backward out of the open door, he staggered to the house's fourth bedroom, reserved for guests back in his youth, and placed his suitcase and laptop by the bed. This room held few enough memories. Perhaps sleeping here wouldn't prove too awkward. He briefly considered staying at a motel, before remembering he didn't have a car.

A few books and other items lay scattered around the room, possibly discarded by someone who'd spent the night. He ran his finger over the cover of *Watership Down*. Talking animals, huh? Shades of blue graced the windows and bed, the patchwork quilt sporting pieces of denim and chambray. A masculine room, but not overly so. Seth found he quite liked it.

With a bed to sleep in settled, he retraced his steps to where he'd left his groceries and hauled them to the kitchen. With any luck, the appliances weren't as ancient as the rest of the furnishings. The stench grew with each step he took. He stopped in his tracks just inside the door. *Oh my God! No wonder the place smelled like garbage!* Although the rest of the house wasn't pristine, a war had obviously been fought in the kitchen—and lost. Monica mentioned a get-together depleting the pantry, but instead of empty cabinets, Seth found empty cabinets *and* an unholy mess. Gnawed, sprouting potatoes lay haphazardly on the floor, and at least two chewed-open bread bags sat on the table, moldy former contents spread over the surface. Remnants of half-eaten sandwiches littered the floor. He wrinkled his nose at the disgusting odor and flung open the windows.

Once he'd regained his composure, he peered into the antique refrigerator. While the crisper drawer might have held rotting vegetables, at least they didn't appear to have been chewed by large rodents. What the hell? Had field rats invaded? Recalling the hair on his aunt's bedspread, he let out a relieved chuckle. If a pet cat had been left in the house alone, of course it would scavenge. But potatoes? Poor hungry kitty. And sandwiches? Perhaps a well-meaning neighbor had left them. Seth vowed to make it up to the poor beast if ever he found it. He'd always wanted a pet, but his stern grandmother couldn't abide anything coming to her house and leaving a mess to clean, barely making an exception for a grandson.

A quick search of the house turned up no food bowls or litter box. Maybe the culprit was an indoor/outdoor cat. Surely it'd come around when hungry.

After finding cleaner under the sink and brooms, dustpans, mops, and cloths hanging on the enclosed back porch or in the pantry, he tuned out the daunting big picture and focused on completing one task at a time.

He'd succeeded in making the room presentable when he noticed a rather large hole in a panel along the wall that he supposed hid the water heater, judging by the occasional burbling whenever he used the sink. The accidental entrance must be where the cat came in. Well, the critter would have to learn to use the front door like everyone else.

Tired and hungry, he stared into the refrigerator, trying to decide on something quick and easy for dinner. Spying a splattered notebook on the buffet, he ambled over and flipped open the cover to reveal page after page of handwritten recipes. "Aunt Bessie's Potato Salad" caught his eyes and made his mouth water. Searching through the refrigerator and cabinets, he found the potatoes he'd recently purchased, eggs, an onion, pickle relish, and everything else he needed to make one of his favorite childhood dishes. The results weren't as good as Aunt Irene's, but sometimes memories grew sweeter with time, right? Only, he didn't remember crunchy bits of eggshell in the original version.

While Seth mopped the floor and bagged up trash, the sun sank lower in the sky, painting the horizon with a brilliant wave of blues and golds, unlike any sunset in the city. He watched the display from the kitchen window until a yawn stretched his mouth wide.

It wouldn't do to have unexpected nocturnal visitors. He blocked the hole in the wall with an upturned footstool from the sitting room. Proper repairs must wait until after a good night's sleep.

He wolfed down a quick dinner of canned soup and a peanut butter and jelly sandwich, along with a few bites of his disappointing potato salad. Later, Seth unpacked his bags, took a tub bath since the one lone bathroom didn't have a shower or even a shower nozzle, and then crawled into bed, exhausted.

CHAPTER 5

DUSTIN made the rounds, flipping on lights and unbolting doors. A quick check through a plate-glass window showed Andy Coleman's Jeep Cherokee in the parking lot. If the world only knew how often patients checked into the doctor's office, only to be shuffled to the veterinarian's next door to hide their true nature. Sometimes maintaining secrecy wore Dustin out.

But the world wasn't ready for proof of shape-shifters existing for real, outside of movie theaters, even if some sectors considered them an open secret of sorts. Exhibit A? Seth's grandmother, who'd deemed Possum Kingdom a quarantine unit for a highly contagious disease.

The bell chimed over the door. Andy's scent washed over Dustin like a cool breeze. Once upon a time, the breeze had soothed him, despite the sharp bite of predator energy. Now the fox shifter's metamorphic ambiance chilled him to the bone.

"Reynard," he murmured the moment the tall blond entered the examining room Dustin prepared for the day. He dipped his head slightly in reverence for a leader, using the formal title.

"Jack." Andy mirrored the gesture. "How's it going? I haven't talked to you much since Irene's memorial service."

"I'm fine, thanks, and hanging in there. She was a good lady. I miss her." Even after two years, greeting Andy with formality and not a kiss—or more, given the time remaining before work—struck him as unnatural. Once upon a time, they'd lived for stolen moments spent together, no matter where or when. Ah, the memories they'd created in the room marked "Storage." Still, at the very least, he could use a hug.

"We all do. She brought stability to the town. I wonder how we'll manage without her."

Dustin heard the unasked questions, but had no clue how to answer. A few years ago, the resident fox skulk, only allowed into town by Irene's good graces, fell into chaos with the unexpected demise of its Reynard. The subsequent rise of a good-hearted but feeble replacement had led to a bloody and painful fight. Although Andy assuming control had brought the battle to a screeching halt, lives were lost, and sacrifices made. Dustin had been Andy's sacrifice. The foxes might have eventually accepted their bi-sexual leader's choice of a male mate, but not an interspecies one. They certainly hadn't approved of the former Reynard's coyote-shifter lover. A female vixen of good family had solidified their support of Andy. Dustin hated politics. He'd love to hate Andy's wife too, but she'd never given him a reason. Damn it.

Seeking to fill an awkward silence, he asked, "How's Roxanne?"

"Fine." Andy flashed a nervous grin. "Anxious to get it over with. The morning sickness is making her a little crazy. Look, have you got a minute? I'd like to talk to you."

Dustin braced himself for bad news. It wasn't like Andy to not simply blurt whatever came to mind. They'd once shared everything. *Stop it, Dustin. Move the fuck on!* "Sure," he pushed out around a lump of uncertainty lodged in his throat.

Andy rammed both hands into his pockets, rocking back on his heels while staring at the floor. "Roxie and I discussed it, and well, we want to name one of the boys after you."

A slap to the face couldn't have surprised Dustin more. "You want to name your son for me? Jesus, man, why don't you stick a knife in me? Did you ever bother to tell your wife what we once were to each other?"

Andy scrubbed a hand through his wheat-colored mane. Normally bound in a tail at the nape of his neck, now the long strands swished loose across his shoulders. Dustin used to love to run his fingers through the lush mass, using the silken strands to guide Andy's head. "I've told her, and she understands. She fooled around with girls in college—one of the reasons I found her attractive. Roxanne doesn't have a judgmental bone in her body." Andy took two long strides, placing him close enough to reach out and touch, but neither man did.

Essence of Andy invaded every pore, creating a steady ache in both Dustin's heart and groin. Andy raised his hand, then dropped it to his side again without actually making contact with Dustin's cheek. "We want to show our support of your claim. The skulk openly backing you will make critics think twice about a challenge."

Oh. Politics again. "I don't want this," Dustin wrenched out from between clenched teeth. "I never wanted it."

"And neither did I. You gotta believe me." Their eyes met. Old feelings lingered in Andy's baby blues, not that he'd act on them. His sense of honor was the thing Dustin had first noticed about the man, back when Andy's cousin had lost control of the skulk and wound up getting run out of town. Andy managed a shy half smile. "I never would have given you up if it wasn't necessary to prevent bloodshed."

"I don't know. We had our moments, but let's not kid ourselves. It wouldn't have lasted. You've always wanted a family, and your attraction is pretty evenly divided between

men and women. Your route isn't an option for me, not a satis-
fying one, anyway." While Dustin wouldn't mind a few kids,
whenever he visualized his future, it didn't include a wife. A
husband, maybe, but not a wife.

"Yeah, that much I'll give you. But, damn, wasn't it good
while it lasted?" Andy leaned down to peer into Dustin's eyes, a
mischievous smile playing across his lips, which coaxed a laugh
out of Dustin.

"Even if I do take over, it won't be permanent. Sooner or
later, succession will have to be arranged. I'll have to pass the
torch eventually."

"Pick someone, or adopt a child."

"I'm not sure the passel would accept someone who wasn't
blood kin." This time Andy did lightly stroke Dustin's cheek
with a callused hand. Dustin leaned into the contact, sighing.

"If you can fill Irene's shoes, nobody, and I mean nobody,
will back anyone else's claim. Irene naming you personally for
the honor holds a lot of weight." Andy jabbed a finger at
Dustin's chest. "The old lady chose you for a reason."

Which didn't make the unwanted burden any lighter.
Dustin's drive not to disappoint Irene and his need to keep
peace in the town plagued his every waking moment. "Yeah,
you're right."

"The skulk is behind you. Every last one of us."

Reminded of how their exchange started, Dustin asked, "Is
showing your support the only reason you want to name your
kit after me?"

Crimson colored Andy's tanned cheeks. "Um… that, and it
rhymes with 'Justin', the other twin."

They shared a laugh, followed by a huffed, "Women!" from
them both. They stood quietly for some time, soaking up each
other's warmth. The moment had come and gone for them.
Dustin held no regrets, though he carried a tiny bit of residual
love in his heart for the Reynard. They'd burned brightly and

hot, but for Andy, Dustin had been a passing fancy and a way for the out-of-town Reynard to gain neighborhood acceptance.

"Thanks, man," Dustin murmured, eyes fixated on Andy's lips.

The tip of Andy's tongue snaked out of his mouth, leaving his lips moist and glistening. Dustin dropped his gaze, knowing better than to entertain dangerous thoughts. "Don't mention it."

He closed his eyes against the pain of Andy's departure, only opening them again upon the bell chiming at his exit. Dustin let out the breath he'd been holding. Close, very close.

And yet still so far away.

Seth fired up his laptop, eager for news for the outside world. He clicked on one of his favorite sites, only to receive the message, "You are not connected to the Internet." What the fuck? Hadn't people in this godforsaken corner of the country heard of Wi-Max?

He clicked the connectivity icon at the corner of his screen and found three networks nearby, all locked. What the hell? People didn't lock their doors here, but they protected their internet?

A man on a mission, he charged through the house, seeking a computer, phone, or any other portal to the world outside. He found a black dial phone (they still made those?) on a small table against the dining room wall. *Why in the hell would anyone put it there?* Oh well, he didn't plan on staying long anyway.

His search also turned up a set of car keys, and a little further reconnoitering revealed a pickup truck in the barn, possibly even older and more dilapidated than Monica's old beater. A valid tag adorned its dented bumper, and the rusting behemoth contained a full tank of gas. Armed with a shopping list and his laptop, Seth took off in the general direction of town. Surely a bookstore or coffee shop would offer Internet connection, right?

It took him driving completely through town, coming to farmland, and glimpsing the "Welcome to Possum Kingdom" sign in his rearview mirror to realize he'd missed his target. He attempted an illegal U-turn, but his aunt's truck forced him to execute a back and forth seven-point turn. While an arrestable offense in some parts of the country, not a single soul wandered by to witness his law breaking, or deep embarrassment, though a sad-eyed spotted cow wished him good morning... or asked for food, whatever the hell her mournful "Moo!" meant.

He returned to the handful of buildings comprising Possum Kingdom, driving more slowly this time, searching for a likely Internet hotspot, a hardware store, or a six-foot Valkyrie to wrestle to the ground so he could recover his iPhone. Several older structures tickled vague memories from his childhood, but two apparently new buildings caught his eye, one bearing a sign that read, "Andrew Coleman, DVM," and another matching sign: "Dustin Livingston, MD." The two buildings connected in the back.

A vet and a medical doctor side by side? Well, he supposed it made sense in a town this size, if the few sparse buildings deserved the title of "town." But why would so small a town need its own doctor and vet? Ahhh... farming community. Must be a lot of sick animals and ailing farm hands 'round about these parts.

An older model mobile home bore a single sign with two inscriptions: "Public Library" and "US Post Office."

The Valkyrie's truck sat outside the doctor's office. Seth whipped in, or attempted to, given the lack of power steering, screeching to a halt near the front door. The sign caught his eye again, momentarily distracting him from his errand to retrieve his phone. Dusty, a doctor. He wondered what changes the years brought with them, although the picture on his Auntie's mantel told the tale of angular planes maturing into handsome features. If the photo was any indication, Dustin had finally grown into his unfortunately large ears.

Dusty. After all these years he'd finally see Dusty again.

Breathing deeply to calm his suddenly shaky nerves, Seth switched off the truck and climbed down. How had his aunt driven the thing, or gotten in and out, with the stump-jumper tires elevating the cab to impossible heights? He tried to secure the vehicle, but gave up after finding the locks to be missing. Unwilling to leave any valuables unprotected, he grabbed up his computer case and strode into the doctor's office with a take-no-prisoners attitude despite the anticipation eating at him. Would Dustin remember him? Recalling some less than stellar moments from his awkward younger days, he amended the question to, *"Do I want Dustin to remember me?"*

An overhead bell alerted a young woman at the counter to Seth's presence, and no sooner had he crossed the threshold than an indescribable sensation swept through him, taking him back in time and bringing to mind freckles and red hair. *What the hell was that?*

"May I help you, sir?" the woman asked, gazing up from a computer screen.

Seth opened his mouth to ask for Monica, but out tumbled, "I'd like to speak with Dr. Livingston, if he has a moment," only then realizing the irony in a childhood buddy bearing the moniker of "Dr. Livingston." How many times had folks chuckled while asking Dusty, "Dr. Livingston, I presume?"

Dropping her eyes to Seth's laptop case and then raising them once again to his face, the woman's welcoming demeanor chilled about seventy degrees. "We don't allow solicitation here. If you'd like to make an appointment, however...."

Following her gaze to his laptop, Seth quickly stammered,

"Oh... oh no. You misunderstand. I'm not selling anything. I'd just like to—"

Anything else he might have said evaporated into thin air, every single brain cell simultaneously declaring a strike. While some of his more catty acquaintances might not have agreed, the man rounding the corner, clad in light-blue scrubs, was a perfect specimen. Not too tall, not too short, not skinny, not fat, and with gorgeous auburn locks slicked back from his forehead, sweeping his collar in back. Clear green eyes locked with Seth's, and for one brief moment in time, he swore no one existed in the universe except the two of them.

The handsome vision broke the spell. "Tiffany, Mrs. Riley needs to reschedule her appointment. Would you check what we have open for next Thursday and give her a call?"

"Sure, Doctor," the lady replied, returning her attention to her computer.

"May I help you?" the doctor asked, the faint hint of a smile turning up his full lips.

Once again Seth detected a magnetic pull, and he wouldn't have been a bit surprised to see lightning crackling between them. "Dusty?" he ventured, closing his mouth quickly lest Dustin notice the drool.

The faint smile blossomed and grew, revealing slightly crooked front teeth. The added touch of dimples and freckles gave the doctor a distinctive little-boy charm.

"Seth?" Dustin's eyes went wide. For a moment, he appeared to be sniffing the air, the gesture quickly changing to a good nose scratch.

Silence filled the space between them for an extended moment. Oh crap! Dustin remembered him, but what if he'd no desire to see or talk to Seth? *Think, Seth, Think!*

After enough time for Seth to break out into a cold sweat, Dustin broke the silence. "I'm sorry about your aunt."

Reminded of why he'd returned to Possum Kingdom,

many years too late, Seth heaved out a sigh. "Yes, and I'm heartbroken for not being here for her, and not having been located until after her service."

"It was a wonderful service," Dustin assured him. "The whole town turned out. Your aunt was a great lady, well-loved." Was that a dig about Seth's neglect for not attending the funeral? He hadn't even known his aunt had passed away until a few days ago. "Anyway," Dustin continued, "I haven't seen you in ages. How've you been?"

Seth ran a hand up the back of his neck. Talking to this man shouldn't be so awkward. Hell, they shared all their secrets as children.

Twenty years ago.

"Okay, I suppose. It's kind of weird being back here. But look at you! You became a doctor. Congratulations!"

The rush of blood to Dustin's cheeks blended his freckles into a solid mass. "It's nothing. I managed to make it through eight years of college without getting kicked out."

"No, doing exactly what you want to do is quite an accomplishment. You always used to say you wanted to be a doctor or a vet...."

"... or both," they chorused and then shared a chuckle.

"Occasionally a dream comes true." Dustin's smile turned shy.

"Doctor?" The woman at the front desk interrupted their staring contest. "Two o'clock was open on Thursday. I've already called Mrs. Riley."

"Thank you, Tiffany." Dustin turned back to Seth. "Now, what can I do for you, Seth?"

Shaken that he'd forgotten his reason for visiting, he managed to say, "Jill, err... A woman named Monica gave me a ride yesterday. She still has my iPhone. I saw her truck parked outside."

"Ahhh." The warm energy seemed to flow back into

Dustin, leaving Seth bereft. "She's my assistant, but she's next door at the moment. Your phone's on my desk. If you'll excuse me, I'll go get it."

He'd been dismissed? What had Seth done to receive the sudden cold shoulder? "Have dinner with me while I'm in town? Catch up on old times. Maybe tell me more about Aunt Irene. You were pretty friendly with my aunt, right?"

The stiff set of Dustin's shoulders melted slightly to a less defensive posture. "How long are you planning to stay?"

"Not long. Just long enough to get her things in order."

All the sunshine left the room with Dustin's dejected, "You're not staying."

A little boy, peddling a bike like mad, trying to keep Seth from leaving. Back then he'd had no choice. Now that he did, he'd leave again. Seth averted his eyes. "No. My life's in Chicago."

"Oh." Dustin paused, his weak not-quite-a-smile spreading across his face but not reaching his eyes. "Then I reckon we'd better make it soon. I'll go get your phone."

Dustin returned a few moments later and handed over Seth's lifeline, along with a neon orange Post-it note. "Here's my number. Why don't you give me a call when you want to get together? I'd love to chat some more, but my next appointment is due any minute."

Seth watched Dustin round the corner.

At the last moment, Dustin threw a shy, backward glance over his shoulder.

Well, well, well. Little Seth McDaniel, all grown up, and he grew up well too. Dustin closed his eyes, took a deep breath, and tried to lose the memory of how damned good the man smelled. The scent of passel enveloped Seth like a fine-fitting jacket, and Dustin bet Seth hadn't a clue that a potent strain of the changeling virus lay dormant inside his body. Had it shown itself? Was the town's secret no longer a secret to the Chicagoan? No, it couldn't have. He reeked of passel, but the distinctive scent of mature jack didn't cling to him.

Seth's open appraisal also spoke volumes. Dustin hadn't been so flagrantly undressed with eyes since he'd marched in a Gay Pride parade in Atlanta wearing only western boots, a Stetson, and a thong after losing a bet. He'd never expected such regard from his childhood friend. Interesting. Very interesting. And also too much a study in futility to even dwell on.

He's not staying. Dustin gripped the edge of an examining table, breathing slowly in and out, trying to reel in his raging lust. He reached one hand down and rearranged his cramped cock. He'd become aroused by the mere scent of someone in the past, but had never sprouted wood in ten seconds flat. The fact Seth was the one whose presence electrified each nerve ending in his body was magnified by the fact Dustin hadn't seen the man in twenty years. The immediate recognition was primal, instinctual, like how he'd somehow *known* Seth's hiding places while playing hide-and-seek as kids. Only now the magnetism was even stronger. He wanted to bend Seth over the exam table, rip his pants off, and bury himself deep inside. The sheer intensity of his hunger frightened him, for he didn't simply want to fuck Seth—he wanted to possess the man.

Was it a territorial compulsion? Dustin would have to ask Andy, who focused more on the town's animalistic side than Dustin. Whatever the cause of his craving, promise of dinner or no promise, he needed to avoid Seth McDaniel like the plague. Any association beyond friendship couldn't possibly end well. Sooner or later, Seth would go back to Chicago, hopefully being none the wiser about the town's little secret.

CHAPTER 6

Ensconced in his aunt's pickup truck, Seth opened the browser on his phone, eager to touch base with life outside of Georgia. His elation at seeing Dustin again crashed and burned in the wake of an outpouring of well wishes for Michael's engagement. Depression turned to anger. How dare they? Michael had practically waltzed from Seth's bed to another man's arms, and they labeled Michael's double-dealing "sweet" and "romantic"? Oh hell no! Just when Seth was ready to hit "send" on a scathing rebuttal, his screen flashed and went out. He punched the power button. Nothing. Crap. Dead battery. Tossing the useless phone on the seat beside him, he turned the engine and backed away from the building. Damn! Why hadn't he asked Dustin for directions to the nearest hardware store?

About to go back inside the office, Seth spotted a sign for Jimmy's Feed and Seed down the street. The business appeared a touch run-down, with weathered boards in need of paint and a rusted tin roof, but if they didn't sell what he needed, they might suggest someplace else.

"Good morning, stranger." A thirtyish man in faded blue

jeans and tennis shoes stepped out from a loading bay. "What can I help you with?" He turned his head to the side, expelling a mouthful of what appeared to be tobacco juice.

"Do you carry plywood?"

"Sure do. How big a sheet you need?"

Seth scratched his head. He never even considered measuring, but had no intention of spending another night in a house with a hole in the wall. "Let me take a look at what you have."

The man stepped aside, allowing Seth to enter the store. Was it Seth's imagination, or did the guy sniff him in passing? The man nodded toward the truck. "You're Irene McDaniel's nephew, ain't ya?"

"Great-nephew, yes. Did you know her?"

The guy cackled. "Everybody in town know'd Ms. Irene. Come on back here, and let's see if we got what ya need." After spitting another carefully aimed stream out the door, the man turned and led Seth through rows of farm implements and loose seeds, ready for bagging. "Too bad about the old lady. You gonna pick up where she left off?"

"No. I'm here to settle her estate and head back home."

Suddenly the man turned around, nose to nose with Seth. His voice dropped to a mere whisper. "You could do a whole lot worse than putting down roots here. There's somebody I'm betting would flat out love to meet ya. Why, together, you and my uncle'd run this whole joint."

"Huh?" Seth took a quick step back.

"And don't you worry none about people giving you no trouble for being gay or nothing. Uncle Junior, well, he likes someone who can give as good as they get in the bedroom, if you get my drift. Folks done learnt not to say nothing against Junior."

Seth took another step back. "How…?"

A greasy smile appeared on the man's face. "You forget where you are. Ain't no secrets in this here town."

"What the fuck?"

"I'll be seeing you again, come next full moon." After a final leer and a wink, the man returned to business. "Now, you need plywood, right?"

The exchange unnerved Seth, sending "Run! Run!" messages to his brain. He forgot about locating Internet access. Instead, he hauled ass back to the farmhouse, where he plugged in his phone and rummaged through the kitchen cabinets for a hasty lunch. Didn't Monica believe in quick and easy? Not a single heat-and-eat meal. But damn if Seth intended to head back into town and risk getting sniffed again. What the fuck was wrong with these people? And damn if he'd understood half of what the guy at the Feed and Seed had said, and it had nothing to do with a heavy accent. It was like these people spoke their own language.

A can of soup later, he searched through drawers and closets, finally locating a rusted toolbox. His patch job wasn't pretty, but at least it might keep animals out of the house until he arranged something better. He'd hoped to simply put the whole estate on the market and head home, but he'd already figured on a new paint job, a floor refinish, and new appliances to get the place in sellable condition. An antique store might take the fridge, but no one would even consider buying a house without a dishwasher. Hell, no wonder Monica bought mostly cookable food—she probably knew there was no microwave. Only two burners on the stove heated, but the oven seemed to work fine. Now if only Seth cooked.

He stared at the scarred kitchen table, picturing his mother, father, Aunt Irene, and, more often than not, Dusty, sitting down for Sunday dinner. There'd been fried chicken, mashed potatoes and gravy, fried okra, stewed tomatoes, and hot buttermilk biscuits. The soup he ate didn't even make a proper appetizer. His mouth watered at the memory of Aunt Irene's macaroni pie. And she'd always had cake or pie for dessert. His gaze wandered to the glass cake plate and cover on the buffet, normally the domain of red velvet, coconut, or some other kind of made-from-scratch masterpiece. He couldn't sell a hand-me-down heirloom, could he? But what use would he ever have for a cake plate?

He wandered into the sitting room, where an ancient console TV took up way too much space, but wasn't hooked up to cable or satellite. How the hell had his aunt survived without network programming?

His phone now somewhat charged, Seth plopped down on the settee, but couldn't get a signal. With no TV, no Internet, and no cell phone, he gave up and went to bed out of boredom at eight thirty.

Once in bed, one thought rose foremost in his mind. Dusty Livingston. After all these years. Seth recalled hiding out with him in a tent fort, whispering secrets. Dustin standing up for him when classmates shouted taunts of "outsider" and "half blood," whatever the hell that meant. "Dusty and Seth, the terrible twosome," a Sunday school teacher once named them.

Damn, but the boy had grown into a fine man. Something about him called to Seth. Maybe his confident stance, the intelligence burning in his eyes, or the lopsided grin that made him appear so approachable. He definitely presented a startling contrast to Seth's self-serving acquaintances back home, or the boyfriend who'd dropped him like a hot rock.

Evicting his fickle ex-lover from his mind, Seth concentrated on the doctor. Firm pecs appeared to be hiding beneath Dusty's cotton scrubs, and the lightweight material had done nothing to conceal a well-formed backside.

He breathed deeply, trying to recapture the scent of Dustin's cologne, or was the intoxicating fragrance the man's natural smell—spicy and sweet with an underlying earthiness? Seth's cock swelled. In his mind's eye, he worked his way up Dusty's sides, sliding eager fingers over strong pecs while burying his nose in the crook of the doctor's neck. Seth's hips snapped up almost of their own volition, sliding his erection to nestle between two tempting mounds of flesh in his imagination.

Seth drew his fingers over his chest, stopping to caress a nipple to full hardness, while he snaked his other hand down to slide beneath the elastic of his boxers. He encircled rigid flesh, slowly pumping up and down before bringing the fingers of his other hand to his mouth to add a bit of lubrication before sliding them down past his balls.

Seth arched his back, thrusting into his fist while creating erotic images involving the good doctor and an examination table. Those stirrup thingies might come in handy, and he imagined lying flat on his back, legs spread, while Dustin stood ready at the end of the table. Seth paused to remove his boxers and fling them to the floor, then resumed stroking, applying moistened fingers to his hole.

Dusty's cock would be long and hard, rising from a bed of copper curls. He'd push in, slowly, green eyes boring into Seth's. Breath caught in Seth's throat and he moved his hand faster to the make-believe pressure of Dustin's entry into his body.

"Oh God!" Barreling toward the finish line and picking up speed, Seth rocked back and forth between the fist in front of him and the finger behind.

Fuck! Fuck! Fuck! He sailed on past the point of no return, body bowing, orgasm slamming into him with the force of a runaway freight train. His grip grew slippery, but still he pumped, come erupting from him in rhythmic spurts. He moaned, thrashing on the bed, aftershocks shuddering through him, too numerous to count.

"That one scored at least a seven on the Richter scale," he muttered, rolling away from the damp sheets to a dry spot and promptly falling asleep.

Dustin lay awake, watching TV with the sound off and trying to let go of the whirlwind of emotions he'd experienced during the day. Seth McDaniel—someone he'd despaired of ever seeing again—in the flesh. He'd often pleaded with Irene to keep contact with her next of kin "just in case Seth gets lonely up there," a mere half-truth. In reality, each week that went by without a letter had driven a spike deeper into Dustin's heart. Every time he'd tried to call, Seth's grandmother insisted Seth wasn't home, even on the occasions when he'd heard his best friend's voice in the background.

Had Seth not wanted to talk to him? Given how close they'd been, Dustin found it hard to believe, and Seth had certainly seemed friendly enough today, if a little reserved. *He came for his phone, numb nuts,* Dustin's conscience chided. Oddly enough, his conscience sounded exactly like Monica, who'd often berated the man she'd never even met for deserting his aunt and the town where he was, in essence, a prince.

Had Dustin made a mistake in sending Monica to pick Seth up? He should have gone himself, but couldn't get away from his practice, and Monica promised to be on her best behavior. But the sister he'd chosen for himself when nature didn't provide one possessed a mind of her own, and "best behavior" could be interpreted anywhere from "I didn't kill him" to "we went out for tea and scones."

Dustin heaved a sigh. Those thoughts weren't getting him anywhere. Seth had come back, announced his intentions to leave again, and would soon be gone. He hadn't come to reconnect and had his own life somewhere else. The proverbial light-bulb came on, and Dustin dashed up the stairs of his log A-frame to what used to be his childhood bedroom, now converted into an office, fired up his computer, and searched for the site Irene had mentioned.

After a few missteps, he finally located Seth McDaniel's profile. Feeling a bit voyeuristic, but rationalizing that Seth wouldn't have created the profile if he didn't want people to read it, Dustin studied the "about me" blurb. Profession: photographer. Status: single. Relief surged through Dustin that he couldn't rightly explain.

He clicked on "Photos" and select an album entitled "Random." His mouth dropped open. Seth took these? The images depicted what must have been older buildings in Chicago. Church spires, an interesting but ill-kept doorway, an aged wall, orange-and-red crumbling brick.

An album marked "Friends" was nearly empty, though Seth's profile stated he had more than a thousand. Did Seth actually know a thousand people? Personally?

A stunning fair-haired hunk identified as "Michael" drew Dustin's attention. Seated with Seth at a restaurant, the blond stared at the camera while Seth's eyes focused on Michael.

Guilt eating at him didn't stop Dustin from reading a few comments from Seth's page, mostly about "Michael" and "marriage." Dustin's heart skipped a beat until he realized Michael wasn't marrying Seth.

His heart broke in two when he found a recent post made by Seth. "My aunt died. I always planned to one day visit her again, but now it's too late." Not a damned soul responded. Over one thousand "friends," and no one offered any sympathy? It took a half hour to figure out how to create an anonymous profile and add Seth with the "Friend" option. Damn. Seth had to accept the offer of friendship. Having never felt the need to spend much time on such sites, only when he tried anyway did Dustin realize he didn't have to create a profile to comment on Seth's post. After ruminating on the right thing to say, he typed in a reply to what he considered a plea for support. He wrote, *"I understand your pain, man, and am right here with you."*

He studied a few more pictures of Seth. Were they self-portraits? In each and every one, Seth appeared somber, nearly depressed, and definitely lonely. Dustin raised his fingertips to the computer screen, lightly brushing them over Seth's forlorn face. "Oh, Seth, life wasn't as good to you as I imagined, was it?"

When at last he made his way back to bed, he closed his eyes, only to find the lonely image embedded on his lids.

The next day, Dustin's resolve to maintain distance gave way and he made a trip to Irene's house "just to be neighborly." He pulled into the yard to discover Seth struggling with a stepladder. "Here, let me help you," Dustin said, climbing out of the truck in time to steady the base for Seth.

"Thanks. A piece of tin up there was flapping in the wind last night."

His only intention was to hold the ladder, eyes focused overhead on the errant tin, but Dustin accidentally placed his hand square on Seth's nicely rounded butt. Despite a layer of denim between Dustin's hand and Seth's skin, Seth might as well have been naked. Dustin jerked his hand away. "Oh my God! I'm sorry."

Seth let out a nervous-sounding chuckle. "'S okay. Been awhile since I've been publicly groped." He slowly ascended the ladder, with Dustin's gaze glued to the twin mounds of flesh undulating under the worn seat of a pair of Levi's.

A few melodic thumps sounded against the metal roof, and a memory returned of a much younger Seth clambering up probably the same ladder, effectively dousing the flames of Dustin's libido. The skinny, awkward Seth of yesteryear had definitely filled out, though he probably wasn't most folks' idea of gorgeous, and height wise, he topped Dustin's own five foot seven by two inches, at most.

Brushing strands of chestnut hair away from his face, Seth didn't visibly display any known style, sporting a more natural look. Brown eyes speckled with flecks of gold blinked down from a face that either lived in sunscreen or never saw the sun, and a slight hint of pudge pooched over his belt. This boy really needed to get outside and chop some wood. From the top of his head down to his worn tennis shoes, Seth McDaniel seemed designed by nature to blend in, not stand out.

"Does this remind you of anything?" Dustin asked.

"Hmm?"

Dustin couldn't suppress a grin. "Remember when we climbed up on the roof and your aunt came running out and caught us?" He pictured Irene storming out of the kitchen door, apron flapping.

Seth climbed down the ladder, chuckling. "She almost wore a flyswatter out on our backsides. I never figured out how she always managed to show up when we were getting into stuff we weren't supposed to."

Dustin knew, but wasn't sharing. Scent. It was all in the scent. He changed the subject instead. "How're the repairs coming?"

"Not bad, but I'm having a hard time finding a contractor in these parts—once I finally located the phone. Can't get a signal out here on my cell."

"It's summer. Contractors stay busy in the summer."

"Yeah. I figured as much. I made arrangements for someone else to take over some assignments for me back home so I can stay longer."

"Assignments? What kind of assignments?"

"I have a photography studio in Chicago. Weddings and other social functions, mostly, the occasional fashion or maga-zine shoot. I do a little freelance work too, for small press publi-cations." A note of pride crept into Seth's words.

"Stay longer" sounded risky. Regardless of Irene's wishes, Dustin couldn't imagine Seth wanting anything to do with a lifestyle so radically different from the way he'd been raised, and it took a hearty soul to deal with the odd assortment of personalities that made up the passel. The longer Seth stayed the more likely he'd be to stumble over the family secrets, if he hadn't uncovered them already. Asking without directly *asking* could prove tricky.

Even among townsfolk, blurting, "Ever feel a little furry?" was considered rude, for some carriers never fully transformed, and walking around in human form with a possum tail one night a month wasn't cause for boasting. However, those individuals did make good perimeter guards, helping to ensure the safety of the passel when they were at their most vulnerable.

"Dusty, let me ask you something."

"Sure. Anything." Folks around there learned to lie convincingly from an early age.

"Did Aunt Irene have a cat or a dog?"

Certainly not a question Dustin expected. "Not in a few years. Why?"

"Well…." A lovely hint of pink tinged Seth's cheeks. "I've found animal hair everywhere inside. And the day I first arrived, it looked like some poor creature got stuck in the kitchen and tore the place apart, foraging for food."

"You don't say." Hmm… Time for a little heart-to-heart talk with the Johnson boys, who'd agreed to clean up the place after the last full moon. And he supposed the missing-pet theory answered the "does he or does he not know?" question.

Out of the blue, Seth blurted, "Damn but I've missed you. While in Chicago, the memories faded, but being here, seeing you again, I remember the good times and the trouble we got into. We wore my parents ragged."

The reference to Seth's parents effectively chilled the atmosphere. Dustin desperately grasped at straws to bring the easy exchange back. The last thing he wanted to do was make Seth uncomfortable. Being back must be weird enough for the poor guy without reminders of why he'd left. "Feel like taking a walk?"

"Huh?"

"Well, you were only eight when you left here. I bet you don't even remember how big this place is. Wanna go check out some cool places where we used to play?"

Seth studied him with his dark eyes, and Dustin couldn't fathom why he'd made the offer. He'd done what he'd set out to do: find out if Seth was okay and get a general idea of when he might be leaving. The smart thing to do would be hop in his truck and leave. Dustin wasn't feeling particularly smart at the moment.

Seth took his time to answer. "I suppose the house won't go anywhere while I'm gone."

Tension melted off Dustin. "Well, let's go." *The less time spent together the better!* his self-preservation mentioned. *Get some distance before an accidental touch turns to a giant zap!* He effectively bound and gagged his nagging inner voice.

The sun beat down, turning the broom sage into a radiant mass of gold. A gentle breeze kept the day from being miserably hot. Out of long habit, Dustin opened the old metal gate, having learned long ago the right way to hold the rusted-out relic so it didn't scrape the ground. Of course, whenever he came here, he usually wore a body small enough to simply crawl underneath.

They followed an old cow path behind the house and down to a creek, the sound of water rushing over rocks growing louder by the minute.

Seth's face lit up. "We used to play soldiers here. We built a log fort beneath the hill over there." He indicated the direction with a nod.

Ah, those were good days, when their biggest cares were not getting caught playing when they were supposed to be doing chores. "We sure did. And we hunted arrowheads under the rocks in the creek."

"I remember the big one you dug out of the bank down by the waterfall. Used to keep it in your pocket. Called it your lucky arrowhead."

Dusty chuckled, revisiting happy days gone by. "I remember. Can't rightly recall what I did with it, though." As clear as if it'd been yesterday, he recalled slipping the quartz fragment into his friend's hand, but he held back on saying so. Would it make Seth uncomfortable to know that the two things Dustin had prized the most had left for Chicago the next day?

"You gave it to me. The day before my grandmother took me away." Seth brought his eyes up from studying the creek bank. A world of pain stared out from their unfathomable depths. "Nana found it and threw it away. Said I didn't need any reminders of this place."

Didn't need reminders? What was the woman's problem? How could Dustin possibly answer without belittling Seth's grandmother? "I'm sorry."

Seth turned away again. "I never had another friend like you. When I first left, I cried and cried to come home. Nana wouldn't listen. Said this place was evil and I should be glad she got me out in time. I never understood why she hated this place, except for maybe being a city girl born and raised. With her tea parties and bridge clubs, she didn't have much use for hay fields and wide-open spaces."

"I'm sure you made other friends." Nausea took root in Dustin's stomach as he imagined what kind of life and friendships Seth must have in Chicago. Seth had listed "single" on his Internet profile, but not everyone's idea of single meant the same thing. Did Seth have a boyfriend? Someone waiting for him back home? The hot blond pictured on Seth's site was a former lover, right? Or maybe Seth liked to keep his options open, had grown into one of those men who liked variety and considered monogamy a bad word.

Personally, Dustin hoped to settle down one day, *if* he ever found someone who met his ever-increasing needs in a partner. Like, "Doesn't mind when I hang with a whole bunch of fuzzy friends every full moon." While the passel included several gay members, they'd either paired up by now or preferred a solitary life. And if the mantle of leadership fell to Dustin on a permanent basis, bringing in an outsider would only create discord. Either way, he'd end up screwed. Or rather, not screwed, and the possibility lessened with each added obligation thrust upon his shoulders. He'd only dated a handful of times since he and Andy went their separate ways.

"Not really. My grandmother was terrified of something happening to me and didn't let me go to other kids' houses to play. She was persnickety about her apartment and never wanted me bring anyone home either. You're the last friend I spent the night with."

For a formerly outgoing child, an upbringing isolated from other kids must have been hell. Dustin viewed Seth with new eyes. "Sounds lonely."

Seth shrugged, focusing his attention on a seedling pine peeking up from a layer of fallen needles. "I thought about this place a lot. You. Auntie. After a while, the memories weren't doing me any good anymore and I gave them up, tried to be what Nana wanted me to be." Seth chuckled mirthlessly. "Listen to me dumping on you. We came down here to remember good times, not for you to become my shrink." His cheeks stretched into the semblance of happiness, but his eyes, when they lifted enough to make contact, carried pain, deep and cutting. "C'mon, let's go find the hill we used to roll down." Off he trotted, but not before Dustin noticed dampness on Seth's cheeks.

They picked their way across the creek and up the bank,

Seth stumbling and nearly falling. Dustin grabbed his arm just in time, hauling him to dry ground and smack against Dustin's chest. Their eyes met and held, and Dustin found himself unable to look away. The chirping birds hushed, as did the babbling of water and the occasional bullfrog. Dustin didn't know who moved first, or if Seth would be receptive, but one minute they stood apart, the next they melded, parting their lips, slipping their tongues inside each other's mouths. Deep, fiery, breathtaking. Seth pulled away first. "I'm sorry...," he began.

"Don't be." Heart pounding, Dustin pulled Seth close again. Please let the unexpected kiss not turn out to be a fluke. The moment their lips touched every doubt faded, the kiss sweet, unhurried, sending an electric current straight to Dustin's groin.

Seth moaned, the evidence of his own arousal pressing against Dustin's leg. This time Dustin withdrew. Seth claimed he didn't belong here anymore, and would soon be leaving. Too much vied for the hours of Dustin's days without adding a short-term fling. Especially not with someone who'd meant to him what Seth had. Hell, he didn't even know who Seth was now. The guy might be an ax murderer, though Dustin's instincts told him otherwise. Nonetheless, the last thing Dustin wanted was another person to turn him away because he didn't fit conveniently into their life. *Love me, love my passel.*

"If...." Seth dropped his gaze, then immediately brought it back up again to lock onto Dustin's. His Adam's apple bobbed with a hard swallow. Voice barely a whisper, he said, "If you wanted to lay me down right here, I'd let you." For a moment temptation reared its persuasive head, until Seth added, "It's been a while."

The quietly spoken words served better than a bucket of ice water dumped down Dustin's back to cool his libido. While Seth might be lonely and temptation personified, Dustin had no intention of being somebody's easy fuck because *It's been a while.*

"I… I have to get back to work. I only stopped by to say hello." Forcing himself not to look back, Dustin left Seth standing by the creek, literally running away before he reconsidered. He'd nearly cleared the driveway when his heart asked, *"Is it too late to change your mind and turn around?"*

CHAPTER 7

"WAY to go, asshole," Seth groused aloud to himself. "You always manage to ruin the moment." Something about isolation coupled with compulsory Internet deprivation forced him to examine his life. It sucked. Big time. Porn and a well-worked right hand marked the limits of his sex life so far this year, except for a quickie or two with Michael a few months back, and the year was half gone.

When was the last time he'd tuned out external clutter enough to even hear his own thoughts? He watched Dustin grow smaller and smaller, and kicked himself, first, for sharing too much information, and second, for offering to drop trou in front of God and everybody. No wonder Dustin ran. Other possibilities occurred to Seth. Maybe Dusty wasn't out and had simply gotten caught up in the moment, or maybe he had somebody waiting for him in town. *Oh my God! Did I try to seduce the dreaded straight guy who somehow manages to send out gay vibes?*

He longed for his phone, to send a message to the world far and wide in hopes of hearing someone reply back—if anyone bothered. At the moment, there weren't enough people in the entire world to keep Seth from feeling alone.

He wound up back at the house, searching for an elusive signal. The front porch yielded up a single bar of connectivity if he leaned way over the railing, holding the phone aloft, while the rest of the house proved a black hole for technology. Damn, why hadn't he tried from the roof while on the ladder? Nearly desperate enough to perch on the weather vane, he considered the next best thing—the attic.

Up creaking stairs he climbed, the narrow passageway provoking a bout of claustrophobia, until he emerged under the eaves of the roof. The stairwell had seemed a whole lot roomier when he'd been eight. Though not terribly tall now, he did have to duck in places where the roof sloped downward. Eventually the space opened up with enough unused footage to add a bonus room, *or a master suite,* whispered the part of his brain that occasionally nagged for a partner and something besides a cramped apartment to live in. He recalled his drunken fantasy of a big house, a porch swing, a red-haired lover, and a kid or two. Well, he certainly had the house and swing, but the only red-haired man he wanted obviously didn't want *him.* He mentally slapped himself in the back of the head, mumbling, "Idiot."

His footsteps left prints through thick dust in a room time forgot. Grime-coated sheets tented out in the shape of chairs or other furniture. Seth passed too close, knocking loose a dust bunny the size of Cleveland, and immediately doubled over in a sneezing fit of epic proportions. "Damn!" he wheezed, hacking and coughing.

More gingerly, he made a careful circuit of the upper floor, forgetting why he'd come up here and losing himself in a whole attic full of things needing sorting. Maybe he'd luck out, like he'd seen on TV shows, and find a priceless painting or other big-ticket item hiding among the castoffs.

A vaguely familiar, steamer-type trunk summoned him like a beacon, and he knelt on the gritty floor beside the wooden box, holding his breath as he cleaned the top with a sweep of his arm. The hinges squealed in anguish when he lifted the lid. Storage for extra linen? No. The shimmery white material sealed in a plastic bag shaped up to be a dress—a fairytale creation displayed in a photo in his grandmother's living room.

His mother's wedding gown.

He wiped his hands on his jeans and carefully removed the plastic bag. Gingerly cradling the elegant garment in his arms, he reveled in the softness of the silk and the slight scratchiness of lace and rows of tiny seed pearls. Damn but he missed his mother. Her smiles, her warm hugs, snuggling up with her to watch TV.

He placed the gown reverently back in its protective covering. Overhandling might ruin a family heirloom. If he kept digging, would he find other treasures in the trunk?

A scrapbook yielded pictures of a lovely blonde girl with corkscrew curls, and with the flip of a few pages, he watched her grow to maturity and eventually to adulthood, where she struck many poses with a dark-haired man. Seth recognized the slightly thin lips, the aquiline nose, and hawk like brows, for he saw them every time he stared into a mirror. While he wasn't gorgeous by any stretch of the imagination, he was very proud to look like his dad, big nose notwithstanding.

The trunk yielded various other artifacts: souvenirs of a honeymoon trip to Acapulco, a pair of worn baby shoes Seth supposed were his own. At the bottom of the pile, he discovered a notebook, pages filled with a neat, flowery scrawl, and settled in to read what he assumed to be his mother's words.

Shape-shifters exist, though I, like most people, believed they were simply fantasy—until I met one.

His mother was a writer? Wow! Nana never mentioned her writing. And as openings went, what a hook! He turned page after page, immersed in an imaginary world where humans

74

transformed into four-legged creatures, some able to alter their form at will, others relying on the power of the full moon.

Had his mother read her work to him as bedtime stories?

Expecting to read about human/wolf metamorphosis, it took him by surprise to read: *With a long, skinny tail and sharp teeth, he didn't resemble my sweet Aaron in the least.*

Aaron? Seth's father's name? His mother named her protagonist after his father? He chuckled. What was dear old Dad's reaction to being included in her story? Seth tried to picture a long, skinny tail and sharp teeth. What fearsome creature had his dad's namesake transformed into at the whims of the lunar cycle?

Brown fur, mottled with cream, and he hissed when another of his kind approached.

Hissed? Like a snake? Seth recalled several stories she'd told him before bed, most involving knights and maidens, with the occasional personified squirrel or rabbit thrown in for good measure. He'd no idea his mother was such an accomplished storyteller and had little doubt she could have sold the contents of the notebook to a publisher.

Riveted to her words, he followed her heroine into the forest, in search of a changed lover.

And there in the moonlight I saw them, more than I'd ever seen in a single place before.

The page ended and he flipped to the next one, heart thudding, to find the word he'd been seeking:

Possums! Cute little things, with naked tails!

Huh? An incredible lead-up, only to have the love interest be a possum shifter? Seth would have laughed out loud if he hadn't found the whole situation tragic. Who wanted to read about the dreaded werepossum?

Though sadly disappointed with the current plot twist, he continued on a few pages to find: *I'm pregnant. Aaron assures me the baby will be fine. Half-bloods sometimes manifest the virus, he says, some-*

times they don't, but we'll have to keep a careful watch. He's taking me to his family doctor....

The house phone rang and Seth darted down the stairs, soon losing himself in details while speaking with a realtor. He forgot about his mother's novel.

"He may be an asshole, but he's not disgusting or anything. Why didn't you go for it?"

Sometimes Dustin wished Monica wasn't quite so outspoken. If she'd have hinted around, made nice, he'd simply have sidestepped the question. He'd never learned how to flat out lie to her direct approach. "Because he's leaving in a few days, will never look back, and I don't want to be remembered as a ten-minute roll in the hay."

"Ten minutes? Damn, been a while, huh?"

Dustin narrowed his eyes. Monica batted hers. "I've got all the complications I need right now, thank you very much. Like, where the hell I'm going to come up with a... with a...."

"Sucker?"

Dustin shot his assistant a meaningful glower. She exaggerated a yawn. "I was going to say 'viable candidate.'"

"Face it"—Monica rested a hand on Dustin's shoulder—"we only have three logical choices. You, Widow Pickens, who's too old, and Junior Timmerman, who suffers from a bad case of heartless asshole. No need to guess what'll happen if Junior takes over: bye-bye, secrecy."

Walking on eggshells his whole life not to slip up and say the wrong thing to the wrong person took a toll on a man. "Living out in the open might not be so bad."

Monica thwacked the back of Dustin's head. "Are you nuts? Do you have any idea what would happen if we suddenly announced, 'Oh, yeah, there's a colony of shape-shifters living in North Georgia. Oh no, we're not cool like werewolves. We're fucking possums!' How long do you reckon it'd take for every predator shifter in the country to beat a path to our door? Or gun-toting lunatics, out to bag the ultimate prize? Or how long before we're denied equal rights? You think marriage equality was a hot topic? You ain't seen nothing yet."

Visions of a happy world where everyone got along vanished in a *poof* of mental smoke. "Yeah, yeah, you've made your point. But Junior does have his supporters."

"Every crowd has a few dickheads. Because a few morons believe his bullshit doesn't make him right."

Dustin took a deep breath and took a step back, ready to pivot and run. "You could do it."

Both of Monica's eyebrows reached for her hairline. "Ain't no way in hell. They wouldn't accept a half-blood whose father was a first-generation possum, and I don't want the headache. It's not in me to play nice."

True enough. From anyone else Dustin would suspect false modesty. Both beginning with "M" was the only thing "Monica" and "modesty" had in common. Dustin sagged down into his office chair while Monica parked herself on his desk, drumming her nails against the wooden surface and attempting to run his life. "Anyhoo, getting back to the original subject, the guy who isn't a troll didn't run when you kissed him, and offered free nookie. If you talk him into staying, and groom some of the insensitive prick out of him, it might sway some of Junior's supporters your way. Old habits are hard to break, and a McDaniel has led the passel since the day they arrived in the area. If folks spotted the last member of a once great family hanging on your arm—"

Dustin's mouth dropped open. "Are you suggesting I use him?"

"What you want, what I want, what Junior wants, doesn't amount to a hill of beans. Someone's got to lead or we'll have chaos. Regardless of how cleverly she lassoed you into the number two spot, Irene was right in giving you the job. You need every tool at your disposal to ensure that her wishes are carried out. Imagine Seth McDaniel as a hammer to build your barn, because, damn it, winter's coming, and we better be ready."

No point denying the truth. Ever since accepting Irene's inevitable end, Dustin had studied each member of the passel without finding a suitable successor.

He blew out a deep breath, leaning back in his chair. "I have three full moons to make a choice, and I won't announce a decision one moment before I have to."

"You're gonna do it, aren't you?" A wicked gleam appeared in Monica's eyes.

Ah, but if Dustin was going down, he'd take Monica with him. "On one condition."

"What?"

"You be my second."

"Bastard!"

"You say that like it's a bad thing." He leaned forward, elbows on the desk, resting his chin primly in his hands. "I'll need every ounce of 'bastard' I can get to pull this off. But I won't, I repeat, I *won't* exploit Seth McDaniel. However, I did promise I'd go out to dinner."

"Nookie!" Monica chortled.

Dustin snorted. "Catching up on old times."

"Call it what you want. Just go get some. You're turning into a grouch."

Determined to do the right thing, Dustin dialed Irene's number. Seth answered the phone on the second ring. "Hello."

"Look, Seth, I want to apologize for running off." *Yeah, apologize, a good place to start.* Dustin swore he heard Seth blushing on the other end of the phone line.

"Umm… about that."

Dustin's heart fell, his carefully rehearsed words curling up and dying a slow, agonizing death on his tongue.

"I have no idea what came over me, Dusty. I truly don't. I'm not one of those guys who goes around hitting on anything that moves." The use of Dustin's nickname offered some reassurance of no hard feelings. Seth attempted some levity, as he'd done in his younger days to relieve awkwardness. "I usually make a guy wine me and dine me first."

A knife twisted in Dustin's belly, but he made his offer anyway. "Don't take this the wrong way, but I'm calling to take you up on your previous suggestion of dinner. Yes, I'd like to wine you and dine you, umm… no strings attached."

An odd sound emerged from the phone's tiny speaker, half laughing, half choking. "But I like strings! Sorry, I'm not helping. You'd like to take me to dinner?"

"Yeah. Possum Kingdom may be a small town, but we have some of the best barbeque you'll find anywhere. What do you say?" Dustin held his breath. Was it his imagination, or did he age four years while waiting for Seth to answer?

Finally, Seth let Dustin off the hook. "I can be ready in a half hour."

"I'll be there."

Dustin hung up the phone to find Monica watching him with amusement in her eyes, and he couldn't fight a grin. "Don't wait up," he chided.

She knitted her brows together, a line forming between her narrowed eyes, and leaned down, nose mere inches from Dustin's. "Remember, if you're not *in* by ten"—she pulled her lips back from her pearly whites in a somewhat feral grin —"then take him home and find another date that puts out.

"Speaking of…." She hopped off the desk. "I'd better get going. Even if you can only manage lukewarm, *I've* got a hottie waiting for me." She spun on her heel and flounced from the room before Dustin managed to stop gaping.

CHAPTER 8

SETH would never have found the quaint little restaurant without Dustin's help. Way off the beaten path, The Pitted Pig managed to attract a lively dinner crowd, despite its remote location. Where had all these people come from?

"Where would you like to sit?" Dustin asked, a plateful of steaming pulled pork in his hands.

"Wherever there's a table." Seth's stomach growled, taunted by the rich scent of hickory-smoked meat, the tangy notes of barbeque sauce making his mouth water. He did love good barbeque.

"Do you mind sitting outside?"

"No. Lead on." Seth admired the view on his trip through the crowded establishment, and if forced under duress to find his way back to the entrance, would have failed miserably. His vision honed in on slender shoulders, a narrow waist, and a well-made backside as he and Dustin navigated tables and tray-laden restaurant staff on the way to the door at the back of the dining room.

They passed table after table of couples and families, many nodding, murmuring, "Jack" at Dustin's passing.

If that was how the town rolled, Seth was not to question.

Finally, Dustin opened the door onto a covered porch holding roughly a dozen tables, mostly empty. "It's getting close to sundown, when the mosquitoes come out," Dustin explained. "During lunch rush it's hard to find room out here to sit."

They settled at a table away from the other occupied ones. From his vantage point, Seth glimpsed the distant mountain peaks. No matter what one might say about Possum Kingdom, it offered spectacular views. The old cane-backed chairs and plastic tablecloths brought back memories of long ago, dining with his family at Aunt Irene's kitchen table. Above their heads, the paddles of a ceiling fan circled in lazy rotation, stirring a slight breeze.

Their server appeared, bearing a tray full of bottles in a wire-bound carrier: one red, one white, and one blue, and two glasses of sweet tea. "Evenin', Jack," the young man said, placing his burdens on the table. "Rolls, Texas toast, or buns?"

Dustin asked, "Can we get some of each?"

"Sure." The pimply-faced teen wandered off, leaving Seth with Dustin and a healthy dose of embarrassment.

"I'm sorry about earlier." Might as well get the humiliating crash and burn out of the way in order to enjoy dinner. Before Seth opened his mouth and inserted his foot, they'd been doing beautifully down by the creek.

"Forget it. To be honest, I'm flattered. I wasn't expecting it. It's not often someone makes an offer here in town. We don't exactly have a chapter of PFLAG yet." Dustin smile.

Damn, but that smile induced one hell of a lot of spine-tingles.

Seth truly hadn't considered small-town scruples when he'd arrived, since staying hadn't been in the cards. But the answer did offer reassurances that he hadn't corrupted what well might have been the town's sole marital prospect for any single ladies.

Back home in Chicago, acceptance of who he was wasn't much of an issue. At least, not after his grandmother's passing. He'd never gotten over his guilt at not telling her about being gay, but she hadn't been the most open-minded of souls. Thoughts of her pursed lips and righteous rebukes had stopped him every time he'd considered disclosing his orientation. All three times. "Is it hard for you here?"

Dustin rested his elbows on the table, the freckles across his nose so much lighter than they'd been when he'd been ten—but Seth could misremember. "It's not too bad. I'm pretty well-respected, and your aunt tended to put people in their places fast if they dared say anything."

Irene. The mysterious aunt of his who'd apparently won, not only Dustin's respect, but hard-nosed Monica's. Monica gave the impression of not granting undeserved loyalty.

The waiter brought bread, disappearing again directly after depositing the basket on the table. Dustin tore a roll in half and piled the inside high with roast pork. "The Southern Sweet is my favorite," he said, nodding toward the white bottle in the carrier. "It's got a molasses base, sweet and smoky. But try the other two also. They're all good."

Seth heeded the advice, tuning out the pleasured moans coming from the other side of the table that added fuel to the fire of his raging libido. Gulping down ice-cold tea didn't extinguish the blaze. He wanted Dustin. Wanted to lie back, squirt tangy sauce on his skin, and have his dinner companion lick it off, much the way Dustin currently licked a dollop off a thumb. Seth's cock swelled, pressing against the unyielding barrier of his jeans. Wriggling as unobtrusively as possible, he attempted a discreet anatomical adjustment. If Dustin noticed, he gave no sign.

"What have you been doing with yourself all these years, Seth?"

Seth swallowed a bite of mesquite-flavored meat. "Nothing

much to tell. I went to school, graduated, started college, changing my major a few times when I couldn't figure out what to do with my life. Nana bought me a camera one year for Christmas, and I found I liked to take pictures. I entered a few contests, won often enough to swell my head and convince me to try making a living out of it. When the money started trickling in, I dropped out of college and started my own business." He bowed his head, heat trailing up his cheeks to his ears. He was bragging about dropping out of school to become a photographer? To a doctor?

"Sounds like you're doing exactly what you want to do."

Well, yeah, true enough. "I am, for the most part. There's always the screaming tantrums to put up with, subjects who won't listen to what you say and afterward blame you for the less than perfect end results."

Sympathy flashed across Dustin's face. "I guess you work with a lot of kids."

"What kids? I'm talking about fashion models!"

Seth spent the next few minutes mimicking some of the more demanding subjects he'd worked with. "No, not my bad side!" he shrilled in a high falsetto. "That's my bad side too! What the hell did you do to my picture? My nose does not look like that!" They both laughed, the tension effectively broken. "How about you? What's it like to be a small-town doctor?"

"I'm not sure how to describe it. It's my life; I've nothing else to compare it to. Born and raised here, left long enough to go to college, and came back. Jobwise, I'm there the moment a child is born, if not before, and I watch them grow. Teens mature, get married, and start a new generation. Occasionally, I'm there at the end."

An invisible fist squeezed Seth's heart. "Were you... were you there for my aunt?"

A furrow formed on Dustin forehead, and he pursed his lips

briefly. "Not at the precise moment, but yes, I was at the house with her. We all were."

Thank God she hadn't been alone. "Who's 'we'?"

"Her friends, those she considered family." Dustin grimaced. "Sorry, I didn't mean that the way it came out."

Seth swallowed hard, once more reminded of his prolonged absence. But what choice had he had? His aunt hadn't reached out to him either.

Dustin changed the subject. "Did Monica tell you how she met your aunt?"

"No. She seems to hate me for being a bad nephew."

Dustin wafted out a sigh, pausing for a draught of tea before continuing. "Monica doesn't hate you. She's jealous of you."

"Of me? Why?" Seth often found himself the object of pity, but never envy.

"Maybe I shouldn't be talking about her behind her back, but I did promise to tell you about your aunt, and Monica's story is a classic example of Ms. Irene McDaniel at her best. You see, Monica's father died when she was about four years old, and her mother moved back to Jacksonville to be with family. She remarried and had two more children.

"When Monica grew older...." Dustin paused, a wrinkle forming between his copper-colored eyebrows. "Let's say she didn't quite fit in. She came to stay with your aunt when she was fifteen, after being rejected by her family."

Fuck! Kicked out? What had the woman done? Likely nothing. Fifteen? Tough age. A load of guilt heaped itself on Seth's shoulders for his rather unkind earlier assessment of The Valkyrie. An image popped into his head a scared and lonely teen, similar to himself. Had her mom kicked her out for being gay? Rebellious? Not eating her peas? In his younger days, Seth had worried about the same thing happening to him if his grandmother ever found out he'd rather have a Sam than a Sue, or if he disobeyed.

"Anyway, Monica grew attached to Irene, wishing they were kin in truth, and she never quite grasped why you didn't come around when you'd been blessed with such a fantastic aunt."

Old remorse slithered awake in Seth's gut. "I would have loved to have spent time down here, but Aunt Irene never once tried to contact me. She didn't even call me on my birthday." Seth hated how childish he sounded, but year after year, he'd hoped for something, and each year he'd eaten birthday cake with his grandmother and gone to bed disillusioned. No party, no gifts except from Nana, and no cards bearing a Georgia return address. Years of disappointment ate at him, leaving him feeling unloved and unwanted. And now, to find out she took in another kid when she didn't even have time for Seth?

"The old harpy never 'fessed up, huh?"

"What?"

Dustin patted his mouth with a napkin and dropped the bandana-print cotton square to the tablecloth. "I'm sorry. I shouldn't speak ill of the dead but, Seth, the only reason Irene didn't contact you was because your grandmother forbade it."

Nana forbade it? Why? "She what? She told me that after my father died, Aunt Irene had no further use for me." A vise grip squeezed Seth's insides. He pictured his grandmother, lower lip quivering when she'd told him the news.

The friend Seth never forgot reached across the table and took his hand. "No, Seth. I'm not sure precisely what she told you or why, but the truth is she threatened Irene."

"Threatened? With what?"

A scarlet flush tinged Dustin's cheeks, revealing more anger than embarrassment. "Irene never told me the exact words, she only said your grandmother wouldn't permit her to see you or talk to you. Irene wrote you letters; I mailed them for her myself. And yes, she did send birthday cards, usually with money enclosed. I take it you never received them."

Do what? All those years of feeling rejected were a lie? The hand holding Seth's burned against his skin, but he didn't pull away. There hadn't been nearly enough human contact in his life. He'd not refuse comfort freely given. "No, I didn't." Seth had witnessed his grandmother's controlling side on many occasions, and yes, she'd resorted to manipulation to get her way. But to keep Seth from his only other living relative?

"Monica saw the situation from the other side, how you received gifts and never sent thank-you cards. She only witnessed how much it hurt Irene not to have you in her life. And Monica, pretty much thrown away by her family, envied you your wonderful aunt. She's not the only one. Over the years, Irene took in many kids in similar situations, some for a short time while she sorted things out with their parents, others on a more permanent basis, like Monica."

Dustin paused to take a bite of his meal, chewing slowly. "Mmmm… this place has the best slaw!"

Seth recognized the stalling tactic. "Why didn't you write to me?" If his heart squeezed any harder, it'd explode.

"I did! Nearly every week when you first left. But you never wrote back, or returned my phone calls. After a while, Mom made me stop calling. Said it broke her heart to see me upset when I didn't get to speak with you."

"You called me?" Seth's mind reeled. All this time he thought he'd been forgotten. He remembered how his grandmother wouldn't meet his eyes when he asked about his old friend. The pieces fell into place. If only he'd had Internet or a cell phone back then…

Dustin finally drew his hand back. Seth missed the warmth immediately. "Seth, people have their reasons for why they make the choices they do. Your grandmother is no different. I'm sure she convinced herself that she was protecting you."

"Protecting me? From what? She knew how lonely I was, how much it hurt me to leave here. Why would she lie to me?"

"I can't speak for your grandmother, but I promise you, you *were* missed."

Twenty years of misconceptions left Seth with a lot to deal with. "My old room is exactly like I left it."

Dustin nodded. "Irene held out hope 'til the end that you'd come back someday."

"Why didn't she contact me after Nana died?"

"She'd been fighting the good fight herself since then. Besides, you lived in Chicago, and via a social media site, she watched you from afar. You seemed happy, and she didn't want to take you away from your home and friends."

Seth recalled his many profile pages, the beautiful lies he'd concocted to make himself appear more interesting, less of a loser. "Oh my God! If she went to my blog, she knew I was gay!" Another possibility presented itself for her lack of interest in Seth—disgust.

"Yeah, and she hoped you'd find the man of your dreams. I told you, she defended me. Irene McDaniel was the kindest, most accepting woman I've ever met. She loved you. Her last thoughts were of you."

Seth's eyes burned, and a knot formed in his chest. He didn't think either had anything to do with spicy barbeque sauce. A tear escaped his control, spilling down his cheek.

"Now look at me. I've gone and upset you." Dustin handed over a napkin. "Are you finished eating?"

Seth bobbed his head, wiping at his eyes with the napkin.

Extracting a wad of cash from his wallet, Dustin peeled off a few bills, securing them under his plate. "C'mon. Let's take a walk."

The sun was beginning to set when Dustin led Seth down a flight of steps, across a neatly manicured lawn, and to the bank of a small lake. A trio of ducks glided across the calm surface.

"The creek behind your house feeds into this." Dustin stopped at a cement bench, sitting down and gesturing for Seth to do the same. "I've always loved it here. So peaceful."

Shoulder to shoulder, the heat radiated off Dustin's body and suddenly Seth felt coldness inside at odds with the sticky summer heat. His own wave of envy consumed him, for Dustin, Monica, and anyone else who'd basked in his aunt's love. "I missed out on a lot."

"Yes, you did, and I'm sorry for that. Did you know your ancestors were some of the first folks to settle here? Hell, half the town wanted to name the place McDanielville."

"And were beaten out by 'Possum Kingdom'?" Seth attempted a feeble joke, trying to regain his balance. Over the course of a few minutes, Dustin had laid waste to the worst of Seth's beliefs. His aunt had never stopped loving him, his best friend had missed him, his grandmother had lied. Inside, a solid block of ice encased his heart and he fought to breathe.

"Beats 'Squirrel Ridge', twenty miles away."

Seth supposed it did. They sat together silently, serenaded by crickets and bullfrogs. The clean scent of the great outdoors, free of exhaust fumes, though occasionally bearing the scent of the restaurant behind them, slowly calmed his nerves. For a moment Seth considered ditching his life in Chicago to fix up his aunt's house for himself instead of some nameless future buyer. But no, he'd never fit in here. *Like you fit in Chicago?*

Dustin wrapped an arm around him, resting a warm hand on Seth's shoulder. "Is this all right?"

"Yes." In fact, in Seth's opinion, it was more than all right. Tonight his world had unraveled—he needed grounding, something to take his mind off the alternate reality he suddenly found himself in.

"Can I kiss you?"

Seth glanced right and left before answering. Behind them sat the restaurant's back wall, secluding them from prying eyes.

"No one can see us." Dustin gave Seth a crooked grin. "Why do you think I brought you here? This bench is pure gold to every high school couple in the county."

"Think we'll shock any teenagers?"

"God, I hope so."

They tilted their heads as one. Seth observed a fleeting sentimental smile before Dustin's lips met his. They nuzzled noses, skimming their lips back and forth. Dustin slipped his tongue inside Seth's mouth, sweet with molasses and spices. Seth moaned, twining his tongue with Dustin's.

At some point he brought his arms up, grasping Dustin and hanging tighter than a drowning man. And still the kiss continued, a lazy, unhurried exploration until they both pulled away, breathless.

"Wow." Seth wasn't sure who'd spoken—him, Dustin, or perhaps both.

Something unfathomable dwelled in Dustin eyes when he withdrew, but it wasn't the raging lust Seth hoped to find. After a moment of intense scrutiny, Dustin said, "C'mon, I'd better take you home."

What? *Was it something I said?*

Dustin remained quiet on the way back to the farmhouse, but he gave Seth a brief glimpse of hope with a scorching hot good-night kiss. "I'd like to stop by tomorrow, if that's okay."

Sensibilities scrambled by turbocharged lust, Seth would've let Dustin have whatever he asked for. The few remaining brain cells that survived their intimate tongue tangle managed to pull together and form a single word: "Sure."

A sleepless night left Dustin horny, tired, and aggravated. Now why the hell had he promised Seth another date? Just because Dustin had revealed his conniving grandmother's duplicity didn't mean Seth would suddenly change his mind and stay. *Stupid, stupid, stupid. Don't get involved with him. He's short term!* the rational part of Dustin's mind told him, quickly shushed by the body part begging him to strip down and let nature take its course.

He slammed a chart down onto his desk, dropping into his chair.

"Mind sharing exactly how that chart pissed you off? Or is it the desk you're mad at?" Monica stood in the office doorway, managing to appear intimidating even in bright pink scrubs. She'd wound her braids around her head, creating the illusion of a fuzzy gold tiara.

"I intended to take Seth out last night, talk a bit about Irene, and take him home. Nothing more."

Monica *tsked.* "Dude, you disappoint me. Was getting laid ever in your plan?"

"No, Monica. Taking advantage of my date was your idea."

"*What?*" Her eyes widened in mock surprise. "And you didn't take my excellent advice? How... wasteful."

Scowling required too much energy. Dustin glared instead. "He's leaving in a few weeks."

"Last time I tried it, meaningless sex didn't take longer than a day or two."

Dustin goggled; Monica snickered. "Gotcha!" Ms. I-get-a-new-boyfriend-every-time-the-wind-blows didn't have to be so damned smug. The town only held so many men. What did she do? Import them?

"I like him, okay? I'm not going to use him, and I'm not wasting my time with a lost cause."

"Okay. Sounds reasonable to me. Why the long face?"

"'Cause, like a fool, I told him I'd come by today."

"And those were your exact words?"

"Huh? Why do you ask?"

A feral grin creased Monica's cheeks. "Why don't you drive

past his house on your way home and keep going. You never said you'd stop, right?"

She earned herself an eye roll and a bad Groucho Marx impression: "That's the most ridiculous thing I've ever heard."

"Not as ridiculous as you avoiding a guy you might like."

Dustin opened his mouth to speak but nothing came out.

Monica threw up her hands and snorted. "Go, get reacquainted, find out what an asshole he is, then you'll be begging him to go the fuck back home."

Yeah, right.

Dustin fretted all afternoon, picking up his phone repeatedly to call Seth and make excuses for not visiting. No doubt about it, however; the closer six o'clock and quitting time came, the faster his heart beat.

With no rational excuse coming to mind, he ended up at Seth's, only to find the man waiting, a cheerful smile on his face. "Want to take a walk again? I promise I won't make any unwanted advances."

Dustin struggled, torn between finding the promise comforting and disappointing. "Sure. Where do you have in mind?"

"The pond."

The spring-fed swimming hole brought back memories.

"Hey, remember that box turtle we found over there by the overflow?" Dustin gestured toward the shallow end of the pond, where runoff flowed down the hill to join the creek.

Seth grinned. "I kept him in a box under the bed until Aunt Irene found him. I thought she'd make me get rid of him. Instead Daddy helped me build a pen." Dustin had planned to keep the terrapin for himself, but seeing the excitement in Seth's eyes had inspired him to hand it over. How he'd lived for the smile on his friend's face. Seeing it now, on a grown-up Seth, brought back those feelings.

A groundhog peeked out from the grass, watching their

passing. Dustin paused, studying the creature, but no lucid thoughts hid within the basic instinct to scratch an itch with a hind foot, avoid the two scary humans, and find dinner. In the meadow, birds chittered and sang. Except for Dustin and Seth, the surrounding tableau had remained relatively unchanged since their last visit here.

Seth sank onto the graded embankment. "I remember coming here when we were kids." He plinked a rock across the water's glassy surface, causing the reflection of nearby pine trees to ripple. "We used to strip down and hop in on a hot day."

Dustin gave a nervous laugh, an image coming to mind of the two of them, stark naked, standing waist-deep in water.

"Remember the rope we used to hang from a tree over there?" Seth pointed to the far side of the pond and the towering oak whose branches nearly swept the surface. "Those were the days." Seth lay back in a bed of clover, arms folded behind his head, staring up at the sky. "The more I stay here, the more I'm in danger of not wanting to leave."

"Oh, really?" A niggling of hope squirmed to life in Dustin's heart. While he wanted Seth here, wanted to rekindle the wonderful friendship of their youth, was it wise to wish him to stay?

"Yeah, really. Down here is where I lived with my mom and dad; it's the only home I remember. My grandmother lived in an apartment, and we moved several times while I was growing up. But here? Here stayed the same. There's something comforting about things that don't change, isn't there?"

You don't know the half of it. Dustin was older than Seth by a couple of years, and, looking back now, he supposed he'd suspected he was gay even at a tender age. His feelings for Seth back then might actually have been his first crush. "When did you first realize you were gay?" he found himself asking.

"I dunno. I guess around thirteen or fourteen. Scared me at

first. The boys at school kept talking about girls, but it wasn't a girl who stayed on my mind."

Dustin wanted to ask, "Who did?" but an eye-locking gaze from Seth kept him quiet. If the two of them hadn't been ripped apart, would young love have grown? A barely audible growl escaped Dustin, aimed at Seth's cold grandmother. He tried to lighten the mood. "I bet you had to beat the boys off with a two-by-four in high school."

The light in Seth's eyes dimmed and he turned away, studying the sky. "No. Not in high school. I was too scared of what my grandmother might say. How about you?"

While the South typically wasn't the most accepting of places, Possum Kingdom defied the norm, except for a few holdouts who managed to make problems here and there. Regardless, Dustin hadn't freely explored the sexual aspect of himself until he left for college. "I dated a bit in college, managed to snag myself a steady boyfriend or two, but never anyone I'd call a partner."

"Me either. Came close once, but it's probably better off we didn't work out." Seth kept his gaze turned away. Did he mean Michael, the guy from the social site? "Woulda been nice not to be alone."

Dustin sidled over to the bank and dropped down beside Seth. The loneliness, the isolation, pulsed off the man. An irresistible force seemed to pull them together. Their lips met, a gentle play of tongue on tongue following. "I missed you," Dustin said, propping up on one arm to stare down at Seth.

"I missed you too."

Their eyes met and held. Fire danced between them. Dustin broke the silence. "Is there anyone waiting for you back in Chicago?"

"No."

"Are you a 'one-night stand only' kind of guy?"

A lovely pink tinge suffused Seth's face. "No. I'm sorry if I gave you that impression. I can count my former lovers on one hand, and still have fingers left over."

The gesture was barely perceptible, but Dustin inched a little bit closer. "Did you mean what you offered down by the creek? That if I wanted to lay you down right here, you'd let me?"

Seth recalled the foolish words he'd blurted. Why had he said anything so asinine? The truth came with all the impact of a brick to the face. He'd wanted Dustin from the moment he'd first laid eyes on the grownup version, but at the creek other things competed for his attention. Now, in their little bubble of calm, he felt safe voicing his wishes. "I've never meant anything more."

Dustin pounced, pinning Seth to the ground. "Mmmmph?" Seth managed around the tongue in his mouth before getting with the program. *Man! Willing!* His brain shut down, his body taking over.

They shoved and clawed, pushed and pulled, until their clothing lay strewn around them on the ground. "Oh God, you have no idea how much I've wanted you," Dustin whispered, blazing a trail between Seth's ear and collarbone with his lips.

Muscles bunched beneath Seth's questing fingers, and he grabbed wherever he found purchase, frantically bucking up, his achingly full cock sliding against Dustin's answering hardness. No gentleness existed between them. They rutted together in frantic desperation, Seth barely noticing the occasional rock digging into his ass.

Sometimes he found himself on top, gazing down into lust-glazed eyes; at others, he looked up from beneath. They rolled and tumbled, panting hot breath into each other's ears.

"Oh God!" Seth exclaimed, pressure building. He redoubled his effort, mind about to shatter to pieces. They groaned and moaned, occasionally cussing for good measure.

Dustin sheathed both their erections in a relentless grip, finding Seth's mouth with his own and sliding their tongues together as frantically as their bodies. The tension built, Seth desperately bucking into Dustin's grasp. He splintered and fragmented, white-hot carnal tidal wave sweeping over him. "Oh God, oh God, oh God...."

A look of intense concentration crossed Dustin's face, and he pumped faster, muscles tensing. He closed his eyes, muttering, "Seth, Seth, Seth...."

Seth came to himself sprawled on top of Dustin, a shit-eating grin plastered to his face. "Well, damn!" he uttered, once he recovered the power of speech, too sated to even consider moving.

"Um... Seth?"

Seth trained unfocused eyes on the man who had just given him the orgasm of a lifetime. "Yeah."

Dustin craned his neck to see over Seth's shoulder. "We need to move." He suddenly swatted at Seth's backside.

"Hey, sometimes I like a little spanky, but during, not after." Seth flinched as Dustin's hand landed again, just as fast but more gently.

"I was too busy to do it earlier." Dustin rolled Seth over and stood, extending a hand. "You can swat your own skeeters if you'd rather. Come home with me?"

Voice scarcely above a whisper, Seth replied, "I'd love to," while allowing Dustin to haul him to his feet.

Dustin bent to retrieve their clothes, his lily-white ass adorned with tiny red mosquito bites.

CHAPTER 9

It didn't surprise Seth that Dustin lived in the small but cozy log cabin he'd been raised in. Now, instead of climbing to the loft and Dustin's old room, Dustin steered him toward the downstairs bedroom, formerly occupied by the senior Livingstons. The familiar scent of lemon oil that he'd always associated with the house lingered.

"Where are your mom and dad now?"

"Dad died three years ago. Mom retired to Florida to be with her sister."

"I'm sorry." Hell, not only had he neglected to be here for Aunt Irene, he'd not been here for Dusty either. Or Dusty's mom. A smiling face came to mind. The Livingstons were in their late forties before Dustin came along, much older than Seth's parents, but they were good people, welcomed him into their home.

"Don't be. To his dying day, Dad claimed he was the luckiest son of a bitch to ever live. He loved life and didn't fear dying—made it easier on those left behind. I only hope I can be half the man he was."

Seth felt confident, even in the short time they'd shared

since his return, that Dustin had left the halfway point a few miles back.

Given Dustin's confident self-assurance, Seth expected something a bit sexier in the way of interior design. Instead, they entered a study in minimalism, with plain log walls and a hardwood floor. A wrought iron bed sat beneath the room's lone window—left open to admit a rose-scented breeze. A worn patchwork quilt similar to the ones Aunt Irene used to sew covered the old double bed. The only nod to creature comforts was the pile of pillows. Two wore matching cases; the other three were covered in plain white cotton. Five pillows? The guy slept with five pillows?

Suddenly an image came to mind: Dustin, curled up in a comfy nest of those pillows, sound asleep. Though they'd taken the edge off at the pond, Seth's cock, semi-hard since he'd arrived at the house, filled completely, demanding attention.

Across from the bed sat a dresser and mirror, the polished wooden top gleaming in the scant illumination of an antique oil lamp, refitted for an electric lightbulb. Again, the faint traces of lemon oil permeated the air. The mirror was perfectly situated to reflect the bed, and for a moment Seth wondered what images had appeared there in the past. A vision of Dustin came to mind, but this time he was neither asleep nor alone, his smoky baritone chanting obscenities as he pounded some willing partner.

How many men had shared Dustin's bed, and had Dustin ever been on the receiving end? Seth certainly hoped so. Though he fully intended to catch tonight, one eyeful of the good doctor's tight ass hiding under those carefully creased dress pants convinced him that he needed to do more than gawk. Normally, Seth bottomed—for Dustin, he'd make an exception. As he stood staring into the mirror, fantasy images filling his head, Dustin appeared behind him, enveloping him in a hug while nuzzling soft lips against Seth's neck. Seth kept his eyes riveted to the mirror. His breath caught in his throat at the erotic display they'd created. He barely recognized his own face, so filled with passion. How long had it been since anyone had seen want in his eyes? Did he always appear slightly unhinged when aroused? If so, he must have looked like a lunatic at the pond.

A firm tug on his shirt pulled the tail from his jeans, and Dustin slid a hand underneath, cool against heated flesh, to stroke Seth's bare skin. The faintest caress traced his abs, slowly moving higher, shooting fire straight to his groin. Dustin ran his other hand down Seth's stomach, inching lower until the barest touch of fingertips dipped beneath Seth's waistband, gently nudging the head of his cock. The wet spot in his boxers must have been apparent, telling Dustin of the depths of Seth's need. Damn, but the man turned him on. He closed his eyes, focusing on the feel of Dustin's fingers against his skin.

When Dustin removed his hands, Seth's body, too long neglected, screamed *no!* A rumbling chuckle sounded behind him. "Not going anywhere," Dustin murmured into Seth's shoulder as he put nimble fingers to work opening Seth's belt, followed by his fly.

Seth opened his eyes and stared at the mirror in time to watch Dustin slide a hand into his boxers, and he groaned at the firm squeeze wrapping around his cock. Watching the two of them like this sent a jolt of arousal through Seth, and nearly brought him to his knees. His cock filled even more, stretching the already taut skin of his shaft. Another scent teased his nose, overriding citrus furniture polish—a combination of Dustin's own natural scent, a light, woodsy cologne, and something else Seth could only name "arousal."

The touch on his flesh felt so different—his own hand had been his companion for too long. *That's Dustin's hand!* beat through his mind like a pulse.

Seth bit back the groan fighting to escape, chewing at his

lower lip with the effort. He longed to shout and let go, but that would end things before they'd properly begun, and he wanted to make this last. They'd wolfed down the appetizer at the pond —now came the main course. As turned on as he was, the best he hoped for was to not embarrass himself and come before he'd even gotten Dustin naked. He hadn't been this horny since his teens.

Meeting lust-filled eyes in the mirror, Seth held Dustin's steady gaze while unbuttoning his own shirt. Dustin stepped back far enough for the crumpled fabric to fall, catching it at the last second and hanging it on the doorknob. Next, he worked Seth's jeans down.

While Seth's breath consisted of sharp, shuddery gasps, Dustin appeared utterly calm, even though the hard length he occasionally pressed into Seth's crack proved his arousal.

Successful in wriggling his feet free of his tennis shoes, Seth allowed Dustin to tug his jeans off. He chuckled when Dustin neatly folded and placed them on the dresser. *So much for ripping our clothes off in reckless abandon.* His smile fell when he caught sight of the simmering hunger in Dustin's eyes. He'd had three lovers in his life, four counting Dustin, and the others had never regarded him with such intensity.

He'd love to have helped with the undressing, but Dustin's undivided attention held Seth captive. All he could do was watch in the mirror as Dustin stripped, revealing a chest more muscular than Seth's, and sprouting a handful of rust-colored curls.

Seth watched, fascinated, while Dustin toed off his shoes, pulling off his belt and peeling his pants down at the same time. Dustin leered over Seth's shoulder, slowly gliding his briefs over the prominent bulge they barely concealed, and then slipping them back into place, putting on a show. When he finally did pull them completely down, revealing a hard, uncut member, Seth unconsciously licked his lips. Damn, what a view.

There didn't appear to be an ounce of fat on the man, every muscle clearly defined, though his muscles were sleek, like a runner's, not the bulging "my muscles have muscles" of some macho types Seth had run into back home.

He let his gaze travel down to Dustin's flat belly. Like the man's chest, and in keeping with Seth's fantasy, a smattering of red hair sprinkled Dustin's groin, his darkened length rising from the neatly trimmed strands.

Self-consciously Seth cupped his balls, hoping his nearly *au natural* state wouldn't be a turnoff. Oh, he trimmed a bit, but nothing compared to the lengths Dustin apparently went to—extreme manscaping. He'd been too enthralled at the pond to do much looking.

Judging from the bodily reaction of the man now standing beside him, his hairiness wasn't a problem. When they were both completely naked, Dustin inclined his head toward the waiting bed. Seth approached and Dustin flipped the covers back, revealing plain white sheets.

Firm hands on his shoulders guided Seth down to the firm mattress, but when he would have rolled onto his stomach, presenting his ass for the taking, Dustin stopped him. "I'm in no hurry, are you?" He turned up his lips in a pulse-quickening smile, lowered his head, and took Seth's nipple into his mouth.

Seth raised his head from the mattress, watching. Dustin smiled around his mouthful and handed over a pillow. Tucking it under his head, Seth settled in for a front-row seat to the show, tangling his fingers in Dustin's perfectly styled locks. As good as Dustin's mouth worked his chest, though, Seth silently willed it lower. Fully erect and aching, he longed for release.

But, damn, that mouth felt good—hot, wet suction working down his torso, sending electric currents jolting throughout his body. Finally, after far too long, moist heat enveloped his cock, as Dustin sank his lips slowly down Seth's shaft. Seth bucked without conscious thought, thrusting his hips, wanting more.

Dustin chuckled, the vibration nearly sending Seth over the edge.

Seth dug his fingers into the mattress. Not yet! He couldn't come yet!

Dustin released Seth's cock and sat back. Oh, fuck. Oh, fuck. Seth sucked in a breath, fighting a battle with pleasure overload. He won—barely. Dustin lowered his head and brushed his lips tentatively against Seth's, nibbling for a moment before seeking entrance into Seth's mouth.

Letting go of his built-up tension, Seth relaxed and let his new lover take the lead. The kiss started slowly, quickly escalating into a primal, needy thing that curled Seth's toes and threatened to consume him.

Dustin eased down on top of him, and Seth pushed up, gliding his slender cock against Dustin's thicker one. Dustin inserted his sparsely haired leg between Seth's more heavily furred thighs, pushing them apart and settling between. He propped his weight on his arms and ground their erections together.

Seth roved his hands over the smooth expanses of Dustin's muscular back and descended to grab handfuls of the solid ass he'd been admiring, dragging Dustin nearer and matching thrust for thrust.

When the kiss broke, Dustin nibbled Seth's neck, worrying a spot beneath his left ear with a gentle application of teeth, and once again, Seth fought for control. Warm breath gusted over his ear, and Dustin grasped Seth's straining erection, working him to full advantage. "I'm gonna come," came out of Seth, more whimper than words.

Dustin rolled off. Seth humped air, whining his frustration. What? No!

"You like to watch, don't you?" It was a statement, not a question.

Seth saw no reason to lie. "Yes," he panted out.

Dustin studied him for a moment before standing and offering Seth a hand. Puzzled, Seth placed his hand in Dustin's and allowed himself to be towed from the bed, too lust-addled to move on his own. Dustin led him back to the dresser and placed a pillow on the hard wooden surface. With eye contact in the mirror and gentle touches, Dustin urged Seth to bend down on the pillow. A drawer slid open and Seth chanced a glance at the contents. It closed before he managed a full inventory, but at least it held condoms and lube.

Mesmerized, his gaze remained glued to Dustin's hands, entranced as Dusty unrolled a condom over his length and liberally slicked the latex. *Oh fuck yeah!*

Dustin worked a slippery finger into Seth's hole, and Seth pushed back with a moan. Soon one finger became two, until Dustin removed his fingers and something longer and harder brushed against Seth's opening. Dustin stilled with the tip of his cock poised at Seth's entrance. Only when Seth glanced up to meet his eyes in the mirror and utter a strained, "Okay," did Dustin proceed, gripping Seth's shoulders and slowly sinking in, never breaking eye contact.

Never had Seth had a front-row seat to his own porn video, and he examined the emotions flitting across Dustin's face. Dustin grinned in the mirror and picked up the pace, thrusting in at a steady rate.

Seth nearly cried when Dustin withdrew. Next thing he knew, Dustin had flung him on the bed, flat on his back with his feet resting on Dustin's shoulders. They locked gazes, never glancing away as Dusty slid back into him, breathlessly murmuring, "Oh, damn, but you feel good!"

Though he'd come once already at the pond, Seth desperately needed another release.

"Stroke yourself," Dustin panted, nodding toward Seth's cock.

Dustin jarred both Seth and the bed, the squeaking springs

keeping time with his energetic thrusts. Thoughts faded away, Seth's world tunneling down to the delicious sensations of Dustin inside of him and the growing friction of own his hand on his cock.

Those intense jade eyes shielded as Dustin closed his lids, throwing his head back in sheer ecstasy. Had any man ever looked so beautiful?

Dustin's rhythm faltered before failing completely. He wailed out his desire, gripping tightly to Seth's waist and burying himself fully. One, two, three hard thrusts, and he stilled, rapture etched on his features.

He held the pose, arms muscles bulging, then opened his eyes with a grin.

Seth's control shattered. He groaned, shoulders leaving the bed. His body bowed, muscles spasming with the force of his orgasm. The first splash caught him on the chest. Suddenly, his grip slid more easily, and Seth rode out wave after wave of shuddering bliss. Yes, yes, yes, yes, yes!

He collapsed, wrung out and exhausted, panting through the aftershocks and heart thudding a reggae beat.

Dustin eased out and reached over Seth's shoulder to grab a tissue from a box on the nightstand. He wrapped the condom, and snatched another tissue to dab at the mess cooling on Seth's chest and abs. Without looking, he aimed for the trash can and scored a direct hit. Impressive.

Ever so slowly, Dustin skimmed his fingers up and down Seth's arms, nibbling at the hollow of Seth's throat. Down and down he traveled, pausing to tease a circle around one crinkly nipple before lapping a swath over the slight bulge of Seth's belly.

More relaxed and comfortable than he'd been in a long, long time, arousal zinged through Seth again. By the time Dustin's mouth reached his groin, his cock had swelled to near-full hardness.

Dustin chucked. "I guess it's true that you can't keep a good man down." He took Seth's cock into the warm cavern of his mouth.

This was no slow lovemaking—this was what Seth imagined happened in the back rooms of clubs, a sucking intended to get him off in the shortest possible time. He stared, fascinated by the hollows forming in Dustin's cheeks. With nothing else to hold onto, he braced his hands on Dustin's shoulders.

Oh, God, yes.

The familiar tingling started low in his belly, and he cried out, filling Dustin's mouth. If anyone had been in the house, they'd have heard him. Right now, who the fuck cared?

Dustin climbed up the bed in one fluid motion and kissed Seth deeply, the taste of come lingering on his tongue. If Seth hadn't already peaked three times tonight, sharing the flavor would have been enough to set him off again.

Dustin pulled the covers over them both. "Good night," he said, caressing Seth's temple with his lips.

While Dustin slept peacefully beside him, Seth lay awake into the night. How the hell could he ever leave this behind to return to an empty life in Chicago?

CHAPTER 10

THAT night became the first of several dates ending at one of their houses, Dustin's work schedule permitting. Having grown used to seeing each other daily, it came as a surprise when Dustin turned Seth down without offering much of an explanation.

"I'm sorry, Seth, but I'm busy tonight."

"Busy doing what? Do you need some help?" Macaroni pie sizzled in the oven, the recipe procured from one of Aunt Irene's handwritten cookbooks.

"Um... thanks, but this is something I have to do on my own. Can I come over tomorrow night instead?"

Only if you like leftovers, Seth nearly said. *Needy much?* Though they'd seen each other regularly for the past week, Dustin had made no mention of being exclusive, or if their being lovers even held any meaning beyond sex. *It's not like he's expecting you to stay,* Seth's conscience justified, pissing him off. His conscience was supposed to be on *his* side.

"Yeah, it's okay. I may go to the library tonight. Use the Internet."

"Don't!"

"Huh?"

"The library's closed tonight. Mrs. Hopkins has the flu."

"The library is closed because the librarian is sick? Doesn't she have an assistant?"

"Assistant is sick too. Nasty bug going around. Highly contagious. She left my office not two minutes ago."

"Oh." Seth breathed a sigh of relief. "You could have told me you were working late. I cooked. Would you like me to bring you a plate?"

"No! I mean, dinner sounds wonderful, but my throat's been kinda scratchy." Dustin coughed on cue. "Maybe you should stay home, not risk catching this bug."

"If you insist."

A relieved-sounding sigh wafted from the phone. "Good. I'll see you tomorrow, and remember, whatever you do, stay home tonight. In the house."

Strange, but maybe Dustin was running a fever, making him delirious. "Okay. Take care of yourself, and call me if you need anything."

"Will do. Good night."

Whew, what a close call. Dustin stood on the roof of his truck in order to get a cell phone signal in the clearing behind Irene's house. The passel gathered, one-hundred-fifty-plus strong around him. Several women scattered the bounty of a late-night run to a bakery thrift shop on the ground. "No one is to go near the house tonight, understand? No one!" He made one more phone call, ensuring the perimeter guards were in place, ever vigilant against attack. A light breeze carried the scent of home cooking to his sensitive nose, adding an additional burden. Seth had cooked. For him.

"But ever since she got sick, we always met at Ms. Irene's

house to eat before heading out into the night," one of the elders protested, bringing Dustin back to the here and now.

"Irene's gone, her great-nephew is living there, and he has no clue about his family." *And he'll be leaving soon and won't ever be the wiser.* Seemed a shame, though, to watch the McDaniel family legacy fade and die. For more than two hundred years, the passel had existed in harmony, for the most part, under the shrewd leadership of various McDaniels. And now the line had nearly died out. McDaniels made great leaders on the whole, but they weren't the most prolific of families. Giving Seth up a second time just might rip Dustin's heart out.

Monica approached, waiting while Dustin climbed down off the truck before assuming an "at ease, soldier" pose to his right, a position befitting the acting second-in-command.

"Are you announcing your intent to take Irene's place?" This from Willie Timmerman from down at the Feed and Seed. Willie's Uncle Junior must have put him up to asking. Willie seldom did anything without direction from his powerful uncle, one of the town's leading citizens and the passel member most likely to issue a challenge. Why Junior hadn't already done so mystified Dustin, but he fully expected opposition, someday soon.

"At the moment, I'm respecting the passing of our leader. When the time is right, I'll recommend a successor or announce my intentions." Aware of the sand trickling away in her hourglass, Irene had spent her last days coaching Dustin on what he'd need to do and say. He hadn't learned nearly enough. If only they'd been given a little more time.

The blood began to sing in his veins, pulsing, exhilarating. He breathed in the scents of fresh mown hay, honeysuckle, and sweet summer evening. After dropping his jeans to the ground, he stepped out of them and neatly folded and placed his lone garment on the front seat of his truck. As interim leader, he fought the change, keeping a watchful eye. One by one, the passel groaned and moaned, their humanity melting away to leave behind a legion of possum bodies foraging in the night.

Transformation was the time the shifter folk were at their most vulnerable, and Irene had told cautionary tales of foxes and coyotes that had nearly decimated the passel a century ago, catching them while shifting and feasting on their members. Occasionally a predatory bird still caused a scare, keeping the leaders ever watchful. When the last of the jacks, jills, and joeys scuttled off to the relative safety of the forest, mouths full of baked goods or insects, Dustin nodded to Monica, who let out a relieved-sounding sigh and released her hold on the beast within. Her long blonde hair shortened, fading to brown and gray, and he briefly spotted the sprouting of a tail. In the blink of an eye, a furred creature with beady black eyes stared up at him as if to say, "What 'cha waitin' for?"

He'd expended too much energy fighting the change. The moment he dropped his guard, he shifted, without even time to register whether or not the process hurt.

Rather than feast on day-old bread, crickets, or grasshoppers, the way the more snippy members of the passel planned to pass their one mandatory transformation of the lunar month, he and Monica took turns with the elders monitoring the group. He patiently waited his turn to slither through the grass while searching for the perfect, juicy June bug.

Close to sunup, he made his final rounds.

Wait! Where was his receptionist, Tiffany?

A scream came from the house.

Scritch, scritch. Seth bolted upright in bed, tugging the patchwork comforter around his chin. His heart thudded a frantic beat in his ears. What was that noise? He inhaled shallow breaths. *Old houses make noises,* he told himself. *It's just the house settling.*

He'd almost convinced himself when *scritch scritch!* There it went again. His heart banged against his ribs. He slipped one hand out from under the covers and snatched at the pull chain on the ancient lamp beside the bed, flooding a corner of the room with light but not chasing back the shadows completely. The bedside clock displayed 5:00 a.m. Something had the nerve to wake him at five freaking o'clock in the morning?

Scritch scritch came again, more insistent this time. Seth took a deep breath, eking it out in a relieved sigh. The cat. Irene must have had a cat after all, and the poor lost kitty wanted in. Or a mouse. Maybe a mouse. He turned out the light, plumped his pillow with a few well-aimed thumps, and nestled back down into the mattress.

SCRITCH SCRITCH SCRITCH! One second horizontal, the next minute vertical, Seth clutched the covers as a shield and turned on the lamp again. He listened. Where had the sound come from? Not his bedroom, right? Right?

Ever so slowly, he placed a hand on the nightstand, easing over the side of the high bed to peer beneath. Nothing but a few dust bunnies, well on their way to becoming dust rhinos. He eased one leg from under the covers. Slowly he wriggled from between the sheets, summoning every bit of his nonexistent courage.

Searching for something, anything, to use for a weapon, he spotted the sword above the mantel, famed to have belonged to his great-great-grandfather. In his youth, he'd been wowed, but grown-up Seth privately suspected the keepsake had come from an auction. Properly armed with the aged relic, he gritted his teeth. Please let the floor not squeak and announce his presence.

Scritch scritch? The nuisance's telltale scratching came again, hesitant, questioning, as though the unwelcome nocturnal visitor daring to disturb Seth's sleep now counted its days numbered.

One careful footstep after the other, Seth tiptoed his way into the kitchen, holding his breath while he flipped the light switch. Whatever lurked out of sight paused mid-scritch, drawing Seth's eyes to the panel sealing in the water heater—the panel he'd replaced.

"Aha!" he told his unwelcome guest. "Can't get in since I covered the hole, can you?" He shuddered. How many times had his aging auntie slept peacefully while a critter ran amok in her home? He recalled the chewed loaf of bread he'd found on the counter, and the massive amounts of decayed food. "You've mooched your last meal, my friend."

Seth raised the sword over his shoulder, aiming to swing it baseball-bat fashion if necessary, and lifted the hook-and-eye latch holding the panel in place. He flung the door open and took a peek inside. "Holy shit!" Seth jumped back from the opening.

"*Eeeeeiiiiiii!*" screamed the thing, before fainting dead away.

Having been transported a few feet away without realizing how he'd gotten there, Seth crept closer, eyes riveted to the humongous rat lying curled up on the floor next to the water heater, the sword point leading him like a divining rod toward the immobile beastly mass.

Was it dead? Had Seth killed the darned thing from fright? "I am the man!" Seth crowed. He hunkered down. He didn't know much about animals except for small purse dogs he'd photographed, but the body lying on the floor wasn't a rat. Was it a… possum? Made sense to find a possum in the house when you lived near a town called Possum Kingdom.

He poked the thing with the sword. Other than jerking with the motion of the blade, the hairy trespasser lay still.

Seth poked again, watching for sides to rise and fall with steady breathing. Nothing. He reached out a tentative hand and snatched the skinny tail, intent on tossing the creature outside and going back to bed. The moment he touched the wormlike appendage the animal squirmed. He let loose. The possum dropped back to the floor, immediately flipping into its "I'm dead, leave me alone" position.

"That's the deal, is it?" Seth screwed up his nerve, grabbing the tail again and then barreling for the door. Both beady eyes flew open, as did a mouth full of sharp teeth. *"Hsssssssssssssss,"* went the possum. Oh, fuck! Seth ran faster, slinging open the front door. Jagged mouth-daggers ripped onto Seth's arm.

"Aaaaaaaaahhhh!"

The possum dropped to the front porch with a heavy *thump* and scurried away into the night.

Seth clutched his bleeding wrist, staring out at the darkness. "It bit me! Son of a bitch bit me!"

CHAPTER 11

A MISSING shifter plus a howling human equaled major damage control needed. Waiting until dawn broke and the passel returned to human form had been sheer agony. Afterward, dealing with passel member's petty grievances ate even more of Dustin's time. The moment he'd extracted himself, he took off for Seth's. *It's my fault, it's my fault, it's my fault,* he chanted, his compact Ford Ranger burning rubber down Irene's long drive. No, not Irene's—*Seth's* long drive. He hoped like hell Monica located Tiffany, and that the woman was okay. If she wasn't, he'd soon hear from Andy.

A million scenarios played out in his head. What would he say, what would he do? How would he explain the sudden need to pay an early morning visit, when last night he'd claimed illness?

He passed the densely packed pine trees lining the drive, then pulled to an abrupt halt in front of the house. Irene's truck wasn't parked in its normal spot at the barn entrance. Dustin beat on the front door anyway. Where was Seth? Dustin's blood ran cold. He visualized Tiffany sinking teeth into Seth's arm, worst-case scenario playing out in his mind. Surely Seth hadn't been injured badly enough to drive to the emergency room over in Crawfordville. Some doctors on staff had grown up nearby and knew the score, but an overzealous young intern might go into conniptions, believing he'd found something medical-journal worthy in Seth's bloodstream.

Calm down. Maybe Seth decided to drive twenty miles to the nearest McDonalds for breakfast. Maybe he'd only screamed because Tiffany startled him.

Dustin hopped back into his truck, checking his watch— ten minutes past nine. He should be at work by now. He hit the speed dial on his phone for his office, in the unlikely event that Seth called or stopped by. Shit! No signal this far out in a hollow. Dustin sped back up the driveway, choking on his own dust. The moment the truck tires tasted asphalt at the top of the hill, his phone rang. "Dr. Livingston," he answered.

A blubbering Tiffany yowled into his ear. "Oh, God, Doc, I'm so, so sorry. I didn't mean to. I really, really, didn't mean to."

"Calm down, Tiffany. You didn't mean to what?" He gave her the benefit of the doubt, though he fully believed he knew what her next words would be. Was it too much to hope that she'd merely broken a window or something at the clinic or double-scheduled a nine o'clock appointment?

She hissed into the phone, probably meaning to whisper. "I bit somebody!"

Dustin's heart stalled, then mule kicked his insides. "I'll be right there." He tossed his phone aside and stomped the gas pedal. Please let him make it to his office before all hell broke loose.

His heart fell the moment he spotted Irene's truck parked outside his practice. He didn't even have to enter the office. Weak as she was, the virus in Tiffany's possum-form saliva had clearly jumpstarted Seth's dormant strain. Pheromones leaked through the windows, the pungent scent of mature male possum calling to Dustin like a siren's song.

Dustin bolted through the door. Tiffany wasn't in sight, Good. Maybe she didn't cry all over Seth, apologizing for something he couldn't understand. Best to break the "Congratulations, it's a possum!" news gently.

He found Seth and Monica in an examining room.

"Quit being a baby," Monica barked. "It's only a scratch."

Seth sat, wide-eyed and blinking on the edge of the table, clutching a bloody washcloth around his wrist.

"He won't let me clean it, doctor." Monica stepped back, dusting her hands together.

Dustin glared; his assistant glared back. "Monica, wait outside until I need you, please."

"Suit yourself."

"Hey, Seth. What happened?" Dustin nodded to Seth's extended wrist.

"Something bit me."

Dustin scrubbed his hands in the sink and applied gloves, though he actually didn't need them. His human DNA effectively killed viruses only affecting animals, and his opossum DNA counteracted human viruses. While theoretically rabies affected both animals and humans, possums were mostly immune—a little known oddity and the basis of the thesis Dustin completed to get into the highly confidential shifter program at medical school.

He peeled back the washcloth, wincing at the severity of the bite. With a delicate hand, he cleansed the wound, gently probing the perimeter of the injury. She'd gotten him good.

As if scent alone weren't enough to go by, the edges of the wound healing faster than normal underscored Seth's virus status. Other changes would come.

In the back of Dustin's mind hung a cloud of worry. With a newly awakened virus in his system, Seth's going back to

Chicago without knowing could prove dangerous. But there was time enough to plan for the future later. The virus alone couldn't bring a shift, and some full-blood passel members lived their whole lives as carriers, never totally manifesting the full symptoms of Channing-Frost. Maybe the same would be true for Seth. One could hope.

"I need to take a blood sample," Dustin said, more for Seth's benefit than for medicinal purposes. He'd already guessed the results.

He moved in close, inhaling a musky whiff. Once more, an overwhelming need to possess Seth raged through him, an inferno out of control. He bit the inside of his cheek, trying to return focus to the task at hand.

"What about rabies?" Seth asked.

"We don't often get rabies." *Fuck! Get a grip, man!* "I mean, possums don't normally carry rabies. Their body temperatures are generally too low to sustain that particular virus."

Seth narrowed his eyes and snatched his hand back. "Who told you it was a possum?"

Oh shit, you've done it now! Dustin backpedaled—hard. "Umm… well, if you'll notice the edges of the bite, the pattern of the teeth. Plus, Irene told me she'd occasionally found one in the house."

Seth relaxed, letting Dustin take his hand again. "Yeah, it was a possum."

Forcing lascivious thoughts from his mind, Dustin slipped into doctor mode, collecting a blood sample and passing it out the door to Monica. Surely she sensed Seth's changed status, probably what provoked her ire. Whoever'd let Tiffany slip off last night had a lot to answer for.

After cleaning the wound, applying a bandage, and issuing a few precautionary shots, Dustin opened the door at Monica's insistent tapping. "Tell him, 'welcome to the family,'" she murmured, sliding the test results into his hand and confirming Dustin's previous conclusion. Welcome to the family, indeed.

He didn't say anything until Monica gave up and quit listening at the door, then swiped his lips over Seth's temple. "I want you to take it easy today, and if you notice anything unusual, call me, okay?" They needed to have a long talk later. For now, damage control.

Dustin spent the rest of the morning luring Tiffany, in possum form, out from behind a trash can in the ladies' room.

By the time Seth left Dustin's office, the steady throbbing in his wrist had lessened to an intermittent tingle. He flexed his arm as much as he dared and it seemed to function fine.

While in town, maybe he should stop by the grocery store for staples Monica didn't seem aware of, like Hamburger Helper and beer.

A mom with two small kids in tow bowed her head and said, "Good morning, jack."

Huh? Was Monica's special brand of crazy catching? Putting the incident out of his mind for his sanity's sake, he perused the shopping aisles. A wonderfully enticing scent hit his nostrils, and as if propelled by some unseen force, he found himself at the meat counter, shoulder to shoulder with three other men. He lowered his face into the cooler case, snuffling deeply. Mmmmm....

"Oops, sorry. That pack's going bad." A white-jacketed man rushed forward, grabbing the rancid hamburger meat and hauling it away.

Three forlorn faces stared at Seth. "Get used to it, jack," one said, giving him a comradely clap on the back. "Happens all the time."

Well, that was strange, but at least he didn't seem to be the target of the hostility Monica reserved for outsiders. Seth finished his shopping and hurried back to the farmhouse. He suddenly found himself craving the sliced turkey he'd considered throwing out two days ago.

A Cadillac Escalade turned in behind him. He parked the truck in its spot in the barn, and returned to the front yard to find a portly gentleman waiting by the front door. "Mr. McDaniel? Hi, I'm Wilson Levitt, and I'd like a few moments of your time, if you don't mind."

Seth had spoken to a realtor or two, but no one by the name of Levitt. "What can I do for you?"

The man grinned, showing nearly as many teeth as the possum from the night before. "It's not what you can do for me, but what I can do for you!" He extended a beefy hand, holding out a "Levitt Real Estate Development" business card.

Seth shuffled his shopping bags in order to take the card. The man seemed oblivious to Seth's predicament. "Now, what you got here, one hundred, one hundred fifty acres?"

"Two hundred seventeen, mostly wooded." Seth had done some homework before his arrival; mature timber enhanced the property's value and made a strong selling point.

Levitt puckered out his lower lip. "Well, I'm afraid those pesky trees'll depreciate your properly values, son."

"Do what? The place is set out with oaks and pines." Seth spent a good deal of time checking lumber prices too.

"Yeah, but to get to the land, we'll have to cut those down and haul 'em off; but don't you worry none. Because I'm a generous man, I'm prepared to offer you nine hundred dollars an acre." He beamed as though he'd offered Seth the moon.

Seth fought hard to tamp down his anger. "Now wait a damned minute. I've done some comparisons, and the going rate for land around here is two thousand dollars an acre. At least fifty acres have mountain views and can pull in as much as

$20,000. And I can sell the timber and bring in one hell of a lot more."

The slimy little shyster rubbed his hands together, shaking his head. "May be prime land, once developed. There's a lot of work to be done here. Build access roads, haul off those useless trees. There's also the little matter of the swampland."

"Swampland? We're in the foothills, there's no swampland here!"

"Oh, yes, there is. Why do think no one's approached you before now? I'm the only one generous enough to take this useless land off your hands. Why, there's rumors going 'round of an Indian burial ground here. Who in their right mind would buy an Indian burial ground?"

Through clenched teeth, Seth suddenly made a spur of the moment decision, hoping like hell he wouldn't regret his rashness later. "The land is not for sale at any price. It's my family's land, and I intend to stay here."

"Okay, you drive a hard bargain. Nine hundred twenty-five dollars an acre, and that's my final offer."

"No thank you, and please get the hell off my farm."

The man opened and closed his mouth a few times, but nothing intelligible came out. Finally, he managed a wavering, "You're turning down my offer?"

"Yep."

Levitt's face turned a horrifying shade of puce. "Mark my words, Mr. McDaniel, in a few months you'll come crawling to me, hand out, begging me to take this useless parcel off your hands."

Through clenched teeth, Seth growled. "I'll take my chances."

"I guarantee no one else will offer anything close to what I'm offering."

"Again, I'll take my chances."

It took another fifteen minutes and behavior bordering on

rude to squeeze the man back into his vehicle and make him leave. "I'm the only one who'll even talk to you," the charlatan claimed in parting.

He was wrong. Four other realtors extended the same "generous" offer the same day. An entirely unpleasant sensation squirmed to life in Seth's gut each time he thought about selling. The land, the house, was all that remained of his family ties. To simply walk away… well, it didn't feel right. In desperation, Seth found a leftover piece of plywood from his kitchen patch job and hand-lettered a sign: *Land not for sale. Realtors will be shot on sight.* He posted the sign by the main road. Let them come now!

I don't want to sell the house.

You need to sell the house.

Seth argued back and forth with himself. What did he need with a huge four-bedroom place in the middle of nowhere? He stalked from room to room; each one would easily accommodate his entire apartment back in Chicago. He liked roaming from room to room. He liked seeing reminders of his family on every shelf. He liked actually owning instead of renting. *But what the hell will I do with it all?*

In a rare bit of good fortune, Seth had found enough signal to operate his phone in the attic. However, his traitorous media sites were now filled with pictures of Michael's wedding attire, venue, choices for flower arrangements, etcetera. He trudged back downstairs, abandoning his phone on a nightstand. He should be cataloging his aunt's heirlooms, or even making arrangements to prepare the house for sale with a real realtor who wouldn't try to rip him off. It didn't hurt to keep his options open, did it? He did none of those things. Instead, he ventured back up to the attic, surfing the internet via his iPhone for possible freelance photo ops in the area.

A hospital in a neighboring town had posted an ad for someone to photograph newborns. But they were probably looking for someone who'd stick around. Photographers were needed for a dance recital in Atlanta. Oh, for yesterday. He hated when job sites didn't update promptly. Another ad drew his attention: *Wildlife photographers needed*. Wildlife? Seth was quite certain he'd find plenty of deer and foxes locally, if memory served. Armed with his trusty Nikon and a 400mm lens, he set off to spy on Mother Nature.

The pond yielded several candid frog shots, and he took a few frames of a ring of stones near a towering pin oak. Laid out in a semicircle around the tree, the gleaming chunks of quartz appeared to have been purposefully arranged. But by whom? Had there once been an old homestead out here?

He drew back in fear when a bundle of gray and brown fur wobbled by. His arm pulsed at the memory of a mouthful of sharp teeth sinking into his flesh. Instead of attacking, this possum appeared mildly curious. The creature approached, twitching its nose in the air. Seth snapped a picture. The animal turned its head, holding the position, as if to say, "Take my good side." Seth snapped, then the creature moved. Was the damned thing posing? He'd just wrapped up a series of candid shots with the possum lounging on a rock when out of the grass came two more. They froze momentarily before dashing over to the third, chittering wildly. The two newcomers inclined their heads, displaying mouthfuls of sharp teeth, but didn't come closer or hiss. Seth, considering the situation reasonably safe, snapped a shot. The trio preened, vamping to put runway models to shame.

In a decided diva moment, one shoved the others out of the way, fighting its way to the center of Seth's camera lens. Another elbowed back. Possums had elbows? Soon the shoving escalated into a free-for-all of ear biting, growling, and tail-tugging.

Throughout the melee Seth stood, squatted, and even crawled on his belly to get the perfect shot. An angry, "Boys!" penetrated the snarling and claw scrabbling. The three possums froze. One spat out a mouthful of fur.

A woman tramped through the weeds, stopping when she saw Seth. "Oh, sorry. I didn't know you were out here." She self-consciously patted errant strands of hair back in place. "I'm Kelly Johnson, your neighbor. I met you at the store the other day. You haven't seen my boys by any chance, have you? I'm afraid they like to sneak down here to the pond and catch crawfish."

From the corner of his eye, Seth observed three furry forms creeping toward a blackberry bush. The woman followed his line of sight. "There you are, you scoundrels. You better march yourselves right back up to the house and finish your chores. Now! Wait until your father comes home and gives you a piece of his mind!"

Three heads bowed, three tails dragged the ground, and three apparently trained possums trooped up the path and over the hill. "Sorry 'bout that, jack, but what can I do? Joeys will be joeys." She shrugged and traipsed off after the critters, leaving Seth bewildered, disbelieving, and with a collection of wildlife shots the likes of which he'd never seen before.

What the hell just happened?

He'd made it halfway to the house before the woman's words hit him like a ton of bricks. "Wait a minute! Did she call them her boys?"

CHAPTER 12

SETH had no sooner made it to the house to research possum behavior when the unmistakable sound of tires on gravel rumbled up the driveway, sounding unusually loud—as did the birds twittering from the magnolia tree, and nearly everything else. He flinched, and though the truck was a ways off, he stepped back from the drive, placing an oak tree between himself and the approaching vehicle.

A shiny white BMW X5 pulled to a stop. The man inside stared into the SUV's rearview mirror, adjusting his tie. Could this man be from Aunt Irene's attorney's office? *Please, God, let it not be another realtor.* Instead of a briefcase, the man stepped down with a box of chocolates in one hand and flowers in the other. "Mr. McDaniel?" he asked, showing a mouthful of choppers, not unlike the three recent possums. He stood at least six foot two, with sandy-blond hair and mustache, both neatly trimmed. The kind of "out of my price range" cologne Seth sniffed at perfume counters drifted toward him on a light breeze.

"You're not a realtor, are you?" Seth hesitated to ask. He'd forgotten junk food at the grocery store, and the chocolates made his mouth water.

"Oh, hell no!"

Good. Seth relaxed a bit. "Can I help you with something?"

"Don't worry, Mr. McDaniel. This here's a social call."

The stranger's well-groomed appearance and expensive clothes hinted at money, with enough age on him for a few permanent crinkles at the eyes. He took a step forward, holding the flowers and candy in front of him. Those truffles hadn't come cheap, and neither had the long-stemmed red roses. "I'm Junior Timmerman, and I thought I'd come introduce myself, seeing as how I knew your aunt. Went to school with your daddy too, but he was a few grades ahead of me. How 'bout we go inside, set a spell. Get better acquainted."

Back home in Chicago, none of Seth's acquaintances dared show up out of the blue without calling first, but he figured unannounced visits might be a Southern thing, like leaving your doors unlocked, although Seth never did. Hadn't the guy at the Feed and Seed mentioned an Uncle Junior?

"Well, the air-conditioning isn't the greatest, but sure, come on in." What could it hurt? The guy seemed harmless enough —thus far.

Junior traipsed along behind Seth, and Seth swore he felt the man attempting to stare holes through his back.

"How long you planning on staying, Mr. McDaniel?"

"Not long. Long enough to get the house fixed up and on the market before I head back home to Chicago." No need to let strangers in on his internal struggle over whether to leave or stay. Besides, the man might know an honest realtor, or a local with an eye on the place.

"You're leaving?" Junior sounded truly disappointed. "But you just got here. If you gave it a chance, you'd find Possum Kingdom to be a nice area to settle down in."

"I remember it fondly from my childhood, but I grew up in Chicago. That's my home now. Can I get you something to drink, Mr. Timmerman?"

"Oh, please, call me Junior. Why don't I step into the kitchen with you, find some water for these flowers?" Junior made himself at home, sidestepping Seth to enter the kitchen and making a beeline for the far cabinets, depositing the chocolates on the counter on his way. He opened a door and extracted a vase, apparently acquainted with where Irene kept things. Seth's anxiety clicked down a notch, taking Junior's familiarity with Aunt Irene's kitchen as further proof of the guy's harmlessness, though Seth remained a bit on guard. Michael had always accused him of having "trust issues." Seth didn't have trust issues; he just didn't trust anyone.

"Sweet tea, Coke, or would you care for a beer?" Seth bent into the refrigerator, shaking the tea pitcher to check for fullness. He might have been displaced from the South at a young age, but he'd still learned to appreciate a tall glass of sweet tea.

"Water will be fine, straight from the tap. Irene's well has some of the sweetest water I've ever tasted." Junior filled the vase, added the flowers, and then placed them in the center of the kitchen table. "They don't have well water up there in Chicago, do they, Mr. McDaniel?"

It seemed ridiculous for a man dressed in a suit, an older man dressed in a suit, no less, to call Seth "Mister" while insisting on being called "Junior."

"Call me Seth."

"All right, Seth." A predatory grin crossed the man's face, and Seth suddenly understood how a T-bone steak must feel right after being doused with A.1. "Let's cut to the chase, shall we?"

Quicker than the eye could follow, Seth found himself pressed up against the refrigerator door, a leering man staring down at him. "We are, without a doubt, the two most powerful men in town."

Seth gulped, forcing out a strangled, "We… we are?"

Junior nodded, his nose mere inches from Seth's. "Without a doubt."

Unable to come up with anything more intelligent to say, Seth replied, "Imagine that."

"Now, surely your aunt's attorney made you aware of how much you inherited, didn't he?"

"I haven't gone over the records thoroughly yet. She left some bonds, a couple of accounts, this farmhouse, and a few acres that con men keep trying to finagle me out of."

"Farmhouse? A few acres? Boy, your aunt owned half of Possum Kingdom! This house sits on over two hundred acres of good farmland. It's been in your family for generations. I don't understand how you could dream of selling and living elsewhere, especially not now given your changed circumstances."

"What changed circumstances?"

Junior plopped a hand on the refrigerator door, and seeing an advantage, Seth ducked beneath and scurried to the far side of the kitchen, keeping the table between them. He glowered at Junior through a dozen rosebuds.

"No need to play coy, Mr.… Seth." The grin came back. "Now, if we combine our forces, we'll be unstoppable. I have hundreds of plans for this town, and with your backing, together we can put Possum Kingdom on the map."

"What are you doing? Running for some kind of office?"

"In a manner of speaking, I reckon you might say I am."

"What do you want me to do? Post flyers? Stuff envelopes?"

A chuckle emerged from Junior's barrel chest. "Oh, a sense of humor. I like that in a man. No, I've got something more practical in mind. There's only one person standing in the way of what I want to do for this town, but if you side with me, the good doctor won't present much of a problem."

The good doctor? "Dustin? What's Dustin got to do with this?"

"Everything." Junior approached slowly, palms up in an "I'm harmless" posture. "He goes with the status quo. Doesn't have any use for progress, much like your aunt, God rest her soul. While it's understandable that a lady of advanced years would resist change, Dr. Livingston is a young man and should make better use of the opportunities at his fingertips."

Seth nearly growled. He wasn't too sure where he and Dustin stood right now, what with Dustin's sudden evasiveness, but he didn't much care for this man talking about his lover/friend/fuck buddy/or whatever the hell Dusty was in such a manner.

Junior continued raising Seth's hackles. "Consider the advances we've made in the last thirty years. Cell phones...."

"Can't get a signal out here."

"Satellite TV."

"Got rabbit ears."

"Internet."

"I go to the library to check e-mails. You're not naming a thing I can't live without."

Junior darted around the table, hemming Seth up against the sink. "You're a nice-looking fella, stuck out here by your lonesome. Whaddya do for company, hmmm? Not only will we rule the whole county, I'll have you throwing rocks at any other man." Before Seth could execute an escape, Junior descended, taking advantage of a surprised gasp to slither his tongue into Seth's open mouth.

Too stunned to react, it took a few rounds of tongue-on-tongue action before Seth pushed Junior away. "What the fuck are you doing?"

"Now, there's no need to play hard to get. We're both grown men. And deep down inside, we want the same thing."

"For you to get the fuck out of my house?"

Junior gave Seth a rueful smile. "I imagine it's a bit over-whelming right now, too much happening too fast. But once you've had time to think things over, you'll agree that I'm the best man for the job. I'll make this town what it should be. No outsiders! I'll get the government to recognize our unique status, maybe even build a casino and make every last one of us rich. You've certainly got enough land to build on."

Anger flashed through Seth, lighting a fire that boiled his blood. "Mr. Timmerman, you've overstepped your bounds and I'd like you to leave." Having already seen how fast the man could move, the only safe place for Timmerman was a few counties over.

"All right, all right." Junior splayed his hands, managing to project a superior air even in a submissive posture. "Give it some time and give me a call. I'm in the phone book. I'll see myself out."

Seth didn't stop trembling until the whine of the BMW's engine faded to nothing. He took a deep breath, hanging on to the counter lest his quivering knees suddenly fail. "What the fuck was that all about, and what's it got to do with Dustin?"

Not only did Seth lock his door before turning in for the night, he slept with Great-great-grandpa's sword.

The next morning a panel van pulled up bright and early, two guys in coveralls hopping out. "Where do you want the satellite dish, Mr. McDaniel?" one asked.

"Satellite dish? I didn't order satellite."

"Says right here, bought and paid for a year's subscription, including the special channels." The guy winked. "Even the X-rated ones."

"A year? I'm not gonna be here a year."

The man scratched his balding head. "Well, somebody paid for it, might as well enjoy it."

An hour later, the men left, leaving behind a listing of Seth's lovely new premium channels and a converter box to allow the ancient TV to take advantage of them. His laptop sat on his aunt's rolltop desk, catching up on several weeks' worth of updates via his new high-speed Internet connection. No doubt lingered in his mind as to who'd paid for the luxury, but why? Nobody coughed up a year's satellite service to buy a vote, did they?

He pulled out his cell phone, planning to head to the attic, hoping to avoid having to stretch across the buffet to make a call from his aunt's oddly placed landline, when he noticed the device showing a full signal. What the fuck? Had Timmerman miraculously installed a cell phone tower near the farm for Seth? Maybe his phone had latched onto his computer modem. Seth wasn't the type to worry about how things worked; he simply grinned when he noticed those five beautiful bars.

Although he'd received mounds of official lawyer-speak letters the day after he'd gotten the phone call about his aunt's passing (requiring a good bit of web surfing to decipher), and understood the basics of his inheritance, some details needed clarifying. Also, a personal letter from the lawyer requested a face to face meeting, "as time permits." The last thing he needed was someone else who'd known the McDaniels forever pointing out how Seth didn't deserve Irene for a relative, but he'd put off the inevitable long enough.

His first phone call was to his aunt's attorney, his second to her stockbroker. His third was to the president of the First National Bank of Possum Kingdom. He sat down hard on the old settee, trying to grasp all he'd been told. Even if only a fraction of what they'd said held true, he was now rich as all fuck, and he needed to pay a visit to the lawyer.

CHAPTER 13

SETH preyed on Dustin's mind. A woman with brown hair, a man with similar eyes or the same height—they all brought back memories of Seth and the nights Dustin had spent with him. He remembered Irene's room, years ago, when he'd found Seth crying. His own heart had broken. How he hated Seth's grandmother for tearing them apart, and for throwing away the arrowhead that he'd hoped might bring Seth back.

If not for that woman, would they have grown up insepara-blc, as they'd been as kids, or would they have drifted, moving on to other interests, other friends? Picturing them lying on their bellies in Irene's room, spilling secrets beneath a quilt draped over the backs of two chairs, Dustin found it hard to believe anything other than physical separation could have kept them apart.

For the past two nights, passel duties had occupied Dustin's time. Yet foremost in his mind was concern over what Seth must think about his absence. Things would be so much easier if Seth knew the whole story. Then there'd be no need for secrets, no need for hiding.

As temporary leader of the passel, the duty fell on Dustin's shoulders, but he didn't want to have to be the one to tell Seth that heading back to Chicago wasn't wise. And Dustin certainly wasn't looking forward to the expression on Seth's face when he learned that from here on out, he might be spending every full moon with a ragtag group of shape-shifters.

On a positive note, for a guy used to not having any family, a "family reunion" held every full moon might hold some appeal. *Dream on!*

In Dustin's lifetime, only a handful of new members had joined the passel accidentally, and a few made a hard transition. Would Seth blame poor Tiffany?

He pictured Seth out at the farmhouse, alone, miles from home, and suffered a hot stab of guilt. Regardless of the circumstances, he wasn't being a very good friend, and for certain Irene sat perched on a cloud somewhere, watching from above, shaking her head at Dustin's lack of courage.

Seth needed him right now. Surely changes were taking place within his body that he couldn't possibly understand— much worse than puberty—and someone had to prepare him for what he might face with the rise of the next full moon.

Well, they had a date scheduled for later, though Dustin wasn't sure if tonight was the right time to come clean. Maybe he should start slowly, ask, "So, Seth. Do you like possums?" He sighed. Dancing around the subject wouldn't work. Once he'd herded a straggling patient out the door who'd wanted to stay and chat with Tiffany, he headed to his office to log in his last chart of the day.

Monica followed him.

"Can this wait?" he asked. "I'm kind of in a hurry."

"Not really."

One glimpse of her thinned lips and creased brow and he dropped in his chair, bracing for the worse. "What?"

"I may not like Seth McDaniel much...."

Dustin's heart sank to his stomach.

"… and I may think Irene deserved a better nephew…."

Dustin's heart plunged further.

"… but you need to make up your mind about who you want running the show. And you need to have a long talk with the guy."

"Why? What's happened?"

"I got wind that Junior Timmerman found out about the bite and has gone courting. And he's pulling out all the stops."

Junior? Well, fuck.

Junior must smell money and opportunity. Dustin let out a bone-weary sigh, good intentions flying out the window. With Junior forcing his hand, he needed to talk to Seth tonight and tell him everything before his rival did. He dialed Irene's home phone number from memory to ensure they were still on for tonight, only to receive a message: "The number you have dialed has been disconnected."

"Shit!" he exclaimed. "It's disconnected and I didn't even get Seth's cell phone number."

The tight pursing of Monica's lips relaxed somewhat. "I have it."

"You do? How did you get it?"

Monica rolled her eyes heavenward. "Duh. I had his phone, remember?"

"*What?*" Dustin stared at Monica in disbelief. "You checked out his phone while you had it? Why that's… that's…."

A perfectly groomed eyebrow arched over Monica's right eye. "Sneaky and underhanded? Guilty as charged. However, since we're dealing with Junior, who'd seize every advantage, one of us needs to be willing to take the less than noble approach."

As disturbing as her logic was, Dustin couldn't argue.

"So, Mr. Morally Upright, do you want his phone number or not?"

"I do."

"Check your phone listing, under 'Asshole'." With a faux sweet grin, Monica spun on her heel and tromped out of the office, leaving Dustin in awe and slightly afraid of his assistant —but exceedingly glad she was on his side.

Dustin hand't fidgeted this much since his one lone attempt to date a female, a hormone-ridden angstfest thereafter referred to as the senior prom. At least tonight he didn't have his anxious father lecturing him on taking precautions during any sexual encounters he might have planned for his date, a lovely young woman whose only amorous adventures for later involved another girl. Dustin would have rather dated her brother anyway.

He fretted, checking his hair in the mirror, more a stall tactic than actual concern over his appearance. How did you tell the man you'd been having sex with, "Oh, yeah, I get furry once a month, more often if the mood hits, isn't that a hoot?" Then waiting for the right opportunity to add, "Oh, did I mention you might get furry too? Remember the sweet little receptionist at the office? Well, seems she followed a snoot full of *eau de* macaroni pie to your house, hunting a nibble and—can you believe it?—bit you instead! Have you ever heard anything so doggone hilarious?"

Dustin cringed. There didn't seem to be a correct way to induct the unaware into the passel. Would Seth hate Tiffany? Would he blame Dustin for not warning him of the dangers?

With less enthusiasm than previous trips, Dustin arrived at the farmhouse far faster than he'd hoped. He needed more time to work things out. *Oh well, no help for it now.* As passel leader and Seth's lover, he couldn't conveniently pass this task to another. He fully believed if he left it up to her, Monica would barge in, yell, "You're a damned possum, get the hell over it," and leave.

Seth answered the door, wearing nothing but a pair of jeans and a welcoming smile, effectively shoving the knife further into Dustin's heart. His news was certain to wipe the smile right off the man's face. "Hey, Dusty. I'm glad you made it tonight. I hope you don't mind leftovers, but I made too much the other night, and since you weren't able to come over, I put it away."

"Leftovers are fine." Dustin's throat felt packed with cotton, the words emerging distant and slurred. He stared down at the floor, unable to meet Seth's eyes.

Seth's chipper demeanor fell. "Is something wrong? Oh my God! You didn't find anything with my blood test, did you?"

"Other than borderline high cholesterol levels? No. But, we need to talk." He hazarded an upward glance.

The color drained from Seth's face. "Sure. Let me turn the oven off. I had everything reheating."

Dustin engaged his inner animal's acute hearing, listening to Seth's footfalls, incoherent mumbling, and then the sound of the stove knob clicking off. Seth called out, "Make yourself at home. Would you like something to drink?"

"Beer, if you have it." Or something stronger. *You might need one too,* went unsaid.

The soft padding of Seth's bare feet across the kitchen linoleum sharpened when he stepped onto the hardwood flooring of the hallway, and then into the sitting room. "Here." He handed Dustin an opened beer.

Dustin guzzled half of it before easing down onto the settee. "Seth," he began. "How much were you told about your family history?"

Instead of joining Dustin, Seth settled with his own beer in an adjacent chair. "Not much. My grandfather died in Vietnam, and my grandmother passed during Dad's senior year of high school. He came here to live with Aunt Irene."

"Your direct ancestor, Braden McDaniel, was one of the town's founding fathers."

"Seems I remember my daddy saying something about a great-great something or other named Braden. But your family's been around as long as mine, right?"

Dustin shook his head. "No. My family settled here in the early 1900s—relative newcomers in the eyes of more established residents." He tried and failed to keep his disgust to a minimum, the constant reminders from folks like Junior that he wasn't "old blood."

Seth voiced Dustin's exact thoughts. "What a stupid prejudice! Anyway, what does any of this have to do with my family? They didn't give yours grief, did they? Were we Georgia's version of the Hatfields and McCoys?"

Taking a deep breath, Dustin ventured out onto a slippery slope. "No. None of the recent McDaniels and Livingstons quarreled, at any rate. Case in point: Irene picked me to be her second-in-command."

"Second-in-command?" One of Seth's brows quirked at an odd angle. "What do you mean? Like in the military?"

Dustin didn't want to do this. He *really* didn't want to do this. Everything he'd rehearsed on the way over vanished from his mind. Best to simply wing it. "You've heard that your aunt was a leader in our community, haven't you?"

"Yes."

Dustin ran his fingers through his hair, gauging his words carefully. He'd only get one chance to do this right, and if he fucked up, he might lose Seth for good. He'd barely survived the last time. What was he thinking? Seth lived in Chicago, and had stated from day one his intentions of going back there. "Your family believed they were unique, and sought out a place where they could live quietly, free of persecution."

"Are you saying they were part of a cult or something? Some kind of religious group?"

"No. Back in the 1700s, though, they probably were viewed as outside the norm. Modern medicine cracked the mystery. It seems they carried a genetic anomaly, a virus, passed from one generation to the next for as long as the family kept a history. We haven't figured out why, but some family members were merely carriers, never showing the full symptoms like others did."

"Symptoms? Like some kind a genetic disease?"

"Not a disease. A virus that works on the central nervous system, making the host stronger and faster. It improves the senses and speeds healing. Bottom line: the virus survives if the host survives. It's in its best interest to take good care of the host. Your father displayed all the major symptoms, while at the time of your birth, your mother wasn't infected." Dustin hated the word "infected." The majority of those with the changeling virus considered themselves "beneficiaries." Blessing or curse, possessing two forms set them apart from the rest of the world, made them special, at least in their own eyes. Some, like Junior, viewed themselves as superior."

"And I have this virus." Seth's words sounded flat, lacking any emotion, and every bit of color left his face.

Dustin rose from the settee. Crap. Poor guy probably thought the worst. Pacing the room allowed Dustin to focus while giving him an excuse not to meet Seth's eyes and witness the expected revulsion. "Many in town do. You, me, Monica, your neighbors, the Johnsons."

"My aunt?"

"Definitely your aunt."

"It's contagious? Is this why my grandmother didn't want me to come here?"

"More than likely." Dustin focused on a picture on the mantel of Irene surrounded by the passel.

"You said my mother wasn't infected when I was born. I

take it she contracted the virus later. Did my father give it to her?"

"Yes. By her choice." Dustin's gaze shifted to a family photo of Seth with his parents, probably taken about the time Seth's mother turned. Not wanting to look, Dustin tore his gaze away and continued pacing.

Seth shot to his feet and quickly overtook Dustin's circuit around the room. He grabbed Dustin's shoulders and held him in place. "She chose to be infected? What is this damn virus? What does it do? Is that why they died? Are you telling me I'm dying?"

"Whoa, whoa! Hold up. Your parents were a very close and loving couple. Your mother wanted to share everything. Your father was destined to take his aunt's place as head of the community someday, and to provide the next generation with a leader. Since the doctor told them you might only be a carrier, your parents intended to ensure any additional children received a double dose."

"What the fuck? Deliberately give kids a disease! That's sick!"

Dustin kept his voice calm as he took Seth's hand in his. "No, it's tradition. If your mother had discovered earlier the whole truth about your father, she'd have done the same for you. Folks around these parts take their traditions seriously. The Channing-Frost virus is the glue that holds the town together. A common bond uniting us all—rich, poor, old, young."

"I've never heard of the Channing-Frost virus. What is it and what does it do?"

"Have you ever heard your aunt referred to as 'the Jill'?"

"No, but Monica's used the term. Though I'm afraid I don't quite understand what it means." Seth wore a puzzled frown.

"Your ancestors named the town Possum Kingdom for a reason, and settled the area, in part, because it provided a perfect environment for the species Didelphimorphia, or North American Opossum. A jill is a mature female opossum, a jack, the male. Young are called joeys, like kangaroos. Around here, leaders and their designated seconds bear the title 'the Jill' or 'the Jack', respective of gender."

Seth took a sip of his beer, releasing a nervous-sounding chuckle. "You folks take the town name a little too seriously if you ask me. And if you're about to share 'One Hundred and One Ways to Prepare Possum', I don't wanna hear it."

Dustin managed a halfhearted smile. "No, they didn't want to eat them, they needed a similar habitat. Those with the virus share a kinship with possums. For instance, remember me telling you about possums not carrying rabies?"

"Yes."

"We're only susceptible to ailments that affect both humans and their animal counterparts." He lifted his gaze to Seth's face and watched a variety of emotions play across his lover's expressive features. Seth released his hold on Dustin, stepping away.

"Stop beating around the bush and spit it out. What are you trying to say?"

Dustin took a deep breath, forcing the words out before he could rethink them. "The virus allows us to transform into animals; some at will, most upon the full moon. Carriers don't change if the virus is too weak in their bloodstreams, though some opt for a fresh infusion. You were tested at five, and while you carry a potent strain, it seems to have stayed dormant. If not inherited, the virus can be transmitted via the saliva of a shifter in their animal form, like the one that bit you. I tested your blood at the office after you were bitten. It seems the virus in your system is active now. And if you've never woken up naked, curled in a ball under your bed surrounded by possum hair, it wasn't active before you came here." Dustin braced himself to intercept, should Seth run fleeing into the night.

"You... I... we... change into fucking possums? That's stupid! I have never in my life done anything of the sort. What kind of sick bullshit is this? Is this some kind of a joke?"

Dustin remained calm, determined to be the voice of reason in an unreasonable situation. "No, Seth, this isn't a joke. Remember when we were kids, how you never beat me at hide-and-seek?"

"Yes. You cheated, didn't you?"

Dustin tapped a finger to his nose. "In a matter of speaking. Between having a keener sense of smell than you, and better hearing, I always smelled or heard exactly where you were. That's also what alerted Irene whenever we got into mischief."

"What are you trying to say? Tell me, already." Seth backed farther away, blinking hard. Even from a distance of a few feet, Dustin heard the rapid beating of the man's heart.

"You were a carrier. The possum that bit you was actually a relatively new shifter. Newbies not born with the virus often lose their human consciousness while in animal form. The poor girl smelled food. In the past, Irene always left food out on full moon nights, and Tiffany attempted to come nibble." Dustin discreetly positioned himself between Seth and the exit. "She nibbled you instead."

Seth's eyes widened and his mouth dropped open.

"She brought your virus out of stasis. Have you noticed lately your sense of smell growing stronger? Have you been able to hear better?"

Seth gawked at Dustin a long moment, finally breaking eye contact to stare at the floor. "Yes," he admitted.

Dustin resumed his pacing. "I believe when the next full moon rolls around, you'll transform for the first time."

"I like a good gag as well as the next man, but this one is wearing pretty thin, and I don't like being the butt of jokes." Seth's face reddened clear up to his ears.

"I'm afraid it's no joke." Dustin rolled his T-shirt up and off his body, dropping it to the settee while toeing off his loafers.

"Not that I'm objecting to you getting naked, but what are you doing?"

"Proving a point." Dustin's blue jeans followed the T-shirt; he wore nothing underneath, figuring Seth to be the type to demand proof. "Now, look at me."

"I am. Am I also allowed to touch?" Seth waggled his brows.

"Not yet. Watch carefully."

Letting his mind go blank, Dustin nudged his sleeping beast awake. It gave grumbling protest, yawned, and wakened, stretching and stretching and stretching until its tiny body seemed to fill Dustin's skin. He opened his eyes to see Seth's feet and ankles jump up onto a chair.

Seth stood frozen on the chair, eyes wide.

Dustin had barely enough time to regain human form and catch Seth before he hit the floor.

Along with superior hearing and smell came additional strength. Dustin hefted Seth in a fireman's carry and trotted down the hall to deposit his pliant form on his bed. He hurried back to the sitting room to dress and then returned to perch on the edge of the comforter, smoothing Seth's hair back from his forehead.

Seth's eyes fluttered open, then widened in horror. He jumped back, knocking his head against the headboard. "Why did you wait until now to tell me?"

"You only came here to get Irene's affairs in order. You didn't need an added burden."

"No, I mean, when we were kids. Why didn't you tell me?"

"I thought your family gave you 'the talk', like mine did. Anyway, I asked my mom why you never seemed to find me during our games like I found you, and she explained that maybe you were a late bloomer, and wouldn't fully develop your senses until you were older. It happens sometimes."

"How old were you the first time you changed?"

"Thirteen."

"And this has been happening in our families for generations?"

Dustin nodded. At least Seth sounded more rational now.

"Are there any more animals around? Werewolves?"

Dustin managed a shy half smile. "We've never allowed predators to stick around except for foxes. There was a terrible power struggle near Atlanta back in the sixties and they were ousted. Irene allowed them to stay until the danger passed, which turned into several decades, but their last change of power didn't go well and left them needing a new leader. The town also needed a veterinarian, and we got both in the same man. We decided to keep him, and by extension, his foxes. He has an office next to mine."

"Are there other towns like ours? Isn't the name a bit blatant?"

"Sure, but we have to be able to find each other some way, though a name like Turkey Run doesn't necessarily mean shifters. North of us, you have Turtletown, Elkton, and Ducktown, Tennessee, though most of the elk folk migrated to Colorado. There's a huge colony up there."

"I want the truth. What happened to my parents? Nana told me they were hit by a car while crossing the road."

Dustin winced. He'd hoped Seth wouldn't ask. "Are you sure you really want me to tell you?"

"If you don't, who will?"

Dustin shared the tale, matter-of-factly, though it ripped his heart out. At one time, he'd been as close to Seth's parents as his own. "Carriers who can't shift are posted as lookouts, to ward off stray dogs and keep the passel—that's a group of possums—out of trouble. Your mother was a new shifter and somehow snuck past the guards and onto the highway. Your dad tried to stop her, and they were both killed by a car. Your grandmother told the truth."

Seth narrowed his eyes. "I recall some comments from their memorial service. They're not actually buried in the cemetery in town, are they?"

"No. Those who die in animal form remain in animal form. They're buried down by the pond in the unofficial family graveyard."

"What happened to Aunt Irene?"

"She turned one last time, too weak to survive the change. She's buried beside your parents."

Seth remained quiet for several moments, staring at the wall. "Dustin?"

"Yeah."

"Would you do me a favor?"

Dustin stopped stroking Seth's hair and clasped his hand. "Anything."

"Would you get the fuck out of my house?"

No yelling: okay, not much. No flung breakables and no threatening of vital parts with sharp objects. Overall, not too bad, Dustin supposed, as far as revelations went.

He climbed into his truck, staring at the light in Seth's window and wishing he'd been allowed to stay. Seth needed watching over tonight while he dealt with what he'd been told. In Seth's state of mind, he wouldn't appreciate Dustin's fretting. Instead he drove to the Johnsons' next door and parked behind their barn. Friends and passel members, they'd never even question the presence of Dustin's Ranger.

He carefully folded his clothes, placing them on the driver's seat, further evidence of his intentions should the Johnson boys get curious enough to investigate, and then slipped into possum form, ambling across the field back to Seth's house to keep watch throughout the night. While most of the passel only used the kitchen entrance, more than a half dozen more existed. Dustin wouldn't use them unless dire circumstance forced his hand.

CHAPTER 14

DUSTIN LIVINGSTON had *not* turned into a possum in the sitting room. Seth had simply averted his gaze for a moment and the creature that'd bitten him had found a way back in. Horror sank in. The possum might still be loose in the house! Grabbing the straw broom from its hook on the back porch, Seth steeled his resolve. He crept down the hall, alert for movement, though what he'd do upon actually encountering the animal he had no idea.

Room by room he investigated, stopping before he entered his aunt's bedroom. He closed his eyes—the essence he'd noticed earlier in some of the townspeople was even more intense here. As he eased the door open, he breathed deeply, his olfactory senses leading him across the floor to the bed. He buried his nose in the quilt, catching the full scent. The beast had been here, evidenced by the hair Seth had found on the bed upon first arriving.

A pet, then. Instead of a cat, Aunt Irene had somehow tamed a possum, which explained everything: the hole in the wall, the food mess, the hair, the appearance of a full-grown possum in the sitting room tonight. Yeah, the neighbor woman had three tame possums, why couldn't Irene have one? Or maybe the tame ones came visiting. Did the women time-share the creatures?

Dustin's words came back to him. *"Have you noticed lately that your sense of smell is stronger? Hearing?"*

His grandmother's words joined Dustin's: *"Your father's family was… well, they weren't natural."* She'd always changed the subject when pressed further.

"Dustin Fucking Livingston! I hate you!" Seth screamed at the room as he moved through like a tornado, sweeping vials and bottles off his aunt's dresser and sending them crashing to the floor. He screamed and screamed and screamed, impotently releasing his temper before the pressure built to critical mass.

His bare foot connected with broken glass, sending pain shooting up his leg. Oh, fuck! That hurt!

His fury ebbed, leaving him empty inside, with an aching throat, and with his aunt's possessions smashed upon the floor. He dropped to an area rug, carefully avoiding the mess. Staring in rapt fascination at his bandaged wrist, he peeled back the gauze to find the bite mark nearly healed. He buried his face in his hands, letting out the hurt, confusion, and bitterness in a relentless wail, unsurprised when strong arms wrapped around him, securing him against Dustin's bare skin.

Neither man spoke. Seth sobbed into the crook of Dustin's neck while Dustin crooned, soft sounds, not words.

Seth's caterwauls gentled as he grew too tired to continue.

At last Dustin said, "You haven't eaten. Can I get you something?"

"Not hungry." The way he felt at the moment, Seth wondered if he'd ever be hungry again.

"No, I suppose not. Is there anything I can do for you?"

Though he'd been furious with the man a few moments ago, now Seth didn't want to be alone. "Hold me until I'm asleep?"

"If you want me to. But first I need to treat your foot. You've cut yourself."

As though Seth weighed nothing, Dustin lifted him and carried him into the bathroom, depositing him on the closed toilet lid. With gentle hands, he probed Seth's wound before applying antiseptic and butterfly bandages.

Seth marveled at how familiar his childhood friend seemed with the inner workings of Aunt's Irene's home, and how unaffected he appeared by casual nudity. "You know your way around here."

"Yes. I was Irene's second-in-command. Even if I weren't a doctor, part of the position's duties included tending minor injuries."

"And the vet?"

"We keep him around in case he's needed. Sometimes it's easier to treat a patient in animal form, and this being a farming community with lots of livestock is the perfect cover."

"Oh." Seth studied Dustin's precise movements as he wound and neatly folded a strip of gauze and secured the ends without using tape.

"Keep an eye on that cut. We're more resistant to illness due to the virus, but we're still at risk of infections, other viruses, and ailments that exist in both species." He handed Seth two ibuprofen tablets and a Dixie cup of water. "Here, take these to help with the pain."

Seth obediently swallowed the pills. "Can I ask you something?"

An intense green-eyed gaze connected with Seth's. "Unless you're gonna ask me to leave again. I've already promised to stay, and I keep my promises."

"Did you plan this? For me to be bitten?" Seth held his breath, hoping against hope for Dustin to tell him no.

Those sad eyes turned away. "No matter what you might

think, I never intended this to happen. In a moment of distraction an elder let Tiffany slip away."

Seth watched for signs of duplicity and found none, only what he believed might be shame. "Take me to bed."

Once more Dustin lifted him, exerting little effort to haul Seth to the bed they'd shared. For now, Seth pushed aside the questions, doubts, and fears, determined to lose himself in the physical. His problems would keep until morning.

Dustin took great care in removing Seth's jeans to avoid his injured foot, and the insistent throbbing slowly faded to a dull ache. Seth's boxers followed the jeans down his legs and off.

When he returned to the bed, Dustin approached from the foot, slowly crawling up the covers, his gaze smoky with longing, tempered with concern. He stopped with his head near Seth's crotch, closed his eyes, and inhaled deeply. "You smell amazing." Dustin brushed his nose against the thatch adorning Seth's groin. "Right now you're scared, but when you learn to appreciate heightened senses...." He let loose a wicked grin. "Let's say they have their uses." Dustin whiffed again, and ran the flat of his tongue along the underside of Seth's cock. "Ummm...," he moaned. "Cock. My favorite meal."

Sumptuous heat engulfed Seth's rising erection, and he fell back against the pillows, closing his eyes. Dustin worked up and down Seth's hardening flesh, humming, hand keeping time with his mouth. He stroked and fondled Seth's balls, occasionally tracing farther below with a fingertip, trailing saliva toward Seth's hole.

"Do you like that?" Dustin paused long enough to ask. "Want me in there?" Dustin the lover momentarily gave way to Dustin the doctor. "Is your foot okay? Need me to stop?"

"Stop now and I may never speak to you again." Seth bowed his back off the bed, chasing the finger, willing it inside his body. A distraction. He needed a distraction, and he needed it now.

Dustin chuckled. "Patience." Slowly he eased the tip of his finger into Seth's opening, teasing more than penetrating.

Seth shoved back, trying to capture the tantalizing digit.

"Is this what you want?" Dustin's rumbling murmur sent a shot a pure lust straight to Seth's groin. Dustin slipped his finger inside and then out again, only to drive past the protective ring of muscle on the next thrust, delving in to ignite a fire deep within.

"Oh God!" Seth exclaimed, writhing on the patchwork quilt.

With Dustin's finger massaging inside and lips stroking him outside, Seth hovered on the edge, passion rendering him incomprehensible. Inanities tripped off his tongue, growls and groans and not quite words. He whined when Dustin withdrew.

"I thought we were immune," he asked, surprised to see Dustin donning a condom and slathering on lube from their stash in the bedside table.

"Not to everything."

Seth spread his legs, welcoming Dustin into his body. They merged on a shared moan, the glide of Dustin's cock through Seth's sphincter muscle an ecstatic combination of pleasure/pain that slowly gave way to pure pleasure.

"God, I love how you feel," Dustin murmured near Seth's ear, descending to scrape his teeth along Seth's throat.

Seth tilted his head back, giving Dustin more room to explore before their mouths met in a flurry of tongues and teeth and heavy breathing. They rocked together, desperation in Seth's faltering motions. He was close, damned close. A few swift stokes of his cock would send him sailing over the edge.

Harder, faster they slammed together, Seth's cock riding a slick of sweat and precum between their bellies, but needing more direct attention.

They grasped randomly at arms, buttocks, and backs, fingers scrambling for purchase as they fought for closer, deeper, more. The bedstead screeched and squalled, the head-board rapping a sharp beat against the wall, keeping tempo with their impassioned coupling.

Deep within the pressure grew, and Seth wrapped his legs around Dustin's thighs, careful of his injured foot, following Dustin's punishing rhythm. Mouth to mouth, Dustin buried inside Seth's body, they crested and plunged, unintelligible cries filling the room.

Out of his mind with lust, Seth slipped a hand between their bodies, frantically stroking himself and using his legs as leverage to force Dustin's cock against that one perfect spot.

"I'm gonna come!" he cried, too far gone to stop himself even if he wanted.

"I'll be right there with you," Dustin replied on panted breaths, never breaking stride.

"Ahhh…. Oh, oh, oh… Damn!" Seth tilted over the edge, hardly noticing when Dustin plunged in deeply and held his position.

Dustin's shouted "Seth!" was lost in harsh inhales and exhales, the bed stilling and quieting. Dustin collapsed on top of Seth, bracing his weight somewhat on his arms.

Silence, save for the *huff, huff, huff* worthy of marathon runners and the incessant twin beats of Seth's and Dustin's hearts.

"That was… that was…." Seth couldn't quite form his thoughts into words.

"Yeah, it was."

"Is it always like this?"

"Excuse me?"

"Me being… infected. Is that what made it so good?"

Dustin raised his head and stared down at Seth. Sweat had turned his hair a deeper auburn, plastering it to his forehead. "The virus has nothing to do with us now. This…." He shoved his hips against Seth, dragging his flagging erection once more over Seth's prostate. "This is pure us."

"Oh." Seth closed his eyes, shutting out the things he'd earmarked for dealing with later.

Dustin slowly slid out, tidied up, pulled the lamp string, and turned off the light.

Seth wriggled into a more comfortable position beneath the covers, resting his head on Dustin's chest.

No matter how hard he tried, sleep wouldn't come. He lay awake, rolling all he'd been told and all he suspected over and over in his head, occasionally glancing over at Dustin's sleeping form. He wanted to believe his lover and somehow manage to stay here forever, but his life was in Chicago. Wasn't it? He wished once more that his Aunt Irene had fought a little harder to keep him as a child.

Recollections of Junior's visit struck him hard, his newly acquired knowledge adding heightened dimensions to Timmerman's suggestions.

Though it pained him to do so, he'd been solo for so long that he needed some alone time to get his head straight and decide exactly what to do next. The last thing he wanted was to make an impetuous decision, or worse, allow someone else to make it for him. He'd allowed others to dictate most of his life. Time to take a stand of his own.

Quietly, so as not to wake Dusty, he tiptoed from room to room, viewing the house with a fresh perspective. Each family photo held new meaning, and he gazed at graying photos of McDaniels past, wondering who were what Dustin called carriers, and who took animal form.

He stared long and hard at his parents' picture, stroking a finger over his mother's curls, down his father's nose. "Why couldn't you be here for me? I need you." They didn't answer, and he placed the picture frame back on the mantel before taking down another that showed two young boys, shirtless, wearing cutoff jeans. Arms around each other's skinny shoulders, they grinned for the camera, one missing his two front teeth.

For hours, he lay on the uncomfortable settee, contemplating running back to Chicago in hopes of waking from this nightmare. Every time he thought about buying a plane ticket, however, his heart ached. For better or worse, Dustin Livingston was all Seth had left, but he couldn't let that color his decisions. He had to decide his future on his own.

Toward daybreak, he gave up the house for the front porch and sat wrapped in a quilt, drinking coffee and watching the sunrise. Not long after, footsteps treaded down the hall. The screen door screeched open, and Dustin slowly approached the porch swing. Gaze studiously fixed on the mug in his hand, Seth forced out the words, "I don't think we should see each other for a while."

CHAPTER 15

DUSTIN left without saying good-bye, but Seth found a note on his bed listing a multitude of phone numbers, e-mail addresses, and other forms of communication, with admonishments to keep an eye on both his bite wound and his cut foot. Instructions for care were included. Seth rolled his eyes. Doctors!

Dustpan in hand, he entered his aunt's room, heart heavy at the destruction he'd wreaked, only to find the room immaculate. Somehow Dustin had managed to clean up the wreckage. Maybe Seth had slept some and simply didn't remember. His anger, or whatever ill feelings he might harbor for the bearer of bad news, clicked down a notch. Relief rushed through him when he found the dog figurine intact; he'd been afraid he'd broken it during his fit of rage.

Determined not to let the bomb Dustin had dropped define the course of his life, Seth returned to the task of setting the house to rights with a vengeance, finding pen and paper and making a list of necessary materials. He avoided Possum Kingdom, driving his aunt's truck to nearby Clayton instead for lumber, paint, caulk, and wood stain, and using the trip to justify his long-overdue visit to the offices of Clooney, Anderson, and Gentry to discuss the finer points of his aunt's will. They said she'd left him "everything," hadn't they? What more did he need to know?

The offices were situated in an eye-catching structure on the edge of town, an old-style plantation house that surely must once have been the grandest in the land, now neatly divided into offices. He wondered, while climbing the steps to the front door, how many of his ancestors might have trod the same path. With his fondness for old architecture, he immediately fell in love with the entryway's soaring ceiling, spiral staircase, and burnished oak handrail and floor, imagining how the structure might have appeared in its heyday. Had any of his relatives attended a party here, maybe, back when the impressive dwelling had likely been the abode of some prominent citizen?

A sign on the wall listed the locations of the various offices, disappointing Seth that he didn't have a legitimate excuse to climb the stairs to the upper floors. He did so anyway, to soak up the ambiance. His explorations brought home exactly why the place held so much appeal—it reminded him of the farm. Niggling guilt took root, admonishing him for wanting to sell something that had held such importance for the family he barely remembered.

No time for self-doubt now. He had enough to worry about at the moment. The staircase effectively hid the entrance to the offices of Clooney, Anderson, and Gentry, but eventually Seth found what he sought.

"Do you have an appointment, sir?" the receptionist asked, taking in his stained Pink Floyd T-shirt and paint-splattered ball cap with obvious disdain the moment he stepped through the door.

Appointment? Seth mentally kicked himself. Why hadn't he bothered to make an appointment? "No, ma'am. Sorry, I didn't realize I'd be in town today and hoped to talk to Mr. Clooney about my aunt's estate."

The judgement ticked down a notch, replace by curiosity. "Who was your aunt?"

"Irene McDaniel from Possum Kingdom."

The woman's entire demeanor changed. "Oh, Mr. McDaniel! Mr. Clooney hoped you might stop by. Have a seat and I'll tell him you're here."

Seth retreated a polite distance, certain he'd be capable of hearing the words she hissed into the telephone if he'd had a mind to. He had yet to decide if his improved hearing amounted to a blessing or a curse. On the plus side, he now had ample warning of anyone coming down his driveway; however, the ability to hear every little night noise, amplified, definitely fell in the minus column. Who knew crickets were so damned noisy?

No one else occupied the waiting room, leaving Seth his choice of overstuffed chairs and well-handled magazines. His stomach rumbled, provoking a watch check. Oh yeah, lunchtime. For a brief moment, he considered calling Dustin and planning an impromptu lunch date. No, he'd been the one to ask for space. Space Dustin seemed determined to give him, as the man hadn't called, or even texted to inquire about Seth's injures. Both wounds had nearly completely healed, or at least enough for Seth to get a tennis shoe on his foot and walk properly. Did Dustin honestly believe "I don't think we should see each other for a while" meant "ignore me completely"?

A few moments later, a distinguished-looking gentleman of advanced years stepped into the waiting room.

"Mr. McDaniel?" The man completely enveloped Seth's hand in his.

Seth rose from the chair he'd sat in for perhaps two minutes, tops. "Mr. Clooney?"

"Please, call me Richard. I understand you wish to speak about your aunt's will." The elderly gentleman let out a gravelly chuckle. "About time you got here. Come on back to my office and let's chat." Richard's pronounced Southern drawl brought back memories of Seth's father and Aunt Irene.

Seth sniffed the air, but not a trace of Possum Kingdom "otherness" clung to either the attorney or his receptionist. What the fuck? Since when did he start sniffing people? He recalled a few noses in the recent past, hovering close to his neck.

Richard chuckled again. "No, Mr. McDaniel, I'm not kin, though I'm fully aware of what you're doing. You're hardly the first to include a good sniff with the handshake."

They entered a spacious office, every available surface covered by paper. A computer sat on the desk, and the documents spread across the keyboard led Seth to believe it didn't receive much use. Built-in bookcases lined the walls, and for a moment, Seth pictured how such an arrangement would work in the sitting room. *You're selling the place, asswipe, stop dreaming*, the part of him longing to return to Chicago informed him.

"You know about...?" Did Richard buy into the lunacy, or did Seth ride the crazy train alone? *Or maybe Dustin told you the truth,* said the part of Seth resolved to put down roots, renovate the farm, and take baby pictures at the nearest hospital. *And sleep with Dustin every night!* his libido chimed in. Yeah, that too.

The attorney eased down into the chair behind his desk, which emitted a startled *squeak!* "Oh yes, I'm fully aware of how your town differs from most. My wife, the late Mrs. Clooney, grew up there, though she somehow managed to dodge the family curse."

"Some might not think it's a curse," Seth replied, honor-bound to defend his heritage.

"Your aunt certainly didn't believe it to be. Called it a gift, and seemed determined to uphold tradition—single-handedly, if need be. Broke her heart when your grandmother carted you off to Chicago. She'd be tickled pink that you finally came home."

Must everyone remind Seth of what he'd missed? "I regret not making the trip while she was still alive. I'd been led to believe she didn't want anything to do with me."

"Oh, she wanted you, without a doubt. Even approached me for legal advice. Your grandmother was a strong-minded lady and threatened to expose the town if Irene didn't back down." Richard narrowed his eyes, peering over the tops of his glasses. "A lot of people made extreme sacrifices to protect the innocent, up to and including falsifying official documents. Irene wouldn't risk exposing those good-hearted souls to possible legal action. I hope you understand."

The lengths necessary to keep the true nature of the town and its residents concealed hadn't occurred to Seth before. Constant duplicity must be a heavy burden on poor Dustin. "I'm starting to," Seth told the lawyer, still somewhat mystified that he was having this conversation. A small part of him still hoped the whole possum thing would turn out to be a joke. Either Richard was in on the ruse or—it wasn't a joke. "How can you talk about this so casually? I mean," Seth said, dropping his voice to a whisper, "we're talking people turning into possums, aren't we?"

Seth half expected the lawyer to gasp and shout, "What the hell are you talking about?" Instead, Richard coolly replied with, "Some say it's the other way around: possums turning into humans, but, yes, you get the gist of it. Now that you have a better understanding of the entire situation, what are you going to do?" He raised one bushy brow.

Oh fuck, oh fuck, oh fuck! It's real, it's not a dream! Seth's last hope of returning to his safe little world—a world devoid of possum shifters—vanished in an instant. "I honestly haven't figured it out yet. I'm hoping you'll help me."

"You've been over the papers I've sent?" Seth nodded. "I'm sure you've noticed how well off your aunt left you."

"I did." A lot of zeroes trailed the five on her savings

155

account balance alone. A *lot* of zeroes. "Do you mind if I ask how she came across so much money?"

One side of Clooney's mouth hiked up. "The family's been here a long time, and I'd love to tell you that they made every penny honestly. However, some of it's moonshine money, dating back to Prohibition, and let me tell you, possums make really good thieves." He smiled more fully. "But one day a friend insisted your aunt invest her little nest egg and encouraged her to buy stocks that caught her eye. Well, she liked apples, so—"

Seth nearly choked. "What? My aunt, who didn't even own a computer, bought tech stocks?"

"Made a fortune off them too. And she left behind a good deal of land—land I'm certain developers are foaming at the mouth for."

Seth shuddered, recalling the men who'd tried to fleece him of the property. "Yes, sir."

"Tempted?"

"If I get an offer that's not insulting—yes."

Clooney let out a weary sigh, gesturing at a chair across from him. "Have a seat."

Seth sat warily, watching the man who knew far more about his aunt's legal matters than Seth probably ever would. Given his recent experience with realtors, how far could he trust anyone?

Clooney picked up a figurine from his desk and rolled it around in his hand—the likeness of a possum mother, young clinging to her back. Back in Chicago, Seth would have considered it an odd thing to have; here it seemed right somehow.

"Now, I don't know how much you know about possums, but they're solitary creatures, keep to themselves. However, your relatives learned early on the benefit of safety in numbers. Your family bought the land in the 1700s, creating a place to live openly and not have to hide. It's been a sanctuary ever since, and kindred spirits—"

"You mean other possum shifters?" Seth interjected, wanting to ensure they remained on the same page.

Richard nodded. "Among a few others. They come here where they can live mostly normal lives. Any other virus and they'd probably receive sympathy, but Channing-Frost inspires fear and revulsion. Hundreds were killed before towns like Possum Kingdom were formed. Your predecessors fought hard for their homes, for their people. Don't throw away their efforts as if they didn't matter."

What? "You… you want to me to stay here?"

"What's your status, if you don't mind my asking? Do you carry the virus?"

"I do." Seth suddenly found the carpet beneath his worn tennis shoes quite fascinating.

"Do you shift?"

"Not yet. I'm told my virus strain was dormant up until now, but I was bitten the other night. Now a doctor tells me there's a good chance I will."

Clooney put the paperweight down. He leaned over the desk and lowered his voice. "I'll let you in on a secret. Your aunt left the majority of her assets to you outright, *except* most of the acreage, which is why I asked to meet with you face to face. I had difficulty phrasing the documents, but the land goes to the current Jack or Jill, as it provides a safe place for the passel to spend their full moons. Whoever is chosen to assume control must answer any challenges, both for the position and the inheritance."

"Challenges?" Seth swallowed hard.

"You're Irene's next of kin. Providing you're able to shift from human to animal form and back again while retaining your right mind, the leadership of the passel should pass to you."

What the fuck? Dustin hadn't mentioned Seth having to fight for the crown of King of Possum Kingdom. And he hadn't been forthcoming with warnings about any challenges either. *Wait 'til I see him again!* "What about the challenges?"

"If other ranking members don't find the leadership suitable, they can contest for the position, beginning with the acting leader she appointed before she died."

"What acting leader?" Seth had a sinking feeling he knew the answer already.

"Dustin Livingston, the town doctor. Of course, rather than oppose you openly, any ambitious member of the passel might try to sweet-talk you into co-leadership."

Oh, yes, Mr. Dustin Livingston, MD. Just wait until the next time I lay eyes on you! Seth staggered out of the mansion-turned-office-complex recalling flowers, chocolates, and casino plans, burdened by more questions and having received far too few answers.

Seth parked the truck in the empty parking lot of the First Baptist Church of Possum Kingdom, staring up at the cross-bearing steeple he recalled from his youth. The ancient structure didn't appear nearly as bleak and oppressing at it had to his eight-year-old self. He bypassed the building and opened the wrought iron gate leading to the cemetery. Tiny white pebbles crunched under his tennis shoes.

He started near the back, with stones time-blackened and names barely discernible. Through a layer of patina on a towering obelisk, he made out an etched "Braden Calhoun McDaniel." The elaborate stone listed the date of death as 1792. Pride welled somewhere deep inside Seth. He'd been a part of an illustrious family. A mere two months ago loneliness and isolation had ruled his life. He moved on, the decay of years lessening the closer he came to the church. How many more generations would pass before the cemetery reached its limit? At last he found what he'd been searching for, the stones of Aaron and Brenda Hynes McDaniel. How young they'd been when they'd died, scarcely older than Seth's current age.

"Hi, Mom, hi, Dad," he began, emotion choking back the things he'd planned to say if he ever got the chance. He dropped to his knees, idly picking at weeds around the headstone. "Dustin told me you're not really here, but buried somewhere around the pond. I wanted to come say hello anyway."

At a loss for appropriate sentiment, he merely said, "Hello," opening his heart and hoping some inner voice might answer him. Nothing came. Freshly turned earth marked the plot next to his parents' grave, where a sparkling white granite stone proclaimed: Irene McDaniel, Beloved Leader. Who'd ordered the stone? Dustin? Monica? For a moment, Seth felt kinship with those who'd mourned the lady's loss when he himself hadn't been there to do his part.

A panicked cry of "Saxon! Get back here!" broke the silence.

Seth glanced up at the terrifying vision of a horse-sized dog barreling straight for him, trailing a leash and an out-of-breath woman. Fear like he'd never known glued Seth to the spot.

He'd rallied together enough brain cells to process "Great Dane" before he fainted or... something, without fully losing consciousness. Every muscle in his body seized. Seth flopped helplessly to his side. A wet tongue slathered the side of his face.

"I'm sorry," the woman said, physically hauling the monster away. "I'm keeping him for a friend, and he's kinda strong."

Seth opened one eye to discover himself curled on the ground in a fetal position, heart pounding. What the fuck? He liked dogs. Well.... He saw the lolling pink tongue from below and his head went swimmy again. Make that, he *used* to like dogs.

The lady extended a hand. Ping-ponging his gaze from the dog to her outstretched hand, Seth replied, "I'd like to stay here a bit longer, if you don't mind."

"Suit yourself. I really am sorry. I told my friend keeping Saxon in Possum Kingdom wasn't a good idea."

The woman strolled away, pulling on the dog's leash. Seth started to rise, but the massive anvil-with-ears head swiveled back his way and he felt faint again.

"You'll get used to it," he heard a deep voice say. "In time, you'll hardly even flinch."

Seth rolled over, spying an elderly couple a few feet away, placing flowers on a grave. A spirit of connection settled over him again. Emboldened, he ventured, "Thanks, jack."

"Don't mention it, jack," the man replied.

Still shaken, Seth climbed to his feet, brushing off bits of gravel and dried grass. On the way back to his aunt's truck, he spotted a playground: swings, a seesaw, and a jungle gym. He aimed his feet toward the parking lot; they carried him toward the jungle gym.

Before he realized his own intent, he found himself hanging upside down from the metal structure by his knees, strangely comfortable.

"Those urges will pass too," the man he'd just met said, moseying by on the path. "Usually only joeys do that."

The woman with him smiled and stopped, patting Seth's arm. "Welcome to the family," she said before tottering off.

The upside-down position did have its merits. Seth's back felt better than it had in weeks. He remained hanging bottom side up, enjoying the afternoon sun, until his belly rumbled again, reminding him lunchtime had long since passed. Once more his thoughts went to Dustin, but the moment he recalled the attorney's words about a possible challenge, and possible pursuit for political gain, the budding fondness grew cold. Was Dustin playing him to get the land?

Seth climbed down from the jungle gym, its bright red-and-yellow paint failing to cheer him. Shuffling along the walkway, he caught a whiff of something delicious. He followed his keen sense of smell to Main Street and found a blackboard in the window of Betty's Diner across the way that announced "Today's special: fried chicken."

The couple from the cemetery, along with a man, woman, and teenaged girl, wandered up, sniffing the breeze. The moment Seth stepped from the curb, a car came around the corner. All six of them froze in place, only reanimating once the car passed. "Sadly, the inborn fear of cars never quite goes away," said the man he'd encountered in the cemetery.

That night Seth passed through the house, turning off lights and preparing for bed. His eyes fell on the notebook he'd found in the attic, what he now believed must be his mother's journal and not a made-up story. He fixed himself a cup of cocoa and trotted off to bed to read. After a few pages, he found his name.

I wish I'd been turned before having Seth. Some of the townsfolk call him an outcast. Irene says when he grows older, he'll show them.

A few pages later he read, *I've asked Aaron to bite me...* and further down the same page, *I'm told I turned last night, but I don't remember. Irene says in time I'll keep my human mind in animal form. Aaron said I ate earthworms. Earthworms! Yuck!*

Page after page chronicled his mother's adventures. It broke his heart to read, *My mother won't talk to me. She won't even answer the phone when I call.* Circular stains dotted the page. Seth reverently stroked his fingers over the tiny round circles, heart clenched tight. His mother's tears?

Around midnight, he reached the last entry. *It's the full moon tonight. Wish me luck. Although Aaron says it's a bit soon, I hope to keep my human mind this time.*

Seth put the notebook aside before his own tears joined his mother's on the pages of her journal. But now, after reading her words, he truly, totally, completely believed.

CHAPTER 16

DUSTIN picked up his phone again, checking the screen for the millionth time. No message from Seth. He wanted to turn back the clock and handle things differently, in such a way that his evenings ended up with them tucked into bed together. Dustin had been alone for years, but was only now learning the meaning of the word "lonely."

"We got trouble." Andy barely paused to knock before storming into the office.

Dustin tore his gaze from his phone. "What? Is someone hurt?"

"Worse. Natalie from the florist shop is dating one of my guys and isn't good at keeping secrets. It seems Junior cleaned 'em out of long-stemmed red roses. He even paid an ungodly amount to have them delivered to Irene's."

"Seth doesn't strike me as the type to fall for empty gestures."

"Junior also hooked up satellite out there and shelled out enough cash for a year's service."

A sensation like a dousing with cold water poured over Dustin's head. "He's being a little blatant, if you ask me."

Andy crossed his arms over his chest, settling one hip against Dustin's desk. "Blatant or not, you need to up your game."

What? "Why? Seth is a grown man and perfectly capable of making up his own mind. Besides, he asked me to give him some breathing room." Dustin sagged over his computer, exhausted from another evening spent as a possum, keeping watch over Seth. Even more exhausting had been forcing himself not to assume human form and hold Seth while he'd cried the night before.

"If Seth turns on the next full moon, he stands a good chance of being the Jack."

"Well, good for him. I sure don't want the responsibility." Squirmy sensations twisted to life in Dustin's gut. If he didn't want to be leader, why did it bother him that the role might fall to Seth? He imagined Seth as a chicken, tossed into a pen of hungry foxes, then changed the image to wolves at Andy's raised-brow assessment.

Andy rounded the desk, bending down to peer into Dustin's eyes. "If Seth chooses Junior, he'll become a puppet. You know it and I know it. Even if you don't care for the guy, think of the passel, or the skulk. Consider Tiffany out front. If Junior takes over, she'll be run off for being an outsider. Do you want to stand back while your friends, your patients, get tossed out like yesterday's newspaper? Do you want to tell that sweet girl at the florist shop she has to leave 'cause she doesn't have the virus?" Andy paused to take a deep breath. "And six months from now, you want to stand idly by while Junior sends your boy packing for not being a full blood, once he decides Seth's outlived his usefulness?"

Dustin sank back into his chair. Ouch! Direct hit! "He wouldn't! The passel would never allow it."

"By then, the passel will be made up of only full bloods, and the casino Junior keeps bragging about building will bring in enough money that they'll do whatever he says. He means to out every last one of you. Go public. And he plans to evict any other shifters besides possums. He has dreams of making full bloods some kind of protected species and turning the town into a reservation, selling the place to the government; that is, if he can get control of the McDaniel lands."

"Where did you hear this?" Dustin didn't think the skulk kept up with passel rumors.

"Let's say I have my sources, and my reasons for wanting to stop his plans. What you and I had aside, you're a damned fine man and one hell of a Jack. If you need to reach some kind of agreement, crawl on your hands and knees to Seth McDaniel and do it. But I'm begging you. I'm a married man with kits on the way. I want to raise them here, in a relatively safe environment. Right now, my family's fate rests with you. And if you don't care about any of those things, do it for Irene."

And therein lay the problem. Dustin did care. He wanted nothing more than to drive out to Seth's, beg him to stay, and help him enmesh himself in the fabric of Possum Kingdom. "After your cousin took over the skulk, you and I met in a bar. You bought me a beer, if I recall, and we wound up out back."

Andy plunked down in a leather chair on the other side of the desk. "Guys hook up all the time. We lasted a little longer than most, and I certainly don't have any regrets." The sincerity in his eyes backed up the truth of Andy's statement.

"Let me ask you something." Dustin held Andy's gaze, silently daring him to turn away. "Did you love me?"

"What?"

"You heard me. Did you love me?"

"Of course I did."

"Others thought you were using me."

Andy narrowed his eyes and fire flashed just beneath the surface. "If you're looking for a reason to say 'poor little me' you won't find it here. I never used you and I never will. When the skulk ousted Cousin Tate, I made a decision based on what I thought best for me, the skulk, *and* you. It nearly killed me to walk away, but I'm happy and want you to be too. And I will always, always have your back, no matter what."

Dustin ended their staring contest first. "Thanks. I suppose I needed to hear you say that, because I'm seeing things from your point of view now. My actions affect not only me and Seth, but the passel. I want to make sure I'm pursuing him for the right reasons. But I'm kinda rusty at the whole dating thing, and I'm not one for grand gestures. Junior is capable of giving Seth everything he wants. I'm not. How can I compete?"

"Question. And answer honestly, don't worry about hurting my feelings or nothing, but how do you feel about the guy?"

"I have no earthly idea. We were friends years ago, and the childhood friendship gets tangled up with how I feel now, as an adult. Throw in a healthy measure of respect for Irene and any of her kinfolk, and you grasp the problem, right?"

"No, I don't. Let me narrow things down for you. Do you think about him a lot?"

Dustin nodded, running a hand over the back of his neck. "Pretty much nonstop."

"About what? The sex?"

"More than the sex." Though sex occupied many of his nightly thoughts. Dustin's ears burned to be talking so bluntly about a new lover to his ex, but he couldn't seem to stop himself. "I may hear a joke and want to share it. The other day I went for barbeque and wanted to call him to go with me. I even sat at the table we'd sat at the night I took him there." He buried his head in his hands. "I'm such a sap."

Andy wasn't finished yet. "Picture him with Junior. Get it good in your mind. Him and Junior sitting at a table—your table—where the two of you sat." The words took on a taunting note.

Dustin glanced up and idly lifted a pencil from his desk, flexing it between his fingers. "And?"

"Imagine him leaning over the table and laying a big, sticky smooch on the bastard." The pencil snapped in half. "Now we're getting somewhere." Andy grinned. "You're jealous. In this case, that's a good thing.

"Now, imagine Seth is working on the house out there and falls off a ladder. He's lying on the ground, grasping his leg and yelling."

Dustin's jaw clicked shut, his teeth grinding together.

"Good. But maybe doctor instincts. Now, imagine Seth sitting alone at Irene's, sad, staring at a picture of his parents."

Recalling the previous night, Seth crying over Brenda's journal, something in Dustin's heart twanged. "Can you get to the point?"

"All these things might well be happening, and you reacted to every one. You care for the guy more than you're willing to admit. Now, I'll let you in on one more secret Junior hopes you don't find out."

"What secret?"

"Ms. Irene left most of the McDaniel spread to the Jack or Jill, not Seth. If Junior worms his way in, pretends to back Seth, only to issue a challenge later, no one will stand up to him. He'll have the power, he'll have the land, and he'll have Seth. And he'll use them for his own gain."

What the fuck? Irene never mentioned any such clause in her will. "How'd you find this out?"

"The receptionist at the law office dates one of my foxes."

Dustin's mouth dropped open. "How many damned single foxes do you have?"

For the first time since he arrived, Andy smiled. "What can I say? Levi gets around. Now, you need to form a strategy. If you want Seth, you gotta stake your claim. And the sooner the better."

"How can I do that when Junior's willing to give him every-thing he wants?" Being a small town doctor wasn't the most profitable field. Junior owned highly lucrative resort properties. How could Dustin hope to compete?

Andy gave Dustin's hand a brief pat. "Give him what he needs."

Dustin considered his friend's advice. What did Seth need? He visualized Irene's house, reminded of Seth's comment about not being able to find a contractor. Calling up a patient on his computer screen, he told Andy, "I have an idea."

"Mr. McDaniel? I'm told you need some work done." Two trucks sat in Seth's yard, loaded down with ladders, cables, scaf-folds, and other equipment.

"You told me on the phone you didn't have a free appoint-ment until October."

"Something opened up," the man replied with a shrug. Doors opened on each truck, and men climbed out. "You need renovations or not?"

Seth pinched himself, figuring he must be asleep. He'd had a dream like this once, of hunky construction workers showing up at his place. His conscience gave him a resounding swat, hissing, *Remember Dustin, you idiot!* Amazing how much his conscience sounded like Monica Sims. "Don't we need to talk? Work up an estimate?"

A blindingly bright smile lit up the man's dark face. "It's already taken care of. Doc taught us boys the meaning of the barter system."

Seth turned sideways to keep from knocking over an enormous

flower arrangement. He loved flowers as much as the next guy, but enough was enough.

"The kitchen next," he told Mari the maid, the latest worker to arrive spouting the virtues of bartering for Dr. Livingston's services. The new microwave she'd brought with her definitely made cooking easier.

Junior had provided satellite and sent roses and chocolate, which Seth had taken to sending next door to the Johnsons. Dustin sent work crews. Irene's house probably hadn't looked this good in thirty years. While he appreciated the gestures, Seth wasn't used to the attention.

His phone rang. "Oh, hi, Junior. Yes, I got them. Sorry, nothing personal, but no, I don't want to have dinner with you." Seth hung up. Of all the nerve! It'd be one thing to have men chase him because they wanted him, but another thing entirely to be chased because of wealth and power.

At least Dustin didn't constantly harass him, though Seth wouldn't have minded the occasional phone call, and his bed seemed so empty at night. *Maybe I should call him* flashed through his mind when the phone rang again. He answered it without checking caller ID, a bit irritated at someone who wouldn't take no for an answer. "Junior, I meant it. I do *not* want to go out with you."

"Junior? Who's Junior?"

Oh, fuck. "Michael?"

At one time Seth would have welcomed a call from Michael, would have crawled through broken glass for the chance to hear the man's sweet tenor again. Those days were long gone. "Why are you calling?" He barely restrained himself from hanging up.

"What? You're not excited to hear from me?"

"Shouldn't you be on your honeymoon?" Seth's teeth clenched tight.

A sigh wafted over the phone. "I need to talk to you."

"The last time you told me that you announced your engagement. You're a married man now. Don't you owe it to your *husband* not to be calling former lovers?"

"I'd hoped we were still friends. Speaking of, didn't you notice when I changed my profile from 'engaged' to 'lost cause'?" Never had the normally confident Michael sounded so small and lost.

"I have better things to do with my time now than surf media sites." Wait. What? Oh, wow. Seth hadn't been on the "All About Me" site in weeks.

"Well, me and Luther broke up."

"What? Last I saw you were selecting caterers. How long have you been married? Two weeks!"

"We called off the wedding." Michael's voice dropped to a murmur. "Oh, Seth, I screwed up. Can you ever forgive me?"

Seth barely bit off the "No!" poised on the tip of his tongue. Was that a sniffle? "Are you crying?"

"It's such a mess! He lied to me! Lied!"

Seth wasn't sure if he really wanted to know the details, but curiosity got the best of him. "About what?"

"He told me he wanted me back, that he'd seen the error of his ways and wanted to make a commitment. The moment I got to New York, he sang a different tune. Nothing's changed; he hasn't changed. When I pressed him to set a date, he came right out and said he'd no intention of marrying anyone, let alone me."

Seth didn't know what to say.

Michael choked sobs shouldn't inspire so much sympathy. Not after the way they'd parted. "I'd really appreciate it if you'd meet with me face-to-face—just to talk."

"Sorry, Michael, but I'm not even in Chicago."

"I know. You mentioned on your profile that you were in Georgia."

Oh shit.

"Optimist that I am, I checked out a local place called The Pitted Pig. Do you know it?"

The gummy worms Seth had eaten earlier must have animated, causing squirmy sensations deep in his belly. "The Pitted Pig? Where are you?"

"I'm in Possum Kingdom. Come and get me before the natives get restless."

Seth staggered and nearly fell onto the settee. Were possums immune to nervous breakdowns?

The barbecue wasn't nearly as tasty without Dustin's company. Seth sat across the table from a man he might have loved once upon a time, but try as he might, he couldn't find any trace of those feelings now in his heart. Head down, hands trembling, Michael brought feelings of pity, nothing more. "I'm sorry he hurt you," Seth said. Please let Michael not read too much into the words. Any chance for them had come and gone, never to return.

"I have no idea why he even looked me up, told me he wanted me back."

"Where are you staying now?"

"My things are still in New York. I didn't know what to do. My family and friends kept asking for wedding details. I needed to get away for a while, so I came here."

"Why here?" Seth hoped Michael didn't want to get back together. The more time he spent with Dustin, the more he realized how little he'd shared with Michael. He pictured the night he'd cried over his mother's journal, how he'd wanted Dustin to magically appear and hold him. And Dustin would have too. Michael? Michael would have been uncomfortable, made excuses, and left at the first opportunity.

"Because you were the only one who ever told me the truth."

"What?"

"You never lied to me and you were always there when I needed you. No matter what I'd done, you'd talk to me. My sister thinks the breakup with Luther is all my fault. She'd been looking forward to having a rich brother-in-law. My so-called friends either laugh and say it serves me right or don't have time for me. But you—even though I hurt you, here you are."

Time to clear the air once and for all. "I know you're upset right now and grasping at straws, but what we had is over."

Michael let out a sigh, staring out over the restaurant's porch railing at the distant mountains. "I know that. I knew that a long time ago."

"You did?"

"Yeah. You don't see it, but you've built this wall to keep others out, and part of it's my fault. Every time I hurt you, you built it higher."

Seth snorted. "I didn't do anything of the sort."

Michael grimaced and nodded. "Every time we had an argument and I walked away, you let me go."

"You had the right to do what you wanted. I couldn't stop you."

"Couldn't or didn't want to? I think you're so used to people walking out of your life that you think that's how things are supposed to be and you don't try to change them. Just once, I'd have loved for you to come after me."

"What?"

Michael cracked a faint grin. "I wanted you to chase me. Is that so bad?"

Actually, given Seth's recent experience with Junior, yes. His thoughts turned to Dustin. Maybe he should break down, call and at least say hello. It'd be the friendly thing to do. Especially since three guys, who called each other "Jack", were currently sawing, hammering, and possibly jackhammering in the kitchen, completing renovations at Dustin's command.

Staring down at the table, Michael quietly confessed, "When I stood you up or you caught me in a lie, I wanted you to put me in my place. I need a firm hand, someone to keep me in line. When we first met, I told you about how Luther treated me, and you were pissed off. I think you even offered to fly to New York and give him a piece of your mind." Michael gave Seth a dreamy sigh. "You were my knight in shining armor." The smile fell. "The months went by, and you let me treat you however I wanted. So I did. I'm sorry now that I realize how badly I mistreated you. In my mind, if you didn't like it, you'd tell me off. But you never did. I acted up to get your attention, like I would with Luther, yet when I ran away, you let me go. I'd come back, you'd let me. You should have slammed the door in my face, made me beg your forgiveness." Michael stared down at his hands, watching a paper napkin turn to bits of shredded fluff in his fingers.

While grateful Michael hadn't delivered an "I want you back" speech, hearing their relationship from Michael's point of view made him cringe. In Seth's opinion, he shouldn't have to keep someone in line. He wanted someone he could trust to treat him like they wanted to be treated, not play some kind of dominance games. Studying the man across from him, as humble as Seth had ever seen him, he didn't feel anger at their breakup, he felt… thankful? Apparently, Luther's appalling behavior was something Michael needed, but with permanence. "Actually, you and I never stood a chance, did we?"

"I suppose not, and I'm really sorry. You're a great guy and—"

"You'd rather I be rich, older, powerful, and dominant?"

Michael paused before answering, still not meeting Seth's eyes. "Yes."

"You also want to be won over by hearts and flowers, don't you?"

Michael gave him a hint of bashful smile. "Right again. See how well you know me?"

Seth's phone vibrated, and he glanced down at the screen. Now would be a really good time for Dustin to call. Damn, a realtor. Seth ignored the caller.

"This really is good barbeque," Michael commented. Seth sighed in relief at the change of subject.

"I like it."

Michael inhaled deeply, then let his breath out slowly. "I love the clean air. I don't see how you'll be able to leave this behind to go back to Chicago."

"It'll be hard." Very hard. Maybe impossible.

Seth's phone rang again, Junior this time. He let the call go to voice mail. The man probably wanted to know how Seth liked the latest flowers. He'd fed them to the Johnsons' goat.

Seth swallowed a bite of potato salad. "What are you going to do now?"

Michael shrugged. "I haven't got a clue. I'm taking this week off to get my head together." He reached across the table to lay his hand on Seth's. "I appreciate you coming to talk with me. I'm sorry I wasn't a better boyfriend, 'cause you deserve the best. There's something else I need to say."

Oh, crap. Bad news coming in five, four, three…

"All your life, you've let others tell you what to do—me, your overbearing grandmother, and you accepted whatever we dished out. Stop doing that. You're too nice a guy to let others run your life. Trust yourself to make decisions and stand by them. If someone else doesn't like it, too bad. Do what's right for Seth.

"Also, the next guy you're with? Don't judge him by me. Let

him in. But if he means something to you, don't give him up
without a fight. I wish I'd focused more on *us* instead of *me*, that
I'd tried harder to meet you halfway. I missed my chance and I
know that. I consider you my friend, a good friend, and I hope
in time you'll feel the same about me."

Their talk turned to other things, and when they parted
company, Seth held out his hand. Michael pulled him into a
hug. "Thank you," he said. "I don't know where I'll go and
what I'll do now, but wherever I am, you'll have a friend." He
drove off in a rental car to who knew where.

The more Seth thought of Michael's words, the more sense
they made. He needed to stop letting other people call the
shots. He needed to take control and stop letting life simply
happen. But how did one change the habits of a lifetime? By
taking chances. From the parking lot of the Pitted Pig, Seth
made a phone call.

"Dr. Livingston's office," a perky voice answered. Tiffany,
the woman who'd changed his life forever. Strange, until now
he'd never even considered a woman capable of changing his
life so dramatically. Equally surprising was the fact the *accident*
seemed more and more like a blessing rather than a curse.
Perhaps he should be sending Junior's flowers to her.

"This is Seth McDaniel. Can I speak to Monica, please?"

The woman squealed, and Seth snatched the phone away
from his ear to avoid permanent damage. "Seth McDaniel! Oh
my God! I'm sorry. I can't begin to tell you how sorry I am!"

Seth spent the next five minutes trying to calm the hyster-
ical woman enough to get a word in edgewise. Remembering
how softly his aunt had once spoken to him when he was upset,
he waited until the wails subsided before venturing a gentle,
"Tiffany?"

Sniff. "Yes?" Her voice wavered, as though she expected
him to yell. Seth didn't think he could be harder on the poor
thing than she was being on herself. If what Dustin said was

175

true, she couldn't be expected to completely control her impulses yet, being a new shifter, right? Attempting to channel Auntie Irene from years ago, Seth lowered his voice, took a deep breath, and tried again. "I want to thank you."

"Tha… thank me?" *Sniffle.* "For what?"

"If it hadn't been for you, I might have gone back to Chicago without ever knowing the truth about my family."

"And you're not mad?"

"No, I'm not mad."

"Thank you! Thank you, thank you, thank you! I was worried! And I—"

Having already spent far longer on the phone than he'd intended, he firmly but politely cut her off. "Nothing to worry about. No harm, no foul. Now, can I please—"

"You want to speak to Doc Livingston?" A bit of hopeful curiosity bled through her occasional snuffle.

"Actually, I'd like to speak with Monica Sims, if she's available."

"Monica? Why do you…. Never mind. Not my business. Hold one moment, please. And thank you again."

"Hello?" a gruff voice asked a moment later, the harsh tones exactly what Seth needed to hear. Thank goodness one person in town wasn't falling all over him, seeking his approval.

"Monica?"

"Who is this?" Ah, lovely, lovely growling.

"It's me, Seth."

"Oh, in that case," Monica said, her voice softening for a second before resuming a hostile edge times two. "What the fuck do you want?"

Ah! Some might find it sick, but Monica's disdain sounded like music to Seth's ears. Maybe a country and western tune about a no-good cheating scoundrel who'd done run off with the truck, but music nonetheless. "I want you to have dinner with me." He could go two rounds at the Pitted Pig, no problem.

"Me? Why me?"

"I've been a bit... overloved lately. I need someone to smack me back to Earth."

Monica hesitated before responding, a little more enthusiastically than the occasion warranted, in Seth's opinion. "I'm your woman!"

Seth got the impression that not much surprised Monica, but from her shocked tone, he believed he just had. He licked a fingertip and drew a tick mark in the air. *That's one for me!*

CHAPTER 17

SETH waited on the back porch at The Pitted Pig, alternately chewing a hangnail and trying to convince himself *that hurts! Cut it out!*

He felt Monica's presence long before her long blonde braids came into sight in the parking lot. She pulsed power, pissed-off attitude, and *fuck, I'm hungry* from a mile away. Seth tracked the trail of white-hot energy through the restaurant, easily imagining people scrambling out of the Valkyrie's way.

I want that! Not Monica, but the command she possessed that made people stand up and take notice. A few months ago, he'd longed to be desired, but having two men competing for his affections was highly overrated. Now he preferred... respect.

Okay, maybe not what Monica had, which inspired submission and fear, and maybe not the respect Dustin commanded without actually posing a threat. Seth wanted respect with a healthy dose of "owns a can of whoop ass and isn't afraid to open it" thrown into the mix. Used only as necessary.

Monica slumped into a chair across from him. "You're

paying." Damn! Even while slouching her presence was commanding.

"Of course. To save us some time, let's get a few things out of the way right now. Yes, I was a lousy great-nephew. No, I didn't deserve a fabulous aunt like Irene. And yes, I'm from She-cargo, and have high falutin' city ways. Did I miss anything?"

"Insufferable asshole."

"Oh yes, how could I forget my favorite nickname? Since we've settled important matters, let's order half a damned pig and proceed to harden our arteries while you answer my questions."

A half hour and a pile of rib bones later, Monica unabashedly licked sweet-and-spicy sauce from her fingers. A smear marred one cheek. She either didn't notice or didn't care. Rearing her chair back on two legs, she rubbed her stomach. "Man, I'm full as a tick! Now that we've eaten enough for a small country, why did you want to meet with me, other than to smack you around and deflate your puffed-up ego?"

Seth grinned. "Because you don't like me."

The chair dropped back on four legs. Monica extended her palms in a warding-off gesture. "Don't be talking no kink at the dinner table. I may be a big woman, but I don't get into whips and chains and shit, no matter how many times I'm asked."

She meant her comment as a joke, right? The mental image of Monica in dominatrix mode—not that it'd be much different than how he normally viewed her—wasn't something he wanted in his head. "Junior and Dustin both have their own agendas when it comes to me, and let's not even talk about my ex suddenly showing up. You'd like nothing better than for me to hop a plane out of here. Personally, I'd like to hop a plane out of here too. But you also cared about my aunt and have your own opinions about local politics."

Monica surveyed him almost clinically. He half expected

her to break out a scalpel and start dissecting. But where disgust had been the only expression he'd read so far, something new crept into place. A softening of the eyes. And did the corner of her lip twitch upward for a split second? Could that have been the beginnings of a… smile? "Why should I help you?"

Seth knew with that one question he'd broken through. It might take weeks or even years, but one day, without a doubt, Monica and he would be friends. "Because you're just about the most invested person in this damn town I've met. Spill!"

In an uncharacteristic display of doubt, Monica nibbled her lower lip, giving her sauce-encrusted nails a thorough examination. "How much of the 'Chandler-Frost Virus and You' lecture did Dustin give you?"

After a quick belch into his napkin, Seth faced Monica with resolution. He needed to be honest if he expected honesty in return. "Dustin tells me there's a good chance I'll go furry on the next full moon." He'd hoped with this meeting to open a door with Monica, maybe a crack. She flung it wide and barged on through, telling him far more than he'd dared hope for.

"The day you arrived you smelled like passel, only not very strong. Since you were bitten, your scent's grown stronger. Even if I wasn't sitting across from you now, I've smelled you on Dustin. I've picked up your scent in the grocery store without even having to lay eyes on you." She tapped a fingertip against her nose. "Hypersensitive sniffers come with the territory."

Since she'd been forthcoming up until now, Seth started in on the list of questions he'd compiled while wondering whether or not she'd show up. "Have you ever wondered, 'Why possums'? I mean, I understand a bear or wolf, to help you defend yourself, but what advantage is there in turning into a possum?"

Monica shrugged a pair of shoulders any high school line-backer would be proud of. "Depends on the threat. If it were another animal, a bear or wolf might work, but what if it were a man? Say you're running through the woods from an enemy. In prehistoric times, he might have a club, or in more recent years, a gun. You turn into a wolf and he kills you. Same with a bear, because you're a threat. But if you turned into a possum and scuttled off into the underbrush, you're home free." While she spoke, she shredded a slice of Texas toast with her fingers, dropping the torn chunks back into the basket. "And I can't tell you how many of our young folks get snapped up by certain government agencies that go by three letters."

"*What?*" Seth couldn't disguise a gasp. "The government knows about us?"

"Yep. And has a vested interest in keeping quiet. You think secret papers about Area 51 might cause a scandal? Wait until the public gets wind of the military using shifters for espionage."

Whoa! Seth hadn't even considered how useful a shifted possum might be. "How about the locals? Is everyone here a possum shifter?"

"Not everyone. But those who aren't have family ties, their own folks to protect."

Her words made a weird kind of sense, in a twisted, sci-fi, B-movie kind of way. "What happens now, to me?"

"Now we wait until the next full moon. If you shift, you'll be expected to assume responsibility for the passel."

He'd been afraid the "gift" came with strings attached. Unfortunately, the only thing, or rather person, he wanted to be attached to was Dustin. "Do you like football?"

Monica gave him an incredulous glare. "I haven't missed a Possums game in five years."

"Good. Now imagine you're the quarterback, and you try to snap the ball to me."

The brow slowly rose over Monica's right eye.

"You hold it out, I ignore it. What do you do?"

"Give it to somebody else?"

"Bingo! I don't want the ball! Give it to Dustin."

Monica's inelegant snort startled Seth. "He doesn't want it either. We're about to lose the game to the opposing team."

Dustin didn't want leadership? Then why send workers to the house, or otherwise try to butter Seth up? "Why not give it to Junior, if Dustin doesn't want it and I don't want it?"

Monica inclined her head toward a boisterous family of six dining a few tables away. "Do you want to walk over there and tell Mr. and Mrs. Sanders that they have to leave the town they both grew up in because they're not 'one of us'?" Her indigo gaze settled on a man with long, sandy-blond hair pulled back in a tail and a woman bearing a noticeable baby bump. "Andy there is Reynard of the local fox skulk. Most of his older shifters are refugees from a vicious power struggle and have nowhere else to go. Want to go tell him and his pregnant wife you're pulling the rug on Irene's promise of protection?"

Seth eyed the two families in question. "Why does Junior want to get rid of them?"

"It's not just them. He'd give me the boot too, for not being 'full blood'. That's the main reason I'd never want to be Jill, the other being that I couldn't tolerate folks calling me at all hours to solve their problems for them. In case you haven't noticed yet, I'm not known for suffering fools lightly." An understatement if Seth ever heard one.

"You're not a full blood either," she continued, "but the name McDaniel carries a lot of weight around here." Monica spat a toothpick onto her plate. "Dustin didn't want the job, but he'll take it to protect the innocent."

From the sounds of the job description, Seth wasn't sure he wanted the job either. What the hell had his family gotten him into? A bit of light showed at the end of the proverbial tunnel. "Can't I name Dustin leader? Give up my claim?" Richard had hinted at such, hadn't he?

"I wish it were that easy. The passel might demand that he challenge you, and he won't, because it's a mark of disrespect. Junior would, and he'd fight dirty."

A boulder lodged in Seth's throat. "What do you mean, 'challenge'?" The lawyer had mentioned challenges, but hadn't fully explained.

"Exactly what you think I mean. A fight, in possum form. Sometimes to the death."

What the hell had Seth walked into? "My choices are either man up or nice folks get screwed?" *Oh my God! When's the next flight out of this crazy-ass place!*

Monica took her frustrations out on another piece of toast. "And don't get any bright ideas about simply handing the town to Junior on a silver platter, those folks over there be damned. He'd lose face, and in losing face, he'd lose support. We're a rather old-fashioned group, I'm afraid. He'll issue a formal challenge."

Maybe Seth still stood a chance of dodging the bullet, though he hated to throw Dustin under the bus in his stead. "What happens if I don't turn?"

"Dustin'll announce his intent to be leader, Junior'll challenge him, and I'll hope for the best. But the challenge might not happen if enough of Junior's supporters are swayed to Dustin's side, or vice versa."

"Which is why they're both showering me with gifts," Seth grumbled. "Junior's hoping to bend me to his will so he can take over, and Dustin wants me to stay here and fulfill my supposed role as a McDaniel."

"Hey!" Monica managed the closest thing to a smile Seth had ever seen on her face. "Enjoy it. You didn't ask for gifts; they gave them."

"I'm a McDaniel."

"So?"

"I found a notebook my mom wrote. She and Dad were

proud to be McDaniels. Aunt Irene was proud. I'm the family screwup."

Monica gave Seth a conspiratorial wink. "Yes. But you can change."

"How?"

"By pulling yourself up by your bootstraps and being the man you were born to be."

What? Was she actually trying to help him? "I'm worried I'll fuck everything up." He expected scorn and ridicule; what he got ran beyond his wildest dreams.

"I'll teach you."

Seth regarded Monica with suspicion. Did he dare hope she'd be on his side? "But you hate me."

"No, I don't. I don't like you, and in my book you're an ungrateful slacker, but I don't hate you."

"Why help me if you don't like me?"

"Number one: I may not like you, but I don't like Junior more. Number two: I love Dustin, and he makes an excellent second-in-command, but he's a doctor and healer first and foremost. He's not a fighter or a leader."

Seth couldn't have been more shocked if Monica had fallen to her knees and proposed. "And you think I am?"

"You can be. Underneath all that city-slicker exterior beats the heart of a McDaniel. Or so Irene always said. If it's under there, I owe it to Irene to help you find it."

At least she wasn't offering to take the direct route through his chest.

And she wasn't finished yet. "A wise woman once told me that you don't have to be perfect to lead; it's more about your heart than your head, and about caring for your people. And you don't have to be smart, just smart enough to know where you're lacking, and surround yourself with folks who'll take up the slack. Dustin played that role for her, and he'll play if for you, too, I'm willing to bet."

Seth took a deep breath and let it out slowly. "The parcel Aunt Irene's house sits on goes back in my family for hundreds of years."

"Yep."

"I have family buried out there."

"Yep."

Although still not totally convinced the whole town didn't suffer from mass hysteria, he finally made up his mind. "I want your help."

Monica beamed a genuine smile. It scared the hell out of him.

After she left, he paid the bill, gathered the torn bread into a napkin, and made his way down the pond to feed the ducks and digest Monica's words along with his meal.

Junior wanted power. The gifts and phone calls were a means to an end. He didn't care about Seth. And though Seth hadn't befriended many townsfolk, he didn't believe any of them should be forced from their homes. Who wanted an elitist who thought he was better than everybody else running the show? That sounded like some kind of crazed dictator to Seth. Junior didn't want him for himself. Did anyone?

An image of Michael flashed before his eyes, a man he thought he'd loved at one time. They'd finally agreed on one thing: they really weren't meant for each other. Michael wouldn't be content living in Georgia; he liked the city's nightlife too much. He'd never give up nightclubs, valet parking, and room service to live a quiet life in a farmhouse.

Wait. Live a quiet life in a farmhouse? Since when had Seth decided not to go back to Chicago? He imagined his lonely apartment, empty, awaiting new tenants, and felt not one ripple of remorse. Next, he envisioned the farmhouse, a red and black "For Sale" sign in the yard. His heart ached, particularly when his mind formed images of families tramping through, criticizing the things that, despite the many years of separation,

Seth still valued. "The ceiling's too high," he heard an imaginary potential buyer screech. "It's too far from town! Hardwood floors! Let's get some carpet in here!" Seth cringed, for the polished floors were the house's best feature, in his opinion.

But it wasn't just the farmhouse he'd miss if he left. The image of Dustin lying in his bed, looking like he belonged there, auburn hair fanned out across the pillow, testified that Seth had grown attached to much more than merely the ancestral McDaniel homestead. Yup, he'd fallen for the man who'd hold Seth if he cried, laugh with him when he was happy, and might yet skinny-dip with him again in the pond. The man who didn't want the responsibility of leadership, but who'd take on the duty to protect the people Aunt Irene had held dear.

Seth tossed a piece of bread to a waiting duck, recalling the group picture on the mantel back at the house. Those people must be the passel he'd heard about, his aunt's surrogate family. Could he fill her shoes? Well, not alone he couldn't. Could he fill them with Dustin and Monica's help and support? That remained to be seen. The only thing Seth could swear to beyond a shadow of a doubt was that he didn't stand a chance without Dustin, *didn't want* to stand a chance without Dustin.

When had the guy started meaning so much to him? He remembered Dustin's comforting arms around him the day before his grandmother had taken him away. In a moment of silence, a small voice answered, *Dusty always meant the world to you.*

Seth waited until after office hours to call and leave a message on Dustin's work phone. "Dusty? It's me, Seth. It's nothing against you or anything, but I'm working through some issues and need the time to get my head together, okay?" Before he could stop them, out tumbled the dreaded words he couldn't take back, but had needed to say ever since they'd first occurred to him while feeding the ducks: "I love you." He ended the call before further embarrassing himself.

I love you? What kind of sentimental mush was that to leave on a voice mail? He wasn't free to say things like that, not with his future hanging in the air.

He sat on the porch of the farmhouse, idly toeing the old wooden swing back and forth, when he sensed his guest's arrival. "I could tell it was you from the magnolia tree."

The plump marsupial body on the bottom step hunched back on its rear paws, its blimp-shaped torso elongating, twisting, and turning until a naked woman stood in its place, skin gleaming ivory by the light of a nearly full moon. "Too close, and I wasn't even shielding," Monica replied. "You aren't focusing."

Unconcerned by her nakedness, she stalked across the porch to stand before him. Seth averted his eyes.

"Look at me."

Seth slowly swiveled his head back in her direction, staring fixedly at her face.

"You can't be bothered by nudity. It's a body, no big deal. Everybody's got one. If you'd been raised here and began turning around thirteen or fourteen, you'd be used to seeing the passel naked. To flinch or get a hard-on will mark you an outsider."

A hard-on! Oh shit! Seth hadn't thought about that. How could he not get hard seeing Dustin? Though he wouldn't have that problem with Monica, he skimmed his gaze down, stopping at her ample breasts and flicking back up to her face again. "I can't."

"You gotta! Now quit being a child. Look at me!"

Hands balled into fists, brain turned to an off-air channel of white noise static, Seth forced himself to study Monica's body from the braids that swept over her shoulder to brush over her backside to the brightly polished toenails.

"Nice color," he said, staring down.

"Good. Your night vision's getting stronger."

Still a bit squeamish about seeing Monica nude, Seth appreciated the lesson she meant to teach, and ran his gaze up her body again, honing in on a dark spot above her navel. Was that… was that Mickey Mouse? He fought back a giggle. "Nice tat." He'd never view drill-sergeant Monica the same way again.

CHAPTER 18

"How's Seth?" Dustin hated asking; however, Monica wouldn't volunteer the information if he didn't.

"He's fine. A little nervous about tomorrow night, but I'll be there." Monica handed over the chart for their last patient of the evening.

"I wish he'd join the passel, let us celebrate his first shifting." Actually, Dustin would take any excuse to cross paths with the man. Only sheer force of will had kept him from turning down Seth's driveway when he passed on his way home every day, despite the fact that he had to go past his house to get to Seth's, then turn around.

"He's not ready to be ridden around on people's shoulders and praised as the next big thing. McDaniels aren't given to public displays."

"No, they're not." Damn the luck!

Monica's voice softened. "He misses you."

"Then why won't he let me help him?"

"Until some decisions are made, he can't be seen to play favorites. For a loser and a wuss, he's now got a pretty good handle on which way the wind blows around these parts."

Dustin twitched up one corner of his mouth. "He should, you're guiding him."

"Yeah, yeah. Flattery will get you everywhere. Now go home and get some rest. Tomorrow is the full moon. I'm sure between wandering Tiffany, the Johnson Boys' Three-Ring Circus, and keeping Junior's knife out of your back, you'll have your hands full."

Another reason to want Seth and Monica with him—to help watch his back. "You have a gift for understatement. You going to Seth's tonight?"

Monica studied her fingernails. "I'm staying there. For now."

"Oh?" She'd been sleeping under the same roof with Seth and hadn't killed him yet?

"It's the safest thing."

Safest for whom? Dustin and Monica had been friends for years, but even he wasn't immune to her acid tongue if she thought him deserving of being ripped a new asshole. "You like him now?"

"Your words, not mine." She wouldn't meet his gaze. Interesting.

Dustin couldn't help goading her a bit. "Why are you working with him?"

"Because I like you, and owe Irene. Besides, he's got Irene's cookbooks and isn't afraid to use them."

A likely story. But at least one of them was keeping an eye on Seth, though Dustin would have preferred to do the honors himself.

Dustin tossed and turned, chasing elusive sleep. No use. He sighed into the darkness. Regardless of how tomorrow night turned out, things would change, for him, for Seth, for the passel. He'd longed for the mysterious McDaniel to suddenly reappear and take the burden from him; now he feared for Seth's survival.

A *bap* sounded against his bedroom window, probably a wind-borne acorn. He listened to the night, sensing a distur- bance outside he couldn't identify. Only one person in the passel besides himself shielded completely enough to create a void where their presence should be. But why the hell would Monica sneak up on him in the middle of the night? He hadn't pissed her off lately, had he?

The *bap!* came again, which he now realized might be a rock hitting the window frame. Seth used to throw rocks to get Dustin's attention when he sneaked over to visit after bedtime. Dustin left his pillow-covered haven behind and trudged to the window to raise the glass.

"Seth?"

A dark blur launched itself at the window; Dustin moved out of the way in the nick of time. The blur landed on the floor, righted itself, and then launched another attack. Dustin found himself flat on his back on the bed, pinned in place, his mouth being devoured.

After an initial moment of shock, he brought his arms up around Seth, returning the man's eager enthusiasm. "Oh, Seth," he murmured against his lover's mouth, "damn, but I missed you."

"Shh... don't talk. Just feel."

Seth shimmied out of a pair of shorts; Dustin slept in the nude. Seth latched his mouth onto Dustin's neck, bathing the skin with his tongue and scraping with his teeth enough to shoot an arrow straight through Dustin's libido. Seth ground an impressive erection against Dustin's rising hardness.

Grasping Seth's backside with both hands, Dustin rocked up, meeting desperate stroke with desperate stroke. Suddenly Seth rolled them, pushing and pulling until they lay lengthwise on the bed, face to face on their sides. Seth brought his leg up and hooked it around Dustin's thigh, anchoring their bodies together. He wrapped a hand around their joined cocks, thrusting hard into his fist. "Tomorrow night, things may change. Tonight, we're equals," he said. "Fuck me."

Dustin squirmed to free himself, but Seth tightened the grip with his leg. "Where are you going?"

"Supplies are in the dresser, remember?"

"Find my shorts."

Dustin rolled away enough to pat the floor, located the discarded garment, and rummaged through the pocket. He unrolled the condom over his ready length. "What about...?"

He swore he heard a grin in Seth's voice. "It pays to plan ahead."

Dustin probed an experimental finger at Seth's opening and found it already well-lubricated. He groaned, his cock hardening further. Damn. Just damn.

"I didn't want to waste any time." Seth rolled to his back, his legs falling open.

Dustin was on him before he stopped moving, sinking in and huffing out a breathy, "Oh fuck, that feels good." A slick, hot tightness slowly yielded to his entry, wrapping around him and stealing coherent thought. Seth. Here. Under him. Opening for him. Nothing else mattered but Seth's fingers exploring Dustin's shoulders, Seth's mouth upon Dustin's own.

Dustin lost himself in the moment and his lover's body, surging forward and back, angling to hit the perfect spot and make things good for them both. Moans, groans, and whimpering cries filled the room, joined by the heady scent of cologne, sweat, and sex.

Seth dug both legs into Dustin's thighs, urging him on. Dustin plunged in again and again, desperate to reach the finish line. The part of his mind still functioning fought the release, determined to cling to the moment and Seth for as long as possible. No telling what tomorrow would bring.

Faster, harder, deeper, he drove, until Seth panted a steady chorus of, "Ah, ah, ah, ah, ah…." The muscles gripping Dustin fluttered. Seth threw back his head, every muscle seizing. "Ah…," he cried again.

Dustin raced to catch him, faster and faster, burying himself completely in Seth's body, his cry of, "Oh my God!" mingling with mindless, wordless shouts of release.

Breathless, sweaty, sated, Dustin crumpled beside Seth and drew him nearer. Their racing heartbeats sounded like thunder in his ears.

"I love you," Seth said.

Dustin wasn't sure whether or not he replied, for he lost consciousness a split second later. He awoke with the dawn, alone and needing a shower.

Seth rolled his eyes. "Not another one!" A buff hunk wearing a bad-boy smile stood on his doorstep, holding a vase of gladiolas and smelling faintly of something that brought to mind a fox. His nametag proclaimed him, "Levi."

"Is there a nursing home on your route, by any chance?"

"No," the delivery man said.

"Hospital?"

"No."

"You got a mother, aunt, wife, or girlfriend?"

The man grinned, appearing more wolf than fox. "I might."

"Good! Now take those"—Seth nodded at the flowers—"to whoever. Just get them the hell out of my sight, okay?"

"Thanks? Umm… how about tomorrow's delivery?"

"If they're from Junior Timmerman, you can have them. The Johnsons asked me to please stop feeding their goat."

The young man returned to his truck, an added bounce in his step. The phone rang a moment later. Shit. Michael. While Seth appreciated the man's determination to *still be friends*, between renovating the house, working with Monica, fending off a wealthy, older, would-be suitor, and worrying about Dustin, he didn't have time to spare at the moment. *A wealthy older suitor?* Inspiration struck. "Hi, Michael! How's it going?"

"Fine. I've come up with a few ideas of what to do next and wanted to talk them over with you. Are you free for lunch?"

If Seth's plan worked, he might get a few moments' peace. "I know a silver fox, loaded to the gills, and available. How about it? Want to meet him?"

Michael didn't immediately answer. Finally, he said, "Is that a trick question?"

Seth huffed out a breath, running his fingers through his hair. Monica would arrive shortly for his possum lessons, and he hoped to avoid distractions by occupying the two biggest obstacles to his concentration—with each other. "Is that a yes?"

"You're kidding, right? Of course it's a yes."

"Be at the Pitted Pig at one o'clock, out on the back porch. The guy's name is Junior." Seth hung up, grateful for a respite and also for the fact that it hadn't bothered him at all to fix up his ex with another man. Had he gotten over Michael so quickly? Or had there truly been nothing real between them to begin with? Should he feel guilty about throwing Michael at Junior? *Nah.*

Junior called five minutes later. Instead of letting the call go to voice mail, Seth picked up on the first ring. "Howdy, Junior."

"Did you get my flowers?"

"About those flowers. Seems I'm allergic to gladiolas." He faked a sneeze for good measure.

"Oh, I'm sorry to hear that. Can I make it up to you, say, by taking you to lunch?"

Ah, the man played right into Seth's hands. Perfect. "I'm kinda busy right now, but listen. I got a friend in town, and I'd appreciate it if you'd keep him company out at the Pig around one o'clock. That work for you?"

"A friend, you say?" Junior's suspicion came across loud and clear.

"Yeah. And you'd better hurry." Seth tried his best not to laugh. "Poor guy can't go anywhere without having to beat off men and women. Says it's a curse to have been born so beautiful. I hate not being there to defend his honor and would take it as a personal favor if you'd keep an eye on Michael for me."

"Beautiful, you say?"

"Like a Greek god." The Greeks had a god for needy exes, right?

"Because you asked nicely, I'll do it. For you!" For the first time in memory, Junior hung up first.

Seth was still smiling over his matchmaking when Monica arrived. "Why're you so damned happy?" she asked, removing a cage from the passenger seat and placing it on her Silverado's tailgate.

"Oh, nothing. Just got Junior off my back for a little while." He couldn't help bragging a little.

"Off your back is exactly where you want Junior Timmerman." Monica waggled her brows. "C'mon over here. I want you to meet somebody."

"Where'd you get him?" Seth stared through the sides of a metal dog crate at a rather fat example of possumhood. It yawned, revealing a multitude of spiny teeth. Seth chuckled. "You're not impressed with me one iota, are you, little guy?"

"This here is Petey the Possum, mascot for the Thurman County High Fighting Possums football team. I'm taking him to Dr. Coleman, the vet, for his annual checkup." Monica dropped a cricket in the cage. The insect didn't even hit the bottom before becoming a possum snack.

Seth stepped away from the cage, overwhelmed with sympathy for the poor jailed beast, and for the cricket. "It's cruel to keep him caged."

"Points for correctly guessing he's male. Look closer." Monica pointed at the beast's backside.

Seth studied the possum from one end to the other. "Oh." A scar wound up one hip.

"Yeah. A teacher found Petey on the side of the road as a joey. His mother was crossing the road with her babies on her back and got hit—an occupational hazard, I'm afraid. Only Petey made it. With his bad leg, he wouldn't survive in the wild." Monica stuck a finger into the cage, rubbing an ear. "I wouldn't worry about him too much. The kids treat him good. It's an earned honor to be given possum-feeding duty. Now, you've probed my mind in animal form. Try seeing into Petey's."

Seth stared at the creature's beady eyes, sensing nothing but hunger, mild curiosity, and the need to… oh crap! Seth jumped back when Petey pissed.

Monica giggled. "Sorry, I couldn't resist. Now this is a regular possum. How can you tell?"

"No human thoughts. Just base instinct."

"Good. Newbies like Tiffany feel somewhat like Petey, here. You have to be careful to watch out for them. They'll get away in a flat minute and wreak havoc."

"Like my mom did," Seth whispered.

Monica lifted her hand to massage Seth's shoulder. "Yeah. After that tragedy, Irene began asking more nonshifting carriers to stand guard. We haven't lost anyone since, although we have had the occasional injury due to a dog attack. Now, try to get Petey to turn around. The secret is to make him think it's his idea. Don't try this on other animals, though. It'll only work on the type of animal you shift into."

After a few unsuccessful attempts, Petey dutifully turned round and round in his cage at Seth's mental commands. Monica grinned. She appeared much less frightening now that she displayed facial expressions other than scowls. "Seth, I believe you might be a McDaniel after all."

A pile of barbequed ribs sat on a platter between Seth and Monica at The Pitted Pig. Seth breathed a sigh of relief when Junior and Michael left without noticing them, or, apparently, noticing much of anything but each other. Their cooing and goo-goo eyes threatened to sap Seth's appetite, and Monica periodically glanced in their direction and made gagging noises.

"The annual convention is a real hoot," she said, brandishing a well-gnawed rib bone.

"Convention?"

"Yeah, every year the small animal, nonpredator organizations meet to keep up with who's where, who's in command, and to work out swaps. The 'furry' movement provides us excellent cover. Before they came into play, we had to be more discreet." She sopped up a blob of barbeque sauce with a roll and popped it into her mouth. "Nothing like a group of grown men dressing as animals to help us blend in."

"What do you mean 'swaps'?" The last thing Seth wanted to hear about was some kind of kinky wife-swapping venture.

"It's a gene-pool thing. If we have too many single ladies, and another town has bachelors out the ying yang, we'll issue an invitation for outsiders to join us, or vice versa. Kinda like a huge annual shifter mixer. But it's not just a singles' club. Say you got a good strong leader type in an area that has plenty, and you're lacking leadership in another. You can find candidates at the cons. Turtletown up north of us found their last leader at a con."

"You said the passel didn't like outsiders."

"We're a bit exclusive, I'm afraid, but that's not the same everywhere. Others view diversity as progress and a way to exchange ideas. Anyway, our vet met his wife at a convention, though typically foxes throw in with the predators."

The only convention Seth ever attended was Comic-Con. What kind of exhibits and lectures would he find at a shifter con? "Burr Removal Made Easy"? "Hiding in Plain Sight, Level One"? "What groups come to the convention, if not predators?"

"Skunks, rabbits, raccoons, squirrels, us. Occasionally the chipmunks send delegates. The reptiles have their own get-togethers."

"Wow! Reptile conventions? Cool!"

"We're a well-kept secret. And we need to stay under wraps. Now, the next convention is in Anaheim—Oh, eat up." She tipped a few more ribs onto Seth's plate. "Full moon tonight. You're gonna need your strength."

Seth stood on the front porch, fully naked. Over the rise, he sensed humans and possums, the possum number rising and the human falling as the townsfolk assumed animal form. In their midst, fighting for control, stood Dustin. Seth's heart lurched. No blood sang in his veins like Monica said it would, no tingling toes heralded a change. He tipped his face up at the sky, a lone tear sliding down his face. It wasn't meant to be. He'd let the family down.

"I'm sorry, Seth. I can't hold on any longer." Monica sat on the lawn one moment, her possum alter ego replacing her in the twinkling of an eye.

Folding himself down on the top step, Seth wrapped his arms around his knees. How he'd hoped to finally find a place where he fit. Was he destined to remain on the outside looking in forever?

Dustin wandered the edge of the yard, furry mind filled with human sympathy.

"But I wanted to be a possum tonight!" Seth screamed at the fickle moon. One moment later, he was.

Night sounds Seth normally took for granted sharpened, and he wondered if real possums appreciated the difference. Wait! He *wondered!* He did a happy little possum flip, if somewhat awkwardly. He wondered! He had his human mind! On the edges of his consciousness, Dustin and Monica conversed before Dustin shrank back into the shadows, apparently satisfied. Monica hunkered down a few yards away, wary eyes sweeping the yard.

Chirp, chirp! What the hell was that? Seth scuttled around, searching the grass for whatever produced cheeping to give a foghorn a run for its money, volume-wise. *Chirp, chirp.* A fat cricket sat a few feet away, singing to lure a prospective mate. Seth stared at the angular, skinny legs, only one thought in his head: *Yummy!* He pounced, as much as his cumbersome body allowed, catching the cricket unawares. *Crunch, crunch, crunch.* Oh! Like potato chips! Also like potato chips, one simply wasn't enough.

Seth spotted another cricket and wobbled over, filling his mouth before his prey hopped away. Stupid cricket. The third and fourth proved equally easy.

I am the crickinator! Seth considered simply opening his

mouth and ambling the length of the yard, scooping up insects like a whale netting plankton.

Eventually his seemingly bottomless belly filled, and he experimented with his new body. Locomotion wasn't a problem if he simply moved without trying to figure out the mechanics. However, the moment he became aware of having four feet to contend with, he stumbled and fell. Should he place the two on the right in tandem, or right front, back left? *Splat!*

A chittering sounded in the general direction of Monica. Did possums laugh?

Oh! Worm! Seth pounced, squealing when his teeth sank into his own tail. Ow! That hurt!

After a while, he grew sleepy and headed for the house. He bumped his nose on the bottom step. How the hell did they get so high? Bouncing his front end lifted his paws an inch off the ground. He bounced again, and again, only succeeding in wearing himself out.

When he'd reached the point of giving up, Monica took pity and led him around the side of the house and underneath. An intricate possum highway existed under the structure, constructed of two by fours and sheet metal. On and on they rambled, entering walls and finally coming out under the bathroom sink.

Weary now, Seth slothed to his bedroom, where he plopped down on the area rug by his bed.

He awoke to sunlight streaming through the window, itchy possum hairs scratching his bare human skin, and the icky sensation that something had crawled into his mouth and died. Wait a minute. It had. Several things, actually. Something scratchy hung from his lip and he wiped it away, only to come away with a cricket leg clinging to his hand. Yuck. Cricket.

❧

Seth slurped his second cup of coffee in a feeble attempt to clear the ick from his mouth. He peeled open one bleary eye to stare at Monica. "You didn't sleep with me, did you?"

Monica snorted into her coffee. "Of course not! I slept in my bed."

Bed? "How the hell did you get in a bed? They're too damned high."

"Didn't you notice how your aunt kept a chair by every bed? You simply climb the rungs, jump to the mattress and tuck yourself in. Umm… in case you didn't know, possums are natural climbers." She narrowed her eyes, staring at Seth with faux concern. "Awww… did the widdle possum s'eep on the cold, hard floor last night 'cause he couldn't get into his big, high bed?"

Not feeling particularly mature at the moment, Seth unwrapped one hand from around his coffee cup to flip her off.

She laughed. "You realize what you did last night, right?"

He shot her a "well, duh!" expression, which sapped his remaining energy—he dropped his head to the kitchen table with a *bang*.

"*He* didn't change until the last of the passel did," supplied a welcome voice from behind. Summoning the few remaining ounces of his strength, Seth lifted his head a fraction and swiveled around to the new arrival. Dustin stood barefoot and bare-chested in the doorway, clad in faded blue jeans, thin spots and holes showing in strategic areas. Even exhausted, Seth found the peek-a-boo display of skin fascinating.

"I fought to hang on, hoping to witness Seth's first transformation," Dustin said as he crossed to the coffeepot and helped himself to a cup. "I finally couldn't control the change any longer. The moment I dropped my guard, *bang!* there you went. Tell me, were you fighting half as hard as I was?"

Fighting? "No. When I'd finally accepted it wasn't happening, *wham!* I'm a possum."

Dustin leaned down, searching Seth's eyes. "Any disorientation? Headache? Nausea?"

Seth shook his head, stopping when the motion made the room spin. "Only due to cricket overload. I'm tired and swimmy-headed."

Both Dustin and Monica's eyebrows shot up toward their hairlines. "That's all?"

"Yeah."

Dustin's wide-eyed surprise met Monica's in a silent exchange Seth worried might be some form of telepathy. He slurped coffee in retaliation for them ignoring him. Was he supposed to have to fight, get headaches, and nausea? Maybe he should rethink that whole "living up to the family name" thing.

"This is un-freaking-believable," Monica murmured.

"What?"

Dustin plopped down in a chair across the table, staring at Seth like some fascinating circus attraction. "Irene didn't have to fight. The moment the last person under her care turned, so did she. If I were meant to lead, remaining in human form, on guard, would be second nature. It's not. If I took over now it might be years before shifting last comes naturally, if ever. Dude, you are the man, literally."

A faint stirring of hope wriggled to life in Seth's heart. "Does that mean Junior can't challenge me?"

"No. He still can, but being top dog, um… possum, won't come easy as long as you're around."

"Are you saying I'll be okay if I go back to She-car… Chicago?" He shot Monica a dirty look for corrupting his vocabulary.

She ignored him to pick up the tale. "I'm not sure you should. In the past, I've heard of McDaniel wives who've carried out the duties for the Jack while husbands fought in wars. While the rightful Jack is alive, however, the designated leader senses them. In fact, one such lady experienced a sudden increase in ability the instant her husband died in combat thousands of miles away."

"What now?" Seth scrubbed his hands over his face, suddenly even more tired.

"Now we get you ready to face the next full moon. Dustin had three cycles to name Irene's successor. We've passed two. In just shy of a month, it'll be time."

"What do I have to do?" Was there a rule book somewhere Seth should be reading? *Shapeshifting 101*? Or maybe, *Werepossum Culture Volume One*?

Dustin answered him this time. "First, make sure the people know who you are, what you stand for, and why you're the only rightful choice. Your family resemblance will go a long way toward ensuring your acceptance."

Seth gave Dustin all the scowl he could manage to muster in his worn-out state. "Are you talkin' 'bout my nose? 'Cause let me tell you, I got enough grief about my nose in grade school." He passed a hand over his prodigious sniffer.

"I like your nose," Dustin inclined his head to say, eyes crinkling at the corners. He leaned across the table and planted a kiss on the McDaniel family legacy.

"Alright, lovebirds, enough kissy-face." Monica slammed her cup down. "Seth holds a legitimate claim, but still can't be seen to be playing favorites between you and Junior. Dustin, between the two of us, we have to make sure he captures the hearts and minds of the townsfolk."

Seth wrenched his attention away from Dustin's suggestive gaze and the promises it held for later. "I thought all I had to do was fight Junior and win."

"Seth, what century are you living in?" Monica gave him "are you serious?" glare. It wasn't pretty. "Everything's political now, and we're off to do a little politicking."

"Damn, I have to post flyers and stuff envelopes after all,

don't I?" Seth groaned, recalling his earlier misconception of what Junior wanted of him. Now, however, instead of Junior's smiling face and a "Vote for Me!" slogan, Seth saw his own somewhat bewildered expression and "Vote for Me... Please!"

"We'll stuff envelopes in the nude," Dustin promised.

The clothes on Seth's image on the imaginary flyers fell off.

CHAPTER 19

"Okay. First thing you gotta learn is the secret handshake."

"The secret what?" Seth stared at Monica. Was she kidding, not that he'd ever seen her kidding before? Or had he?

"The secret handshake." She approached, hand outstretched, a twitch at the corner of her mouth the equivalent of a caution flag.

After wiping his sweaty palm on his gym shorts, Seth slowly, slowly, brought his hand up toward the woman he half expected to pull some kind of kung fu move, leaving him sprawled on his ass. Particularly when they now stood in the barn, where she'd insisted they spread a layer of hay as padding before beginning Seth's training.

"Now," she explained, "the extra something the virus provides that allows us to shift gives off energy. That, along with a slight change to your natural scent, is how the folks in town can tell you're now a jack." Did she add "ass" or was that Seth's imagination? "The stronger the energy, the more respect you'll get from the passel. Remember how the Johnson boys toed the line in the grocery store? Well, they didn't want to be on the receiving end of another jolt from me."

"You're going to shock me?" Seth jerked his hand back, cradling the appendage against his chest.

Monica's lip twitching grew more pronounced. "Nothing that will do permanent damage, and like shifting at will, you can learn to control the amount of power, hide it if necessary, or amp it up to warn an enemy, though you seem to have inherited a natural shield. A minimal dose of shifter mojo is like taking a hit of some really good shit for these people, if that's what you intend. Or you can deliver a hard swat, like I do occasionally to the triplets. Wins them over, or keeps 'em in line, depending on what's needed. Now, quit being a wuss and give me your hand. I want you to concentrate, focus inward on your animal. He knows where the energy lives and will help you find it."

This couldn't possibly be a good idea. Seth raised his hand, mentally poking at his inner marsupial. It growled, rolled over, and hissed, *Go away! I'm sleeping.*

Monica rolled her eyes. "You're the host body, your animal is a symbiont. You're the boss."

Seth poked again, harder this time. *Yeah, yeah, yadda, yadda,* his inner beast seemed to say, yawning and stretching a many-toothed mouth wide. A sensation began in his fingers and toes and moved inward, a mass influx of raw power. Every hair on his body stood on end.

"Good, good." Monica nodded encouragement. "Now, concentrate that power to your hand."

Imagining a movie poster he'd seen of Iron Man, Seth shoved the tingling sensations toward one palm. Confidence surged through him, and he no longer hesitated to slap his palm against his teacher's.

The smirk left Monica's face. She sailed backward, smacking into a stack of hay bales. The hay tumbled to the ground. One long braid stuck out from beneath the pile.

"Monica! Monica! Are you all right?" Seth flew across the

barn, grabbing bales and flinging them aside. Dear God, let him not have killed the woman.

Monica lay flat on her back, staring at the rafters. "Holy shit!" A dazed grin split her face. "I can't wait to see the sparks fly when you hit Junior!"

They practiced a few more times, until Monica stumbled out of the barn. "Okay, enough for one day."

Was she drooling a little? Seth swore the tips of her braids smoldered.

She gave him a coy smile and approached her truck. "One more for the road?" She held out her hand. Had she forgotten she was staying at the farmhouse?

Daaaaammmmmmn!

"I thought you said we were going to work out." Seth shot a puzzled glance from the fallen tree to the ax slung over Monica's shoulder. Dressed in a red flannel shirt with the sleeves ripped out and overalls with only one gallus fastened, she could have posed for a certain paper towel maker should they ever feel the need to be more inclusive in their advertising.

"This is a better workout than any gym machine can give, plus you'll be killing two birds with one stone."

Personally, Seth held firmly to a motto of "live and let live" when it came to bird killing, but he'd keep his mouth shut, particularly when Monica hefted a weapon capable of dismembering errant teens in horror flicks.

"Put your gloves on."

Seth obeyed, choosing to pick his battles. Dustin trusted Monica to teach Seth the ins and outs of shifter-hood, though how chopping wood related to turning furry he hadn't yet worked out.

"Swing with your shoulders, but take the hit in your arms.

You don't want to jar your back." She demonstrated, neatly cleaving a limb from the tree.

Seth winced in sympathy for the poor tree. Monica swung the ax easily and with deft precision. Exactly how much practice had she had, and on what... or whom?

"Here, you try." She handed over the ax.

Seth raised the weapon of moss destruction over his shoulder, baseball-bat fashion, hoping he'd still have all his toes at the end of the day. He brought the blade crashing down. The head bit into the tree trunk, wedging in deep. Shock waves traveled up his arms and into his shoulders. "Oh shit!" He released the handle and attempted to shake sensation back into his fingers and arms.

"Don't aim for the middle. That's what a chainsaw's for. Instead, hack the limbs off."

Seth pulled and pulled, but the ax wouldn't give up its hold on the tree. Monica snorted and lent her substantial strength to the effort. The ax jerked free, nearly sending them both tumbling to the ground.

Monica wrapped her arms around Seth, guiding the next chopping motion, and together they neatly liberated a limb from the tree. "Perfect!" Monica exclaimed. "Once you've chopped the limbs off, cut them into pieces about fifteen to eighteen inches long."

Seth couldn't figure out whether to exult at the praise or be pissed with himself for seeking this woman's approval. It was as though Monica somehow channeled his aunt's spirit, and by pleasing Monica, he might win his late aunt's "atta boy."

His self-styled tutor wrested the decision from his grasp. "I'll be back in a few hours to check your progress. Have fun!"

Leaving Seth no time to react, Monica hopped into her truck and scratched tires out of the field, pissing him off beyond reason. He took his frustrations out on the tree.

Monica returned two hours later, bearing a jug of sweet tea

and a smile. A pile of chopped wood sat beside a tree trunk now devoid of any limbs. "Now, let's go win over one of Junior's strongest supporters, who'd probably issue a challenge herself if she weren't too old. Help me load the truck." It seemed "help" actually meant, *"You load the truck while I supervise."*

"Where are we taking the wood?" Seth visualized a roaring fire in the fireplace at his aunt's house, and himself cuddled with Dustin on the settee. What? Where were his delusions of domesticity coming from?

"You'll see."

Seth gulped down the tea, enjoying the breeze coming in through the open truck windows. Twenty minutes later, they pulled up in front of a small frame house that, in Seth's by no means expert opinion, could benefit from some repairs.

Monica backed the truck up to a shed. "Unload now. I'll be right back."

Though his arms felt like jelly and even his blisters sported blisters, gloves notwithstanding, Seth did as told. Not without more than a few grumbles.

A few moments later, he glanced over to find a shriveled, wrinkled face scowling at him.

"Aah-ahhh!" He jumped back before he realized the one who'd scared him stood only about four feet tall.

Monica practically yelled, "Ms. Pickens? We've brought you a load of firewood for this winter. I'd like you to meet Seth *McDaniel*." If she'd stressed *McDaniel* any harder it might have snapped in half. "He's Irene's nephew."

"Nephew?" the woman shrieked, unnecessarily loud. "Can't be no nephew. Aaron McDaniel died long 'bout twenty year ago. Didn't think there were no more McDaniels."

From over the woman's shoulder, Monica grimaced, jerked her head, and then mouthed, "Say something!" She thrust her hand out and winked.

Seth slid his right hand out of the glove, wincing when the rough leather abraded his blistered fingers. "Afternoon, ma'am." He attempted to add a touch of the South to his distinct Yankee accent. "And how are you today?" Holy shit! Monica wanted him to use power on this tiny woman? What if he hurt her?

Badgering his possum into wakefulness, he dialed the force down to its lowest setting, taking a wrinkled hand in his newly roughened one. He gritted his teeth at the sudden jolt that jarred nearly as much as a swing from the ax landing on the tree trunk. Seth interpreted the gesture as the equivalent of the woman trying to out-squeeze his grip. He amped up his own energy level a notch or two. Still the woman frowned, hanging onto his hand.

"That all you got, boy?" A gimlet eye accompanied the matron's taunt.

Seth raised both an eyebrow and his metaphysical signal. A dreamy smile appeared on the old woman's face. He continued to pour on energy until the woman released his hand, collapsing against Monica with an undignified giggle.

Through a nearly toothless grin, the woman proclaimed, "You can come back and visit me anytime."

Monica waited until they reached the main road before clapping Seth on the shoulder. "Well done. With Widow Pickens goes the rest of the Pickens clan."

"Do you mind explaining what you just said in English, please?"

"Sixteen Junior supporters down, about fifty to go."

For the next few days, Seth worked on the house every morning, grateful to Junior and Michael for seeming to have forgotten him, and visited passel members every evening with Monica. He'd been practicing his cooking skills with the help of his aunt's cookbooks, and Monica always managed to show up in time for dinner. "No offense," he asked over shepherd's pie one evening, "but why doesn't Dustin go with me occasionally?"

Monica swallowed down a mouthful of peas, carrots, and mashed potatoes. "It wouldn't do to show favoritism right now. Rest assured he's doing his part."

Seth had been wondering if perhaps Dustin suffered second-thought syndrome. He missed the guy—not merely the sex, but the quiet moments, the "us against the world" camaraderie begun many years ago as kids, and apparently still alive and kicking.

"Once you're installed as head of the passel, he'll come back 'round again."

More and more, Seth worried about taking over the passel. Two months ago, he'd been hanging out in Chicago, giving doormats everywhere a bad name. Overnight, he'd become some kind of big bad *something*, with a destiny, purpose, and a kick-ass female sidekick, though Monica might argue the point of who played second fiddle to whom.

"Who are we visiting tonight?" Let it not be the Widow Pickens, who seemed to have developed an addiction to Seth's handshakes.

"The Martins. A young couple with a new baby." A worry crease appeared between her eyebrows. "For the life of me, I can't figure out how to impress them. They're comfortably financed, and don't seem to need anything."

Seth's ears perked up. The great Monica didn't have a plan? And he did? What started as a smug smile bloomed into the proverbial possum-eating-briars grin he'd heard about but had never fully understood until then. "Leave it to me."

Two hours later found Baby Martin giggling and cooing while Seth snapped pictures. The fake grin on Monica's face showed signs of strain. Taking pity, Seth wrapped up the impromptu photo shoot. "I'll upload these at home and e-mail them to you," he told the beaming parents. "If you'd like, I'll also send the web address of a guy who'll give you a discount on an eleven-by-twenty canvas. It's been nice meeting you, but we should go now. Monica has an early morning at the office."

Back in the truck, Monica declared, "Those were the last of Junior's direct supporters. Now, we need to solidify your claim with the rest of the passel. And we're running out of time."

"What do you mean 'running out of time'?"

"Only a few more days until the next full moon."

Idly caressing his camera case, Seth thought back to the happy parents, and the three posing possums he now recognized as the Johnson boys. It couldn't be that easy to impress people, could it?

"Monica? Is there a church social hall or something I can borrow for an afternoon? Set up a studio?"

CHAPTER 20

THEY came from far and wide—singles, couples, families. Against a background of the Jordan River painted on the wall of the church basement, Seth set up his equipment. He'd driven all the way to Athens to rent reflectors and other necessary items he hadn't brought with him.

Each subject posed and preened before stepping behind a curtain to change, returning a moment later in animal form to pose and preen some more.

"What a stroke of genius," Seth heard someone purr into his ear. He looked up into Dustin's welcome smile. "Everyone in town turned out today, didn't they?"

"I'm not sure, but I've been snapping pictures forever." Seth grinned like a lovesick schoolboy, unable to conceal the thrill of simply being in the same room with Dustin. "What are you doing here?"

"Why, I've come to take you to lunch, if you'd like."

Seth glanced around, grateful to see his last appointment shuffling out and no one left waiting.

"Monica told everyone you needed a break. Shall we?" Dustin extended his arm.

Seth checked his cameras before packing them away. "I suppose we shouldn't be seen together." Right now, though, staring at the object of his nightly fantasies, he couldn't quite recall why.

"We won't be." Seth cocked a questioning brow. Dustin answered with a grin. "C'mon, truck's waiting."

Dustin drove out past the farmhouse and turned down a dirt road. "This is the rear entrance to the field at the back of your property," Dustin explained, "where we've been parking for the full moon." He hopped out and removed a picnic basket from the bed of the truck. "Would you mind bringing the tea?" He nodded toward an insulated plastic jug.

Seth snatched up the jug and followed Dustin a ways down a dirt road and through a metal gate into the field. From his vantage point, he spotted the roof of the farmhouse. Summer insects chirped and whirred. Soon fall would set in. The trees would be beautiful once the leaves turned.

Gazing at the distant mountains, breathing in the fresh country air, Seth made up his mind. After the full moon, no matter how the night went, he'd make arrangements to have his few meager possessions packed up and moved down. He'd seen his last of Chicago, though while strolling through broom sage and buttercups in Dustin's wake, he didn't think he'd miss the city. He belonged here, and come hell or high water, here he'd stay. That was, if he survived any challenges. Only now, with Dustin's support and his heritage hanging in the balance, failure wasn't an option. Regardless of how cowed he'd been by his late grandmother, he needed to step out of her shadow and "grow a pair," as Monica might say.

He didn't ask where they were going, somehow guessing it'd be to the pond. Dustin stopped on the bank, near where they'd recently acquainted themselves with each other's bodies. A crane turned a baleful stare their way and took wing. Seth imagined the bullfrogs breathing a collective sigh of relief.

"The Johnson boys sometimes come here," Seth warned, in case Dustin planned any amorous adventures—adventures Seth wouldn't object to, providing they didn't have an audience.

"Monica took them to a movie in Clayton. Won't be back for hours."

"Really?"

"Really."

They placed their burdens down and came together in a flurry of tongues and hands and flying clothes. "What? Mr. Neat isn't folding everything and hanging it on a tree?" Seth couldn't help teasing.

"A time and a place for everything. And this time and this place is for something else." Dustin grinned, revealing his imperfect front teeth. "Last one in is a rotten egg!" He turned and ran to the deep end of the pond, launched himself from the bank, and landed with a splash.

Not to be outdone, Seth took off after him, sending jets of water up into Dustin's face with his spectacular cannonball.

They laughed and splashed like happy youngsters. Their eyes met and the kidding ended. One minute they stood in waist-deep water, the next Seth found himself lying in the shallows.

"How much did you miss me?" Seth asked, craning his neck to gaze down his body into Dustin's eyes.

Dustin's smirk evaporated a moment later as he lapped the crown of Seth's length with his tongue. "Damn, that's good!" Seth exclaimed, closing his eyes and resting his head on his arms. Up and down the moist heat of Dustin's mouth worked him, a startling contrast to the cool water caressing his hole with each of Dustin's movements. As long as it had been, he feared he wouldn't last five minutes.

He wanted more, but didn't have the strength to ask. Besides, he hovered too close to the brink. Dustin's magical mouth disappeared and wet skin caressed wet skin as Dustin climbed on top of Seth. Sealing their mouths, they thrust frantically against each other, and Dustin slipped one hand between them to slide their cocks together.

Uncalled, Seth's inner circuitry summoned power from deep within. The hairs on his arms and legs rose, Dustin's energy meeting and matching Seth's.

"Oh, God!" Seth moaned, pushing into Dustin's fist. He found the rounded mounds of Dustin's backside and pulled him closer, urging him on. Harder and faster, they shoved against each other, lost in the moment. Dustin stroked Seth's ear with tongue, teeth, and hot breath, moving down to his shoulder and the most sensitive parts of his neck. Hands scrabbling for purchase on Dustin's wet skin, Seth whined, cried, and begged wordlessly for what only Dustin could give. Every nerve ending felt on fire, their joined essences mating as surely as their bodies.

"That's it, baby, come for me," Dustin murmured, shattering Seth's control. Their lengths slid together more easily, both men crying out together.

They lay half in and half out of the water, catching their breath.

"I love you, Seth," Dustin finally said.

Seth scraped together enough blissed-out brain cells to reply, "I love you too, Dustin."

"No matter what happens at the next full moon, it won't change how I feel."

"I hope not."

"I know not."

Before Seth had time to dwell on what might happen in a few days, Dustin rose, offering a hand up. "C'mon. Let's eat. Afterwards, I want you to meet some people."

∾

Your grandpa is over there, here's your grandmother, and over there is your Aunt Irene." Dustin pointed out the flattened stones marking the graves of the elder McDaniels. He took Seth's hand, led the way around the pin oak, and knelt beside two more stones. "Here's where they buried your parents." Dustin had been too young to attend the passel burial, though he'd been to the bogus one in town, but many times he'd visited this place, remembering Seth and their friendship.

"Deep down, I always hoped you'd come back someday. My mother told me that even if you did, you'd be changed." He gave Seth's hand a squeeze. "You were, but it's not a bad thing."

"It's peaceful here," Seth said.

"Yeah. That's why they chose this spot, and why I come here."

"Junior wants to build a casino."

"Yeah." The thought turned Dustin's stomach.

"I don't like Junior much. Seems like he should be a wheeler-dealer on Wall Street, not out here in the country." Seth lifted Dustin's arm and slid beneath, staring deep into Dustin's eyes. "Help me stop him?"

More than mere passel loyalty prompted the reply: "I'll do whatever I can." Dustin kissed Seth, soaking up the tranquility before it came to an end. Sooner or later, they'd have to return to town, face their problems again. But for now, maybe one more round....

"No! Out of the question. Absolutely not." Seth shook his head. He couldn't believe Monica would actually suggest such a hare-brained scheme.

"It's a way to solve the issue of the challenge without a single drop of blood being spilled." Monica's unasked-for dinner guest said. Tall, sporting a tail of flaxen hair, the guy's otherworldliness raised Seth's hackles. The town veterinarian seemed nice enough, but Seth's inner possum spat and hissed, hell-bent and determined to intimidate the Reynard's fox alter ego.

"Stop it!" Monica snapped. "Andy's here to help us; he's not a threat."

"No, I'm not," Andy agreed. "I'm fighting for my people as hard as you're fighting for yours. I don't understand what you have against the plan. A coyote shifter friend of mine agreed to help. He shows up, growls a little, you run him off, you're a hero."

"I can't wait to watch Junior tuck tail and run." Monica's nefarious grin scared the living daylights out of Seth. He was glad her scheming wasn't directed at him.

This time. He'd keep his eyes open, though.

The Reynard's plan sounded viable; however, he didn't want to win by trickery and be forevermore goaded by a guilty conscience, doubting his ability to lead. No, he had to play fair and win honestly. "While I appreciate what you're trying to do, I can't allow it," he finally said, wiping the grins off his would-be coconspirators' faces. "I'll face Junior head-on, and may the best man, I mean, possum, win."

Later in the evening, reevaluating the wisdom of his decision, Seth realized that, in all his life, not only did this mark the first important decision he'd ever fully made on his own, but he'd actually stood up to two people he'd have been cowering from a few months ago. Even more surprising, he didn't doubt for a minute he'd made the right choice.

"You suggested what?" Dustin's mouth dropped open. How could Andy suggest such a thing?

"I told him about my coyote buddy, and how to win the passel leadership without a challenge." Worry wrinkles appeared on Andy's brow. "The man turned it down flat."

Dustin let out a shaky breath. "If he'd stoop to sneaky tricks, no matter what my personal feelings for him, or Irene, might be, I wouldn't back Seth to head the passel." He should be angry, take Andy to task, but he couldn't. The Reynard fought for his family and his people.

In his shoes, Dustin might do the same.

Seth didn't ask Monica where they were going, she wouldn't answer anyway if she didn't want to, though he hoped Southern pit barbeque waited at the end. He'd learned her by now; she might be gruff, but hid a good heart beneath her porcupine quills. However, when she pulled her truck into the parking lot of the Athens Fertility Clinic, his hackles rose.

She turned off the ignition, huffing out a breath. Fear and uncertainty pulsed from her.

"Is something wrong?" Why the hell had she brought him to a fertility clinic?

"No. We're here as a precaution."

"A precaution against what?" Seth swallowed hard, heart dropping to his stomach.

"You are, without a doubt, the last member of Irene's family. If anything happens to you, your family ends." She glanced up, her sky-blue gaze holding the promise of rain. "I loved Irene. She took me in when my family kicked me out, gave me a home, and convinced me I wasn't a mutant. I want some part of her to go on. We have an appointment in there," she said, nodding toward the building, "in fifteen minutes."

"What is this place?"

"The best fertility clinic in the South." She held up a hand to ward off objections. "Tomorrow night is the full moon. You can say no and we'll leave now, forget I mentioned it, but I'd like you to go in with me, let them harvest your sperm." Until then, he'd no idea Monica possessed the ability to be shy. She stared down at the floorboard. "If anything happens to you, or if someone challenges your leadership on the grounds that you can't produce an heir, I'd like permission to carry your child, keep the McDaniel name alive."

What. The. Fuck. What the hell could Seth say? She'd sprung this on him so suddenly. She wanted to carry his child? Keep the McDaniel family going? Should he be flattered or horrified? After a few moments he organized his scattered thoughts enough to form words. "Why? You don't even like me."

Monica shrugged. "You're not too bad, for a city boy. You just needed me to kick your ass into shape. I'd be lying if I said I was doing this totally for you, 'cause I'll be giving up the ability to turn for nine months, as well as any position in the passel I might hold at the time. I'm doing this for Irene, for myself, and for Dustin, in the event you manage to build something permanent with him." She managed a brief flicker of a smile.

Seth cringed. Kids. He imagined some of the more nightmarish examples of childhood he'd photographed. The images morphed into the sweet face of his own future child, freckles running across a too big nose. Once more, he recalled his fantasy: big house, porch swing, a partner and kids. Did he dare hope to make the dream come true?

Wait a minute! "While I wouldn't mind a son or a daughter, I don't think I'm ready for triplets. That's not a passel trait, is it?"

"Sometimes."

Seth swore his heart stopped, only starting again when Monica added, "But not in your family or McDaniels wouldn't be so scarce. Multiple births happen mostly when the virus goes back for generations in both lines, like the Johnsons. To avoid power struggles within the passel, McDaniels usually found their mates elsewhere, and some married nonshifters who later turned. My mom wasn't passel either, so chances are we'd have a single birth if we left things up to nature. However, with a fertility clinic, we stand the same chance as any other couple who comes here."

Oh. What would his parents think? His aunt? His friends back in Chicago? *What friends? Have any called you since you've been here, besides Michael?* his conscience asked. *Good point*, he silently replied. "Did you mention this to Dustin?"

"Do I need to?"

"Maybe later, not right now." He considered a few more minutes. He'd rather be safe than sorry, and answered her question by getting out of the truck and marching toward the clinic's entrance. Let Monica's fears not come true.

Only after they arrived back at the farmhouse did she say, "Thanks, Seth. No matter what happens, if I ever need to take a trip back to the clinic, I promise you I'll be a good mother."

A tight knot formed in his throat, but he managed to squeeze out, "Thanks, Monica. If it's a boy, will you name him Aaron, after my dad?"

She nodded, the tips of her braids slithering over the top of her thighs. "And Irene for a girl?"

He considered for a moment, thinking of the pictures he'd found of his mother as a child, with her golden ringlets bound by ribbons. "How about 'Brenda Irene'?"

"Works for me."

Monica continued coaching him for the "big night," but she didn't mention kids again.

～

Dustin lay awake, an all too common occurrence lately, hoping to hear pebbles against the window. Around 2:00 a.m., he gave up and fell into a fitful doze.

The world might completely change tomorrow night.

And he could lose Seth.

He should have just accepted the damned leadership.

CHAPTER 21

SETH showered and shaved. Why go to such effort when most of his evening would be spent on all fours, terrorizing crickets and earthworms? His stomach heaved. The grandfather clock *bonged* five times. Only five o'clock?

He donned a pair of blue jeans, *sans* boxers, per Monica's instructions, and paced the sitting room before plopping down on the settee, only to hop back up and begin pacing again. Where the hell was she?

Desperate for a distraction, he logged on to his media site profile to post an update. What would he say? "Turning into a possum tonight. If you don't hear from me again, check under the oak tree by the pond"?

He wound up doing research instead. After typing "possums" into a search engine, he read up on possum kind, hoping to gain some kind of advantage. Instead, all he found were more possibilities for marsupial munching.

One hour before sundown, his coach arrived.

"Should we eat first?" Seth asked, though he doubted he'd be able to force anything past the lump in his throat, or if he did, it wouldn't stay down with all the churning in his belly.

"No need. There's more protein in crickets than in ground beef. Plus, we always spread baked goods out on the field, have ourselves a feast."

Seth felt his face go green.

"What? Don't tell me you're gonna wuss out on me again and be squeamish."

"No, I'm okay. Just a nervous stomach." A *very* nervous stomach, as in, every cricket he'd eaten a month ago suddenly reanimated in his belly and proceeded to kick him with six legs each.

"That's to be expected."

Seth had a hard time reconciling this kinder, gentler Monica with the bloodthirsty harpy he'd imagined her to be the first day he'd met her. Then again, if she spoke too loudly or made any sudden moves tonight, he might start running and not stop until he reached Chicago. He peeked out the window at the sun, now a mere sliver showing over the treetops. His heart beat double-time. It wouldn't be long now. "Is it time to go?" Any chance of him waking up from the really weird dream he seemed to be having?

Leaning against the doorframe, the picture of icy coolness, Monica replied, "Yes. Are you ready?"

"No."

"Wrong answer. If you don't believe in yourself, the passel won't either."

Forcing his shoulders back, Seth exhaled slowly, letting the tension seep out with the breath. He squared his shoulders, forcing his head as high as his five-foot-nine-inch height allowed.

"Bring up the aura a bit, let everyone waiting out there tonight see what you're made of."

Seth poked the possum and snickered, thinking how much that sounded like "choking the chicken." His inner critter grinned. *Crickets tonight!* it chirped.

"Dustin will address the passel, announce you as his choice for Irene's successor, and ask if anyone contests his decision." Monica rubbed his shoulders like he'd seen managers do to boxers before a prizefight.

"What'll I say?"

"Nothing, unless someone asks you a direct question. Campaign season's over—tonight's the election. Now, if you're ready, let's go." Instead of her usual jeans, scrubs, or overalls, tonight Monica wore a strapless sundress, held in place only by elastic at the top. Her hair hung in waves down her back. She looked... pretty. But he didn't dare tell her that. "Some of the weaker shifters will be feeling the moon by now."

Together they marched out the front door and past the barn. Frogs called from the direction of the pond; an owl hooted from the woods. "We need to watch out for him," Monica warned.

Seth nodded, his own personal possum spirit giving a brief shudder—Seth distracted the anxious critter by tuning in to cricket song, promising an upcoming feast.

This close to sundown, the humid heat of September in Georgia eased, forecasting a bit of chill later on. Despite a cooling breeze, sweat beaded on Seth's forehead. He'd tuned into Dustin's unique essence before stepping foot off the porch, and picked up Junior halfway across the yard, followed by Widow Pickens and a few elders while opening the gate. Monica's energy hummed around him like a swarm of angry bees. He imagined the two of them stepping into a wrestling ring, posturing to intimidate their opponents.

At last they came to the edge of the field. Seth stopped, closing his eyes and recalling the times as a kid when he'd stayed with a babysitter. He imagined his parents and great-aunt standing in this same field. How he'd love them to be here for him now.

The air seemed to vibrate with nervous anticipation,

emanating from a circle of possum shifters. Dustin stepped into the circle. "Tonight marks the third full moon since our beloved leader passed beyond. As is my duty as her appointed, I'm prepared to name her successor."

It seemed as though even the crickets and frogs fell silent, waiting for Dustin's verdict. "Jacks, jills, and joeys of the passel, I give you Seth Aaron McDaniel, our former Jill's only remaining kin, and heir."

Seth took a deep breath, his heart pounding out a punishing rhythm.

"Are there any here who disagree with my decision?"

Junior stepped forward. "I do."

"On what grounds?"

Seth longed to smack the smirk off Junior's arrogant face.

"The line dies with him. He won't father an heir and has no brothers or sisters to provide one." Yeah, and Junior had an imbecile nephew—big deal!

Monica stepped into the circle. "Not true. He will be a father." She patted her belly—her flat belly. Granted, she didn't actually lie, she merely made creative use of the truth, for they had planned for future McDaniels, hadn't they?

Uncertainty passed over Junior's face, gone in an instant. "You're carrying his child?"

Seth got the feeling Monica wanted to stick out her tongue at the asshole. "Not yet, but I will. More than one way to skin a possum, Junior."

Junior scowled, taking a step closer to Monica. Dustin neatly inserted himself between them. "Seems your argument is invalid. Do you have any other objections?"

"This man is a stranger here, to our ways. How can he make decisions affecting the passel if he doesn't even know us?"

A good point.

"He's a McDaniel, he can learn," Dustin replied with icy coolness. "Who would you name in his place?"

Junior responded with, "Myself."

Dustin directed his attention to those forming the circle. "Do any of you have any reason why Junior's challenge shouldn't be accepted?"

Seth held his breath. The good deeds of the past few weeks hadn't gained him a champion, apparently, though none spoke up on Junior's behalf either.

"The challenge stands. May the best man win." Dustin stripped off his jeans, and the rest of the passel followed suit, Seth going last. The dark shapes hovering at the edge of the field suddenly disappeared, though their energy remained, hidden in the knee-high grass. Only Seth, Monica, Dustin, and Junior maintained human form.

Seth watched Junior's transformation, then Monica's, then Dustin's. Satisfied all was as it should be, he turned his consciousness inward. One moment he stood on two feet, the next on four. Between clumps of grass, possums crept closer to witness his upcoming battle with Junior.

Out of the corner of his eye, he registered a dark blur streaking across the field. Damn it all to hell! He'd told Monica not to send the coyote shifter. He'd deal with her later! He turned, ready to send the mutt packing. The passel noticed the intruder, some hissing and running, some flopping on the ground to play dead. Junior scurried into a groundhog burrow. The coyote made a beeline for Seth, who stood his ground. A toothy mouth opened and snapped shut.

A scant second before impact, Seth realized no human awareness existed within the canine's skull. This was a real fucking coyote! He closed his eyes, expecting to be snapped in two. An agonized squeal split the night, and he opened his eyes to the horrifying vision of Dustin clutched in slavering jaws. With no time to consider the danger, Seth acted.

He latched all fifty-two of his teeth onto the dog's ear. The monster dropped Dustin, then whipped around to snap and growl at Seth. Searing pain shot through Seth's naked tail. The beast shook its head, weakening Seth's grip. If Seth let go, the bastard would surely kill him.

Suddenly the attacker yelped, his thrashing dislodging Seth and sending him flying. Seth started to run for the trees. A pained moan stopped him in his tracks. A few feet away, Dustin lay on the ground, bleeding from a wound in his middle. A furious Monica crouched over his body, ready to fight to the death, by the looks of it. Seth's blood boiled. How dare the son of a bitch coyote hurt one of the passel! Worse yet, hurt his lover!

He whipped around, ready to single-handedly tear the beast limb from limb, to find he no longer fought alone. Three juvenile possums joined the fray, two hanging from the creature's ears like bizarre matched ornaments, the third clinging to the beast's tail. All the flailing, whining, and barking in the world wouldn't dislodge the Larry, Curly, and Moe of the possum shifter world.

Seth went for the jugular. The coyote yelped, instincts turning from fight to flight. Seth chittered for the boys to let go, and he felt the relief in the beast's mind, as well as the triplets' reluctant compliance. He reached out mentally, hoping to find the Johnsons far away, along with Dustin and Monica.

A solid wall of possum power stood at his back. None too gently, he released his hold on the coyote's throat, dropping to the ground and regaining a fighting stance, lest the brute hadn't yet learned its lesson. As one, the passel surged; the coyote tucked tail and ran.

Tired, sore, and anxious, Seth staggered toward where he'd last seen Dustin, trying his best not to show the passel his weakness, and worried how he'd ever defeat Junior in a fair fight tonight. He hunkered down next to Dustin's too-still body. Even in animal form, his heart somersaulted when he took in the puncture wounds on his lover's side, heard the painful-sounding rasps. Monica's gaze, when it met Seth's, held no promise.

I've got him, take care of them, she communicated, tossing her snout toward the passel.

Too weary to think straight, Seth limped back to the people, determined to be the leader they needed now. Rather than cowering like frightened animals, one by one they approached, starting with the Widow Pickens. She performed a possum bow at Seth's feet, offering her cheek. *Lick it*, she murmured, possibly sensing Seth's bewilderment. Seth obliged, giving her reddish muzzle a quick flick of his tongue. She ambled away, allowing the next elder to make a public statement of support. One after the other of the senior members of the passel acknowledged Seth's claim to leadership. After the third one, he discreetly wiped a paw across his tongue, spitting out loose hair. Did possums hack up fur balls?

The Johnson boys toddled up, their toothy grins a bit alarming. Their parents attempted to herd them back, allowing more senior members to pay homage first. Seth stopped them. *Let them come*, he said. *They deserve this place in line.* He didn't understand how he was talking, only that, with a series of odd vocalizations, his desires seemed to be heard. More reverently than he believed possible, the boys paid their respects, one winking and giving Seth's paw a playful nip in passing. Seth didn't scold him. The boy had earned the right.

Junior was noticeably absent. Seth decided a public reprimand would be in order next full moon. Furry bodies wandered off into the field to do what possums did until dawn. Seth joined Monica in cleaning Dustin's wounds.

The first light of dawn brought a fox to the meadow, and Seth braced for another attack. The fox crept closer, head down. Throughout the field, possum bodies morphed into human. Seth waited, worried what the shift might do to Dustin, but Dustin remained in possum form. The fox shifted and grew into Andy.

"He's not going to change. He's too weak," now-human Monica said. Seth nodded, reaching within to his inner man. One moment he was in a four-footed body, dew clinging to his fur, the next he stood on two feet, gazing down at his injured lover.

"I'll take him," Andy said, bending to scoop up the battered creature. "I guess you've figured out by now why the vet and doctor's offices are joined."

Seth's heart broke anew. Surely Dustin wouldn't survive such heinous injuries. Seth stroked a tiny ear, earning a barely audible sigh.

"I'll do my best for him." Andy cradled Dustin to his chest as he turned to leave.

"I'll go with you." Seth's place was with Dustin.

Monica placed a restraining hand on his arm. "No. The passel needs you right now."

She bent and murmured into his ear, "He'll be okay. Andy and I will take good care of him. Reassure the people, solidify your position, and go get some sleep."

He nodded, fighting the moisture in his eyes threatening to spill over his lashes. Dustin was hurt. Maybe critically. If only Seth had acted quicker, realized the coyote was real sooner. Shoulda, coulda, woulda rolled around his brain. "Keep me posted."

With a heavy heart, he returned his attention to the passel, *his* passel.

"Jacks, jills, and joeys," he began, "we've suffered an unnecessary tragedy tonight. Rest assured measures will be taken to prevent such a situation from happening again."

Already the wheels turned in his head: perimeter fencing, more guards, motion sensors....

As one the people bowed, then fell into step to escort him to the farmhouse. He imagined the scene played out with his aunt at the head of group, his grandfather, his great-grandfather, humbled at his new sense of purpose.

He was a McDaniel. Carrying on the family legacy.

Once the passel members left him, he placed a call to the vet, only to hear the ominous "No news yet, and if you dare come down here without getting some rest first, I'll shoot you full of tranquilizers. You'll be no good to anybody dead on your feet." He showered and fell into bed, his dreams marred by slavering jowls and snapping teeth.

Seth rose a few hours later. He pulled into the vet's parking lot promptly at noon, a bit banged up and sporting a few bruises, but nowhere near as bad off as Dustin. Andy let him in, rubbing bleary eyes. "I've got him sedated. I won't lie, it's really bad."

"It is?" Oh God, no. He shouldn't have listened to Monica, should have come here sooner. "Where... where is he? Can I see him?"

Andy expelled a sigh. "We have to airlift him to a hospital in Tennessee."

"Tennessee! Is he...? How do they...."

"Relax. He's too weak to turn. A university hospital up there specializes in injuries of this kind. It's easier to treat him this way, and whereas he'll get bigger if he shifts, his stitches won't grow, and though we heal faster than most humans, he'll heal even faster in possum form. It's better this way." The vet placed a comforting hand on Seth's shoulder. "Come on back for a few minutes, but please don't be shocked if he doesn't appear to recognize you, okay? It's not personal. Sometimes when we're hurt, we lose our grip on our human side, let the animal take over."

Bracing for the worst, Seth followed Andy down the hallway, taking in the doorway adjoining the two practices. "Makes sense now, doesn't it?" Andy commented. "The human doctor on one side and the animal doctor on the other?"

Although yipping and meowing emerged from deep inside the bowels of the building, Seth detected no human consciousness behind the door marked "Kennel."

A barest hint of humanity brushed his senses when Andy stopped and unlocked a door marked, "Storage." Instead of containing shelves or cages, the space resembled a hospital room. A bowl-shaped pillow sat in the center of the bed, a brown and tan body lying in the depression. An IV stand stood next to the bed, one end of the plastic tubing running into Dustin's leg.

The room smelled of blood and antiseptic. A swath of bandages, stained crimson, hid most of Dustin's middle. One paw was wrapped, as well. Seth damped down his fear—it wouldn't help his lover.

He felt awkward talking to a possum, but only for a moment. This was Dustin, whom he'd known for years. "Hey, you," he said, crouching down to be nose to nose with the injured animal. "How ya doing?" As gently as possible, he reached out to stroke a bare ear. Dustin forced out a contented sigh, canting his head to give Seth better access.

Andy chuckled. "He's not a total goner if he can still get off on an ear scratch. I'll leave you two alone for a minute and go check on the chopper."

Dustin whimpered, but not in pain.

"Yes, Junior showed his true colors. The whole passel is calling him a coward. They denied his claims." Seth scrunched his lips in a rueful smile. "I may be totally out of my element, but for good or bad, they've named me the Jack."

A sharp yip escaped Dustin.

"Whoops, sorry, didn't mean to scratch too hard." Seth

switched to Dustin's other ear, listening closely to chirps and squeaks that translated to *"Are you really going to have an heir, or did Monica say that to shut Junior up?"*

"That much is true, well, sorta true," Seth replied. "Monica took me to a fertility clinic to make a deposit, wants to be my surrogate when the time comes—for Irene's sake."

If and when the time came, would Dustin be there? He didn't want leadership. Would he want fatherhood?

Now wasn't the time to consider such things.

Seth stroked a finger along Dustin's neck, carefully avoiding his injuries. What soft fur. Until recently, Seth had never really thought about possums, hadn't even seen one since leaving Georgia, but Dustin? Dustin made one damned fine specimen, in either form. "There's one condition."

Dustin cheeped.

"Seems Monica had ulterior motives announcing she'd be the mother of my child. Suggesting that she'll soon be pregnant excuses her from passel duties. Why she doesn't want anything to do with leadership beats the hell out of me. She's so damned good at it."

Possum Dustin gave a weak nod, cheeping out, *"She lacks social skills and knows it. But she makes excellent backup."*

That she did. And a hell of a teacher too. Maybe he should assign her to work with Tiffany and other new shifters. "That she does. But her declining second duties means you've got no choice but to get better soon, 'cause the people get kinda antsy if you mess with their leadership structure. And until you get better, Widow Pickens insists on filling the role." He shuddered, recalling the old lady's leering grin and her cackled "Hit me, big boy!" while reaching for his hand.

The sound Dustin made might have been the possum equivalent of a snicker.

"Will you be okay?"

Dustin extended his tongue, giving Seth's hand a quick lick.

"You scared the hell out of me."

The concern in twin button eyes seemed to say, *Me and you both, pal!*

Seth inclined his head, placing a kiss on Dustin's snout. "You get better and come back to me. We got us some celebrating to do."

It might have been a trick of the light, but it seemed to Seth that Dustin nodded.

Andy appeared in the doorway, two strangers in flight gear behind him, their uniforms emblazoned with "Channel Four Action News." One reeked to high heavens of skunk, the other of chipmunk. "Y'all set? We need to get moving."

"Huh?" Seth's gaze traveled from the new arrivals to Andy and back again.

"It's our cover. These boys have an excuse to be up in the air—no explanations needed."

"Oh." Seth kissed Dustin's nose again. "I'll be waiting."

He watched the men prepare Dustin for the journey, then stood in the parking lot and stared at the heavens long after the helicopter lifted.

An arm fell over his shoulders. "You can't help worrying, but these next few weeks are critical. Prove to the passel you're the right choice. Dustin would tell you the same thing if he were here. I'll keep you informed, and he'll be back soon, I promise."

Seth reached up and patted Andy's arm. "I hope you're right, man, I hope you're right."

"I'd love for you to come up, but the hospital doesn't allow visitors." The sound of Dustin's voice was sweet music to Seth's ears. "This is supposed to be a veterinary clinic. Their secret wouldn't last long with humans traipsing in and out, visiting."

Seth sighed. "You're right, but I'm dying to see you."

"Yeah, I'd like to see you too, but a man driving up from Georgia to visit a wild animal involved in a hay-baler accident would look too suspicious. We've got to keep our secrets."

"But I'm just one man. No one would notice."

"Maybe not, but if they let you visit, then the hospital would have to change their rules, and families would start flocking in by the dozens. And some shifters have very large families."

Yeah. That was Dustin, the voice of reason; a trait Seth believed made him an ideal second-in-command.

But didn't help at all with Seth's desire to see Dustin, hold him.

"Anyway, I'll be home in a few days, I'm told. In the mean-time...." Dustin lowered his voice to a seductive murmur. "What 'cha wearing?"

Seth crept down the hallway to his bedroom, even though Monica wasn't due for lessons for a few hours, too busy helping the temporary doctor fill Dustin's shoes in town. He lay back on the bed, popped the top button on his shorts, and eased the zipper down. "Just a pair of cut-off blue jeans."

A groan emerged from the phone. "Good. If I were there, I'd run my hands all over your body. You do it for me."

Seth activated the speaker function and placed his cell-phone beside him on the bed. He slid his fingers over his stom-ach, less pudgy now than it had been before he began doing physical labor on the farm. He reached a nipple, giving a quick flick. The nub stiffened.

Oh, damn. He needed Dustin's hands, not his own. "How about you? Are you naked?"

"Oh yeah," came the breathy reply. "And I've got about a half hour before they bring lunch."

Seth hadn't thought of the possibility of someone walking in on Dustin. It worried him and excited him at the same time.

"I want to be in you," Seth said, voice gone husky. "Wet your finger and play with your hole."

A sharp gasp reached Seth's ears. He ran a lazy hand up and down his erect shaft. "Good. Now, stroke yourself with your other hand. Imagine it's my hand, that I'm stroking you as I push in."

Dustin and Seth both groaned. "Damn, you're tight," Seth improvised, locking down a clenching grip on himself. He pushed into his fist, imagining Dustin's pucker flaring to let him in.

He increased his speed, pressure already starting to build. Behind his closed eyelids, he watched his cock disappear inside Dustin, and then reappear again when he drew back.

"Damn, Seth. I want you here."

"And I want to be there. Cup your balls and stroke yourself. I want to hear you come." Seth words came out a bit breathy.

He'd save any embarrassment for later. Never had he even dreamed of phone sex like this before. So out of character. Or maybe, out of character for who he used to be, before Dustin came back into his life.

He panted, pumping into his fist and imagining Dustin doing the same, miles away.

"I want to fuck you, Dustin. I want to pound your ass. I want to feel you come, your muscles gripping me, milking me." Seth shut up, too far gone to form words.

"Harder," Dustin pleaded over the phone. "Fuck me harder. Make me feel it."

Conversation changed to grunts and profanity, the sounds of Dustin getting closer.

So good, so damn good, just to hear him, know he'd be okay, they'd be together again… Oh, God! Oh, God! Seth cried out, "Dustin!" Cum spattered his bare chest. He lay on the bed, heart hammering in his ears.

A moment later, Dustin shouted "Oh damn!" loudly, even with the speaker away from Seth's ear.

Seth continued to convulse even after he'd quit spurting. Damn. Just... damn. He grinned the grin of the sated. "I can't wait until we do that for real."

"Heh. You've given me added incentive to heal quicker."

Heal. Yes, Dustin needed to heal from injuries that could have taken his life, and come home. To Seth. "I love you, Dustin."

"Love you too. Don't worry, I'll be back soon."

Seth drove his aunt's bush hog the final lap around field, ensuring no tall grass remained for predators to hide in. A new electrified fence marked the edges of the passel's gathering place, strung between cedar posts with a little help from the Johnson boys. Seth had also lined up interviews for more full-moon guards, and a game warden to advise him on preventing owl attacks. Now all he needed was a steady job to bring in income, for he felt funny spending family money. He might need the McDaniel legacy for the passel.

All in all, he didn't think he'd done too badly for his first two weeks on the job as the Jack. He parked the tractor in the barn and went inside his house—*his* house—to fix dinner.

"I've got it!" he told Monica a few hours later over a dinner of pot roast, stewed potatoes, and green beans—with a fair imitation of Aunt Irene's buttermilk biscuits, if he did say so himself. "What if I turn the place into a bed-and-breakfast and invite city shifters to come out and enjoy the full moon in the great outdoors? We can advertise at the conventions. Not only will the farm generate an income, we can engender a little goodwill with other changelings." He also had his eye on a vacant storefront in a perfect location for a studio. It seemed his alternative family photos were a hit, and he'd already secured space at the Anaheim convention. He'd had no idea the money to be made from unconventional family photos. Not to mention the nice check he'd received from a conservation magazine for pictures of the shifted Johnson boys. That reminded him. He needed to talk with Andy. An outdoorsman's e-zine offered good money for candid fox photos.

"Oh, speaking of other shifters—" Monica turned her lips up in her most evil grin. "I heard today Mr. Big Shot Junior Timmerman is moving to New York." She pronounced the town "New Yawk."

"Really? Why?" Not that Seth wasn't eternally grateful.

"Seems Widow Pickens called him out for running away and leaving the passel defenseless, and his new boyfriend gave him an ultimatum: move to the city, or else."

Seth nearly choked on his green beans. "Michael? And Junior?" Damn. He'd hope they'd distract each other, but he'd never dreamed they'd turn out to be more than a brief fling. Didn't Junior look down on Michael for not being a possum shifter? If so, Seth might have to confront the man. Then again, if Junior planned to move to New York for Michael, they must have started something serious.

"Yep."

Seth hadn't seen that one coming. "Ha! That's a match made someplace unpleasant." He hoped for Michael's sake that Junior learned some manners. Then again, why did he even care? Unless he'd developed some kind of residual, "one of mine to take care of" thing for his ex, like he had for the passel members. Once he'd duty-bound himself to worry about a town full of people, what was one more? Well, with the exception of Junior, who could damned well take care of himself.

Seth and Monica shared a grin and some homemade apple pie.

After they'd washed and put away the dishes, they headed

out to the front yard for Monica to share more possum wisdom. Seth scrunched up his face, trying to squeeze his muscles into possum shape.

"Not like that, you moron! What're you trying to do, bust a spleen?" The only woman in Seth's life stood, hands on hips, a glower pasted on her face. "Reach down inside, like you do for power, only instead of concentrating on your hand, send it evenly over your body. And don't scowl! You look constipated."

Seth focused on sending out the energy more uniformly. His inner critter laughed—he swatted it with a metaphysical hand.

One of the Johnson boys (Eddy?) came trotting across the yard, wearing bright orange board shorts and a dingy white T-shirt. "Nah, that's wrong. Imagine you're playing Skyrim." He held out his hands, miming working a game controller. "You know how your whole body tenses up? That's the way to do it."

A second Johnson appeared, dressed too similar to the first for clothing to be much help with identification. Was this one Freddy or Teddy? Seth considered labeling them for future reference. "Don't listen to him, he's an idiot! Imagine you're listening to heavy metal and the music kinda vibrates through you."

"They're both wrong. What you gotta do is meditate, blank your mind." That advice came from the third brother, now emerging from the trees separating Johnson land from McDaniel.

"I'll show you how to meditate!" the second shouted, grabbing his sibling around the waist and slinging him to ground in a squirming mass of knobby elbows and knees.

"Fight, fight," taunted the first, taking a flying leap to join the heap of twisting bodies and hurled insults.

Monica rolled her eyes heavenward. "As I was saying...."

Seth raised a finger. "A moment, please." Although he had no idea what Skyrim was, he closed his eyes, raised his air guitar, and belted out a rousing rendition of "Back in Black." He hit the ground a moment later, with a tiny mouth full of pointy teeth trying to sing "Ba-a-ah-ack!"

"Hey! You did it!" Monica exclaimed. She turned her attention to wrestling the boys apart.

"I am the possum!" Seth crowed, struggling to extricate himself from his jeans. "I changed at will!" He rewarded himself by wading into a patch of azalea bushes in search of prey, and was crunching his third cricket when his ears perked up to the sound of tires on the driveway. He froze momentarily, then waddled out from under the shrubs, rolling his view up, way up, to Dustin's truck.

"Dustin!" he squeaked, waddling as fast as his nonaerodynamic body allowed.

Andy opened the driver's door and stepped out. Seth stopped in his tracks, smile falling, until....

"Seth?" Dustin rounded the hood from the passenger side.

"Okay, boys, time to go home," Seth heard Monica say from a million miles away. Seth sat back on his haunches, imagining AC/DC in concert and him with front-row seats. The next minute, he was wiping assorted cricket parts from his lips as he closed the distance between himself and the man he'd worried he'd never see again.

Dustin met Seth halfway, attacking Seth's mouth with his own. "Mmmmm...," he exclaimed as he came for air. "Cricket!"

CHAPTER 22

Eighteen Months Later

"DON'T make me come over there!" Seth aimed his best "the Jack" scowl at the trio of teens vamping it up on the football field—with blatant disregard for the rest of the team.

"He started it!" Eddy yelled, reaching around Teddy to smack the back of Freddy's head with a football helmet.

"Did not!" Freddy shot back.

"Did too!" chorused Eddy and Teddy.

"I don't care who started it—I'm ending it!" Seth backed away from his tripod, hands on his hips. To the other students in the group Fighting Possums photo, he probably appeared to glower. However, goose bumps rose on the arms of the Johnson boys and a few other players, a strong enough warning to back down.

"Oh! I'm just in time, I see," the nearly deaf Widow Pickens shouted, beaming up at Seth from her vantage point more than a foot and a half below him. She placed a hand on his arm, a beatific smile adding more wrinkles to her dried apple of a face.

Seth huffed. The last thing he needed was his own personal ninety-year-old fangirl. "Now, now, Ms. Pickens," he said in his most placating tone, wresting her hand from his arm, "not in front of the kiddies. What brings you here, anyway?"

"How many times must I tell you to call me Estelle?" She batted her lashes. "My granddaughter is one of the seniors you're taking pictures of today. She spilled spaghetti sauce on her blouse at lunch and asked me to bring her another." Estelle held up a folded garment for Seth's inspection. "But please, continue, I wouldn't want to hold you up." She nodded toward the football team, gathered for their yearbook photo.

"Thank you." Seth bent to peer into his camera. A hand swatted his ass.

"Oops, must've slipped." The old lady cackled her way across the field.

The Johnson boys, amply chastened by their leader's power play, resumed their positions within the lineup, allowing Seth to finish the photo shoot.

The coach approached after Seth snapped the last shot. "Okay, seniors. Now go get prettied up for your pictures."

Seth packed up his equipment, lugging several heavy cases to the Thurman County High auditorium to render yearbook likenesses. Easy money, and not a bad job—until....

"I can't believe my grandmother brought this old thing!"

Thoughts of the family waiting for him at home allowed Seth to survive the next few hours. The Johnson boys loaded his SUV and he set off, pleased with the fruits of his labor.

He stopped by his studio next to the public library/post office and dropped off his equipment. Before powering down his computer for the day, he took a tiny little peek at his profile on "All About Me." Oh my! More than one hundred comments on his latest uploaded pic. Unsurprising—everyone loved baby pictures, it seemed. But… he nearly choked when he noticed a familiar icon and a message stating:

Awww… how cute! He looks just like you. Congratulations.

Michael? Paying a compliment? In the year and half since Seth had introduced the man to Junior, he hadn't heard much from Michael except for the odd comment online. He clicked on Michael's profile to read: "Engaged" listed under "Status." Under his "Latest news" heading, he'd posted: *Guess what, peoples? We're getting married! In New York.* A picture of a smiling Junior accompanied the announcement. Getting married? Good for them. Nothing poked at Seth's heart while reading the engagement announcement; in fact, it inspired relief—providing the couple remained in New York.

Widow Pickens putting Junior in his place for cowardice in front of the entire town might have contributed to the man's sudden desire to relocate. How did Junior like scuttling around Central Park every month, dodging joggers and little frou-frou, bootie-wearing dogs?

He drove home with one hand on the steering wheel, the other flying up to greet oncoming drivers (he still shivered at approaching cars), a woman walking her dog (Seth barely even cringed now when faced with canines), and a man getting mail out of his mailbox. In a short amount of time, he'd gone from stranger to one of Possum Kingdom's leading citizens, which still made his head spin.

Two vehicles occupied the back yard when he arrived home —Dustin's Ranger and the old Silverado Monica refused to replace. Seth parked in his usual spot in the barn and checked the progress on the new garage on his way to the front porch. "I'm home!" he called, stepping inside.

Dustin greeted him with a glass of tea and a kiss by the door. "We've got guests checking in tomorrow. A family of skunk shifters down from Cleveland. I've put them in the new attic suite. And a pair of honeymooning bunnies are set to arrive next week."

Bunnies? "Better put 'em in the back bedroom. Keep us from hearing 'em."

Dustin laughed. "We can always give them a run for their money." He swatted Seth's ass.

"Hey, you two. Cut that out! There's an impressionable child here!" Monica rose from the settee and strolled out to join the men in the hall, handing Dustin an empty bottle. "Here, go wash this." She placed six-month-old Aaron on her shoulder, lightly swatting his back until he belched. "Oh! There's Mommy's little truck driver."

Dustin brushed a quick kiss against Seth's neck. "Sure you won't stay for dinner, Monica? We have plenty."

Monica held out the baby, and Seth grinned, taking the little boy with his mother's light-colored hair and father's nose. "Thanks, but I really need to get home."

"Well, I'll see you at work tomorrow, then." Dustin rose up on his toes to kiss Monica's cheek. "If you'll excuse me, I need to get supper on the table." Dustin ruffled the baby's golden curls on his way out of the room.

"I've finally found a suitable babysitter for full moon nights, didn't I, widdle Aaron-rarin'," Monica singsonged, the sudden display of maternal affection taking Seth aback. Even after nine months of pregnancy and six months of co-parenthood, it still amazed Seth what a great mother Monica turned out to be. If he hadn't seen the evidence with his own eyes, he never would have believed she possessed a maternal side.

Clutching the sleepy child to his chest, he walked Monica out to her truck. A cricket perched on the hood. Aaron snatched at it, gurgling. Seth laughed, snagging the bug and stuffing it out of the baby's reach into a pocket. "No, son. You can't have the hoppy critter. You can have one when you're bigger."

He hugged Monica. "Thanks for him," he said, trying and failing to keep the soppy grin from his face. "From me and Dustin both."

Monica replied with a bittersweet smile. "Irene would be happy, about the baby, about you and Dustin, and about you heading the passel." She nuzzled noses with her son. "Isn't it amazing, Aaron? Your daddy's all grown up now. Who'da thunk it possible?"

She climbed into her truck. "Take care of Aaron and Dustin."

Seth stood in the yard and watched her leave, Aaron drowsing in his arms. When the sound of the truck faded into nothingness, Seth murmured, "C'mon, little guy; let's get you to bed."

He entered the house. Dustin's off-key singing came from the kitchen, and the scent of cabbage and corned beef announced another foray into Aunt Irene's cookbook.

Careful not to disturb the baby, Seth eased down the hall to his old bedroom, now converted into a nursery. He placed his son in the crib and crouched beside the spindles to croon, "Back in Black."

ABOUT EDEN WINTERS

You will know Eden Winters by her distinctive white plumage and exuberant cry of "Hey, y'all!" in a Southern US drawl so thick it renders even the simplest of words unrecognizable. Watch out, she hugs!

Driven by insatiable curiosity, she possibly holds the world's record for curriculum changes to the point that she's never quite earned a degree but is a force to be reckoned with at Trivial Pursuit.

She's trudged down hallways with police detectives, learned to disarm knife-wielding bad guys, and witnessed the correct way to blow doors off buildings. Her e-mail contains various snippets of forensic wisdom, such as "What would a dead body left in a Mexican drug tunnel look like after six months?" In the process of her adventures she has written fourteen m/m romance novels, has won several Rainbow Awards, was a Lambda Awards Finalist, and lives in terror of authorities showing up at her door to question her Internet searches. When not putting characters in dangerous situations she's a mild-mannered business executive, mother, grandmother, vegetarian, and PFLAG activist.

Her natural habitats are airports, coffee shops, and on the backs of motorcycles.

Keep up with Eden and Rocky Ridge Books by joining the newsletter.

edenwinters.com
Edenwinters@gmail.com

A Bear Walks Into a Bar

The Urso of Ballantine Mountain thinks he'll run a rag-tag band of shifters out of his territory. He doesn't expect to find a family.

Two Bears and a Baby

Sawyer and Dillon are the only two bears of the Ballantine Mountain Sleuth—until baby makes three.

The Ballantine Bears Box Set

Get both novels in one handy volume for a double dose of bear shifter love.

Otter Chaos

When otter shifter Lon meets Corey on the slopes, they're in for some good times in the mountains. Until the werewolves show up.

❧

Keep current with the Rocky Ridge gang by joining the newsletter.

Chapter One

Dillon wiped down the bar with one hand, holding his cellphone to his ear with the other. He tuned out his friends' guffaws and squawks as they horsed around when they should've been bringing in cases of beer from the cooler.

"Sis, we've been over this and over this. I can't abide by the rules back home. I need to be free to live my own life. I've got my friends, I've got the bar, that's all I need." Except maybe another bear. The wolves and fox were fine to play with, but nothing cranked his shaft like a bear with a hard on. But another bear meant going home, where Dillon would be expected to follow old-fashioned guidelines. She must not know that the Urso had told him to leave and never come back. Better for her not to know—she still had to deal with the asshole.

All because he couldn't keep it in his pants.

Bears were sexual creatures. Not using his dick until being

officially mated wasn't going to happen for him. Who'd ever heard of uptight bears?

His sister snorted. "Your *friends* are irresponsible. You know it as well as I do. Who's going to look after you all winter?"

Dillon sighed and rolled his eyes. *Crash!* came from the storeroom. His friends, irresponsible? Well, yes. "I'm a big boy and can look after myself."

"Oh fuck yeah!" somebody out of sight yelled. Assholes better tone it down before the neighbors called the cops again and complained about the "loud porno" the bar played all day on a non-existent TV.

"You know it's not only your opinion that matters. What if something goes wrong? You're young and unpredictable. What if you lose control? What then? We can't risk humans learning about us."

Dillon turned his back so he wouldn't have to see the claw marks in the door frame—claw marks he'd inflicted the last time he'd gotten drunk and shifted. Shifting took care of the alcohol in his system, but for a few seconds... Some things his sister didn't need to know.

"I'll just have to make sure nothing happens, then, won't I?" No matter how much he might lie, not having a place in the world, not being part of a bear sleuth, ripped at his guts. He wouldn't go crawling back, begging to be let back into the sleuth. He wouldn't. Ever.

But so much stuff he didn't know. His friends weren't much better off, and sooner or later someone was going to do something stupid, like challenge a car on Main Street. He'd learned a lot from his pals, and they from him, but even so, they couldn't even keep the local elk from shitting in the front yard. You'd think the four-legged nuisances would leave an apex predator alone, but no... Pellets everywhere.

If he and his friends couldn't handle a few elk, how would they ever manage a tour bus full of wolves?

Fucking uptight Urso!

A shifter's world was no place for wusses. Still, the celibacy and "species purity" his former leader dictated didn't fit into Dillon's world. Fucking made him happy. As long as he didn't hurt anybody, what was the harm in getting off with his friends? If he *did* hurt somebody, it was only because they'd asked.

And without him, the guys had no one. No options. They'd make it here or nowhere. Dillon couldn't leave them.

"Isabel asked about you," his sister said, in a singsong voice that suggested future cubs for their mother to dandle on her knee. That's what his siblings, with the combined total of sixteen cubs, were for. Dillon's world was officially a cub-free zone.

"We've talked about that too." Hard to hold a conversation about female mates when he'd have to shift before work to ease the pain in his over-worked ass. *"On the outside chance you change your mind and leave,"* his friends had told him, *"we wanna make sure you don't forget about us."*

As if.

Now came his sister's turn to sigh. "Okay, okay. I'll admit defeat on you finding a nice woman. But what about winter? Where are you going to den up that's safe?"

Good fucking question, and one Dillon couldn't answer. His friends would do what they could for him, but he really needed his own kind when hibernation set in. He'd never been through this alone, and going bear and staying bear was a good possibility for the untrained—or wreaking havoc on those around him. And gay bears that bucked the system weren't trained in his former sleuth. The Urso didn't give a rat's ass if he lived or died.

All the more reason to live.

"You'd better make a decision and soon. The snows have

already started here. You need to be tucked into a proper den before the storms hit Colorado tomorrow."

Fuck. Give a guy some time, why don't you? His friends had quieted down. Someone must be getting a blowjob, the asshole. Leaving Dillon to do all the work. Probably Jerry, who'd recently been drooling and practically humping a barstool over a construction worker he hadn't worked up the nerve to talk to yet.

It never failed. Troy came in, Jerry salivated, Troy left, Jerry ran in the back to whack off or talk Brad into some lip service.

Damn, but Dillon would like to be in the back, playing too.

His sister's voice grew more grating, refocusing his straying thoughts. "What about local sleuths? Any out there that won't resent a new male showing up?"

Pick an excuse, any excuse, to let Dillon stay where he was. "There's another bear over the mountain I've heard about." Yeah, one lone bear didn't exactly count as a sleuth. Probably an old miner, forty-niner type who'd be damned if a few lousy hunters would run him off his land like they had the other bears. But the lack of potential rivals had attracted Dillon to this area, where he could pretend to be human most of the time.

"One bear? Only one?"

"Yeah, and just because he bought a mountain or something. It's now a private wildlife preserve."

"So, no sleuth." Sleuth. What an awful name for a shifter group.

"No. But he's invited other shifters to share his sanctuary, as long as they obey his rules." Thank Mother Moon they were miles away, up near Nederland. The last thing Dillon needed was more shifter bullshit. He'd had enough to last a lifetime.

"I still wish you'd come home."

Dillon loved his sister, he truly did, but now was time for him to venture forth from the family cave. "I've got a good life here. A bar to run. I'm taking classes online to learn to run it better. With folks driving out this way to watch the aspens change, we've done pretty good business." Later, The Bear Claw would take advantage of snow bunnies on their way to the slopes. They might not stay in this Podunk town, but lots of tourists drove through on their way elsewhere.

"I gotta go. Skype me when you can and let me know you're okay." His sister made a "mwah" kissing noise into the phone.

Okay. Shit, Dillon might never be okay again. No family, no sleuth, and the local elk leaving calling cards all over his lawn.

What he needed was a distraction.

"Guys!" he hollered. Time to start his "happy hibernation" party.

Sawyer Ballantine stalked through the conference room, shrugging out of a too-restrictive jacket. One more minute and he'd have these guys for lunch. Literally. "Might I remind you who owns this company?"

"You do," his board of directors chorused.

"Who bought it as a financial fuckup and turned a profit the first year?"

"You did," they responded.

"Yes, I did. I call the shots. And I say that you'll listen to Rudy here"—he hiked a thumb at the stocky-built guy at the far end of the table—"while I'm taking a six-month sabbatical."

Sabbatical, hell. Six months out of the year he wasn't fit company for humans. Mother Nature was a cruel bitch.

Rudy sat up a little straighter, not that he needed to try to be intimidating. At two inches shy of Sawyer's six feet six, and with shoulders linebackers would kill for, the man commanded attention in his own right, and occasionally needed swatting down to keep him in line.

Not too much swatting though. Kinky little asshole might get off on that shit, though Sawyer wasn't above a subtle release of power to remind the guy of the pecking order.

"Now, Carson, where are the financials I asked for?"

"Scanned and e-mailed, sir." The wizened accountant scrunched further down into his chair.

Of all the humans who called Sawyer "boss", only Carson showed the proper nervousness in his presence, as though the man sensed a predator nearby. Reminded Sawyer of a rabbit.

Sawyer turned and swallowed a mouthful of drool. One mustn't think of employees as food.

"If that is all," he growled, leaving no doubts the meeting had ended. Without so much as a backward glance, he strode down the hall to his office and slammed the door. Assholes. They made money hand over fist, thanks to him, and yet tried to dictate his regular presence in the office. Not happening. He'd stayed too long already.

Cold weather sweeping in made him antsy, set off warning bells in his head, calling him home.

Damned fucking tie. Trying to choke him. He ripped off the offending silk and tossed the tattered remnants to the floor. Oh well, that's why his housekeeper bought them by the dozen. His button down dress shirt hit the floor a moment later, and he'd peeled out of his crisply pressed slacks when the door opened and closed behind him.

Only one man dared to enter his sanctuary without knocking, and if he'd not been expecting Rudy, the wolf would be pinned against the wall.

"I think some of the pack should go with you." The most daring of Sawyer's employees stepped into viewing range, the jacket Sawyer had discarded in the conference room slung over one shoulder.

"And I say I go alone." Sawyer opened the private quarters he'd built into his office, and donned the pair of jeans hanging from the back of a chair. A massive bed took up some of the space, and through another doorway a Jacuzzi tub beckoned. Sometimes situations warranted his full attention, no matter what time of year. The hidden rooms allowed him to function as much as winter allowed. Damn it all. Why couldn't he be like Rudy, not needing so much down time?

Oh right. Then he'd be a wolf instead of a bear. He pulled on a T-shirt, emblazoned with the name of the local Harley dealership. Next came his boots and chaps. Ah, so much more comfortable than a suit and tie.

Rudy blew out his breath. "You're taking the Harley then?"

"Might as well get one more ride in while the weather holds." Mother Moon knew when Sawyer would next be able to cruise the mountains with the sun shining down.

"You don't know what you're up against. You really need a few of my wolves with you."

A few wolves to know my business, you mean. "Truce means I tolerate the pack living on my lands. We're not partners, and you don't question me." Sawyer flexed his fingers.

Rudy's scowl would've sent half the pack scurrying for the hills.

But not Sawyer. Oh how many times he'd dreamed of wiping out the entire pack in payment for their crimes against his kind. "There's four shifters encroaching on my territory, and I'll see to them myself." Four unknown shifters were no match for a full grown bear, no matter what their species.

Pursed lips and a tapping foot were the only outward signs of Rudy's displeasure, though the thin trickle of power dancing over Sawyer's skin might as well have been Morse code for "I'm pissed."

Sawyer spun, catching Rudy in the jaw with his fist and sending the wolf flying. "Don't make me repeat myself. You're currently second-in-command, but that could change." And would in a heartbeat, the moment a better candidate appeared.

Rudy righted himself and kept quiet.

Good. While Sawyer had to teach him a lesson every now and then, a pack leader shouldn't kowtow too much. The other wolves would tear an incompetent Lobo to shreds. Shifter politics.

Sawyer grabbed his leather jacket and strode out of his office, down the hall, and into the elevator. He didn't wait to see if Rudy followed. The scent of wolf gave the man away. Wasn't a shifter born that Sawyer couldn't sniff out, though he'd learned to hide his own nature—especially when one of his biggest projects involved a herd of Rocky Mountain sheep shifters who'd contracted for a new condo complex west of Denver.

Business was good, and for business to stay good, Sawyer pretended to be human, and kept the wolves and other local shifters out of sight, except for Rudy—who never got near the sheep.

Which was why Sawyer planned to make this trip alone. No telling what, or who, he'd find.

The parking garage housed a variety of vehicles, but the reserved section held only two: a late model Bentley and a Harley Davidson.

"Rudy, you're not going and that's that." Sawyer tightened the saddlebags on his Harley Road King. "Besides, how am I gonna hook up with some hot young stud if he keeps sniffing around for the wet fur coat?"

"Hardy-har! But I still think you shouldn't ride into an unknown situation without a proper honor guard. Give me an hour and I'll round up Ricky, Jordan, Clancy—"

Werewolf Bikers. Sounded like a bad B-movie.

If you have to announce your position, then you don't deserve your position, Grandpa used to say.

But even now the trees beckoned. If Sawyer strained, he could hear the rivers miles away, imagine silver trout flashing in the dappled sunlight peeking through the trees, smell the rich scent of loam and decaying leaves. Soon he'd reach that tranquil haven, leaving behind exhaust fumes and the beep, beep, beep, hurry, hurry, hurry of the city.

A man of both worlds.

"What if something happens to you?" Rudy whined.

"All the more reason for you not to go. Say something does happen"—fat fucking chance—"I need you to keep things together. Do you have any idea how fast an idiot like Brian would destroy the pack?" Rudy needed a better second-in-command, and a fresh infusion of new blood to shore up an aging pack.

Of course, Sawyer being the last bear within a hundred miles didn't help his own situation. Rudy's age would soon tell on him, though at the moment he'd still whip any challengers —except for Sawyer. Brian became a bigger threat with each passing day.

The Lobo sighed. "I worry. What if you run into trouble? For you and for the pack. We can't take another war."

No, not with the fragile peace between the predators and elk, who'd slowly begun to encroach on Sawyer's territory since their last eviction. Elk, tasty things. Eat one, the rest fell into line—for a time. And leave it to Rudy to worry about his precious wolves only, and not the many others depending on Sawyer's generosity.

"Do you honestly think I'd let anything better me? I'm going to take care of four shifters who haven't asked permission to cross into my domain." Besides, the elk might have sent them, and the message he'd gotten only said four shifters, not what kind. They must be desperate or stupid.

"I still don't like you traveling alone."

No, you don't like not knowing what I'm up to. Sawyer's fist and

Rudy's face were seconds away from meeting again. Sawyer cracked his knuckles.

Rudy winced, but persisted. "You're the last bear on the mountain. As you said, maybe I can lead the wolves, but do you think for a moment that the deer, beavers, otters, coyotes, and foxes will accept my lead if you don't come back?" The Lobo folded his arms across his designer-shirt-clad chest. "The possums are stubborn, you know."

"So growl at them, and when they fall over and play dead, make any decisions before they come to." Sawyer so did not need this shit right now.

Rudy tapped his foot. In alternate form he'd have his ears laid back, snarling.

"I'm just going to take the long way home. You and the guys go on ahead." Sawyer added the sinister smile known to get him his way—and make the rabbits shit their pants. "Leave the lights on for me." What he really wanted was to get laid—repeatedly, to tide him over while he stayed close to his den and spent most of his time sleeping, and waking up with the hard on from hell with only his own paw to solve the problem. Damned hibernation.

"But—"

"No buts, Rudy." Sawyer turned up the heat, physically driving Rudy back with shifter energy. "You're the leader of the largest predator group under my protection, and my employee. You keep the business going when I can't be too visible. I need you. But at the end of the day, my word is law, got it?" If not for the weight of responsibility, they might have been friends.

Sawyer couldn't afford friends. Rudy hadn't been party to the extermination of Sawyer's clan, but he was still a wolf.

Rudy nodded, eyes downcast. Asswipe needed to alpha up before some upstart kicked his butt and seized power —like Brian.

Of course, that might prove interesting. This close to

winter, Sawyer's animal instincts were spoiling for either a good fight or a good fuck, and wasn't too particular of which.

"Where exactly are you going? Would you at least tell me that?"

"A town nobody's heard of about thirty-five miles from home." If Sawyer needed to hide, he'd find a similar out of the way spot. Too bad this particular spot sat on the border between elk and predator. Just because they lived off vegetation didn't mean his rivals weren't a threat—an expert marksman had joined the herd a few years ago. He'd been tough and stringy, but ceased being a problem.

Conversation grew impossible when Sawyer fired up his bike. Mother Moon, but he loved the rumble of the big Harley between his thighs, the wind on his face, tempting his sensitive nose with a million different scents: moss, pines, rabbit, clover, chicken barbequeing on a grill at a campsite downhill, all awaiting him once he reached his mountain.

Fluffy clouds overhead cast shadows over the scenery, and the crisp scent of snow drifted over the highest mountaintops. Colorado. No greater place existed on earth.

Occasionally he caught a whiff of human emotions: anger, fear, sorrow, lust. Especially lust.

Damn, he needed to get laid.

Read the rest!

www.ingramcontent.com/pod-product-compliance
Lightning Source LLC
Chambersburg PA
CBHW052040240626
47153CB00006B/2169